D0916579

HOME TO CURRAHEE

For ***Home to Currahee by Beverly Varnado***

"A genuine slice of Southern life, chocked full of heartache and healing—with a side of humor."

Marion Bond West,
Author, Contributing Editor, *Guideposts*

More praise for Beverly Varnado

"Beverly Varnado spins a wonderful and touching tale, weighted with the folklore and beauty of St. Simons Island. . ." —Rusty Whitener, *Author of A Season of Miracles, A Season of Mysteries, Christy Award Finalist,* for *Give My Love to the Chestnut Trees,*

"Beverly Varnado writes with the passion of a bygone era. Her characters leap from the page!" —Elizabeth Ludwig, Author of *The Edge of Freedom* series, for *Give My Love to the Chestnut Trees,*

"It's not often I'm surprised by a book, but this book captured me from the beginning. . . . out of the hundreds of novels I've read, I'd rank this book in my top 10 fiction books." —Eddie Snipes, Author and President of Christian Author's Guild, for *Give My Love to the Chestnut Trees,*

"Ms. Varnado writes in a lyrical . . . style . . ." —Rose McCauley, author of *Christmas Belles of Georgia,* for *Give My Love to the Chestnut Trees*,

" . . . easy to understand why this book was one of ten semifinalists in Christian Writers Guild Operation First Novel." —Ada Brownell, author of *Imagine the Future You,* for *Give My Love to the Chestnut Trees*

"Beverly Varnado has succeeded in delivering a truly heart-warming story. Her attention to detail creates a lovely tapestry, weaving together place, history, memorable characters and a timeless message." —Jacalyn Wilson, author of *Heaven's Mountain and Mountain Girl, f*or *Give My Love to the Chestnut Trees*,

"Beverly Varnado knows how to make readers care about her characters." —Mary Hake, freelance writer and editor, for *Give My Love to the Chestnut Trees*,

Home to Currahee

When her tragic past intersects with a hero's mysterious legacy, what she does next can change everything

Beverly Varnado

xulon
PRESS

Home to Currahee
by Beverly Varnado

Printed in the United States of America

Library of Congress Info

ISBN 9781629523545

www.xulonpress.com

Contents

Author's Note

Currahee Mountain, as a *Home to Currahee* character claims, is the wallpaper in my brain. Though, I have not lived in the area for many decades, I was born within sight of Currahee and have climbed it more than once. I have stood on some of the highest peaks the Rocky Mountains boast, but there is no scene more thrilling to me than the vista from atop Currahee Mountain.

It did not seem fair to choose one small town business over another for this manuscript, so I have taken creative liberties in the names of business establishments and of course, all of the characters are fictional. Though set in the present, this is a Toccoa woven from elements of the past as well as the imagination, but this place and these characters are real to me and I hope will be just as vivid to the reader.

Welcome to the foothills of the Blue Ridge Mountains. Its rich biodiversity makes it one of the most beautiful and winsome areas in the world, and its people make it a place one longs to linger.

Welcome home.

For my sister, Tammy,
whose persistent love and encouragement
have helped sustain me and my writing through many years.
For my dad, who gave me Currahee
and for the men of the 101st Airborne Division.

Chapter One

Jump

"I have full confidence in your courage, devotion to duty and skill
in battle. We will accept nothing less than full victory…
Let us beseech the blessings of Almighty God
upon this great and noble undertaking."
—General Dwight D. Eisenhower (1890-1969)

Somewhere over the English Channel

June 6, 1944

C-47 engines roared in Silas Braham's head—still he nodded. He tried to keep himself alert, mentally reviewing the jump procedure, though he should be able to do this jump in his sleep, having practiced it so many times.

His buddy, Les, punched him on the shoulder. "Hey, Silas—you gettin' sleepy?"

"Yeah, must be those new motion sickness pills we took." Imagine taking a pill to keep you from throwing up.

"That's what I was thinkin'." Les gave him a grin that betrayed the seriousness of the mission. "You know, this ain't no practice. It's the real thing."

"The real thing," Silas mumbled, rubbing his sweaty palms on his legs.

He and the men in the seats around him hated the relentless exercises back at Currahee, which included three-mile runs up the mountain. Now he was thinking they weren't such a bad idea. In spite of the training, his confidence wavered, and he wrestled with icy fear. Before them were variables for which no amount of drills could really prepare them. Somehow he had already outlived his feelings of indestructibility.

"You scared?" Les asked with another grin.

Silas debated on whether to admit it. "Yeah. How about you?"

Les shrugged and looked away.

Words floated in Silas' brain—General Eisenhower's before they left.

"Full victory. Full victory."

The phrase rattled in his brain like the engines in his ears. Much rested on the success of this mission.

Silas pulled on his gear to test its security. The packs dragged on his legs—cargo almost equal to his body weight. He patted his left breast pocket and felt the rectangular outline inside—her picture.

He'd never forget the day almost a year ago when she bumped into him at the village market. *"Excusez moi, Monsieur."*

"Excuse me, ma'am." Delighted over a collision with such loveliness, he scrambled to the floor to help pick up market items that had spilled from her basket.

Wisps of wavy brown hair fell over her face as she placed a potato back in the basket on her arm. "I am, how do you say—clumsy—not watching where I was going," she said in heavily accented English.

"Sounds like you might be from France, ma'am." He dropped several more potatoes in her basket and helped her to her feet. "How long have you lived in England?"

"Ma mere et mon pere sent me here to live with *ma tante* years ago. She is married to an Englishman. They were afraid German forces would occupy France and of course, they did. I have not heard from them in a long time."

Her eyes grew sad and an intense desire washed over him to right what had dimmed their light. He longed to see those brown orbs dance with joy. The bustling in the market behind them faded and all he knew was her face.

"I do not know when I may go back," her voice a whisper now, "or if my family is still alive."

He nodded, yet knew he couldn't possibly understand the extent of her pain. "My name is Silas."

"Je m'appelle Anne Marie." She touched the sleeve of his uniform, "You are an American soldier?"

Her touch sent a current up his arm and with it, he knew she was the one. He couldn't explain what happened. It was as if he had loved her all his life.

He saw her every time he had a pass to leave base and two weeks ago, he obtained permission from his Commanding Officer to marry. That same evening, he knelt before the most incandescent beauty he'd ever known.

"I know I don't have much to give you right now," he'd said, "but you'd make me the happiest man in the world if you'd marry me."

"Mais, oui," she cried as tears spilled down her cheeks.

The base chaplain married them the next day. He last saw her two days before this mission.

"Where are you going?" she asked before he left.

"I can't tell you." He touched her face—her beauty now creased with worry. "I don't know when I'll see you again." He couldn't tell her about the danger of the mission before him. Somehow, he felt she knew. After all, he was a paratrooper.

"If we become separated, I will come to you in America when this war is over, and I am able to find my parents. I have to know they are alive. They will want me to have the things in my dowry, if the Germans have not taken them."

He held her close and felt her tears against his cheek. "Anne Marie, I'd do anything in my power for you."

They had exchanged one last kiss, and then he had left.

Now he checked his watch once more. They should be getting close.

He thought of her parents under German oppression. He joined the Army paratroopers because he wanted to do his part to serve his country, but she had made this a personal war for him. Down there lived people who were loved by someone he loved. He had seen their picture and heard their stories.

Shouts went up as an explosion to the left of the plane almost knocked him from his seat. His heart raced like an express train as they began to take enemy fire.

"Man, that one was close," Les said, wiping his forehead with the back of his hand. "Them Germans must've waked up. We were countin' on them sleepin' longer than this."

Silas nodded. This was not good.

He peered through the open door of the plane at the small arms tracer fire and explosions in the air. He tried to calm himself by searching for the strobe lights of the drop target set by the pathfinders who'd gone before them. He found them just before the plane veered sharply and then finally, the red light that signaled for them to "stand up and hook up" came on.

Along with his comrades, he stood and reached up to tether his static line to the anchor line above him that ensured his parachute would automatically open. The check equipment command came: "Twenty okay, nineteen okay, eighteen okay."

Les called out, "Seventeen okay."

After patting himself one more time, he called, "Sixteen okay," and listened as the rest of the paratroopers checked off.

They waited for the green jump light, constantly trying to steady themselves against the violent rocking. His heart leaped to his throat—more thundering explosions.

The green light flashed. The jumpmaster screamed, "Jump!" Those ahead of him hurled into a nightmare, their parachutes illumined by fire all around.

Les turned to him one last time. Silas peered into his eyes and nodded. Les pivoted and fell forward out of the plane.

His turn next.

He touched his hand to his left pocket once more.

For her, for them, for the folks back home, pushing his fear aside, he jumped.

Chapter Two

The Discovery

"Here is the world. Beautiful and terrible things
will happen. Don't be afraid."
—Frederick Buechner

Toccoa, Georgia

Present Day

The first time I saw the blue-green peak of forested Currahee Mountain, its magnetism drew me to it with a force that seemed stronger than destiny, and somehow I knew I'd live in sight of it one day. What I didn't know is how once there, the unwinding of a story would guide me to other destinations I'd never imagined.

"Linnea, I'm fine. Really." I spoke into my cell phone as I scanned columns of corrugated boxes around me in the kitchen and wondered how long it'd take to make sense of this moving disaster.

"But Mom, you're alone and you don't know a soul," Linnea said from her apartment in Athens.

"I know a soul, two souls—my real estate agent and the mail carrier that came by yesterday. Wait, three; there was that nice closing attorney, too."

"That's not what I mean and you know it. I knew Jason and I shouldn't have enrolled for classes this summer—"

"No way are you and your brother getting derailed. I'm a big girl." I sighed and leaned against the table. "Listen, focus on your studies, and we'll catch up later in the week, okay?"

A silent moment. "Fine, but I'm texting you tomorrow."

I hung up the phone, raked a cleaning rag out of a chair, and plopped down. Linnea was right. After Three Guys and a Trailer pulled out of the yard yesterday with an empty moving van, I knew I was in trouble. I didn't think my real estate agent, the mail woman, and least of all the lawyer who closed on my house purchase were going to come over and unpack boxes for me. The real estate agent was so busy, it usually took her two days to return my calls, the mail woman only nodded as I threw up my hand and she sped off down the street, and I couldn't even remember the name of the closing attorney.

However, one thing was sure, my children needed to stay on track as much as possible at the University of Georgia, especially after the last few years we'd had.

Ice cubes in a glass on the table beside me clinked as they melted, and a trickle of perspiration inched its way down my back. I stood and crossed to the hall to click the thermostat down a bit in anticipation of some heavy lifting. Even in the foothills of the Blue Ridge, late July could deliver scorching days here in Toccoa, Georgia.

As I passed the open door to the basement, I tried not to glance down the stairs, because even a glimpse at the hoarder's paradise below put me in high anxiety—clutter resulting from decades of the house being in rental with absentee landlords and renters leaving their discards behind. The creepy chaos was almost a deal breaker for me, but in the end, the sunny bay windows in the kitchen and the house's rock bottom fixer-upper price won out. To the real estate agent's credit, she'd helped arrange for essential repairs to be done before I moved in. However, to save money, I planned to do some projects myself.

Now a day of reckoning was upon me.

I didn't want to live in a house that possibly included a hidden rodent infestation underneath the junk down there. I shuddered. Thankfully I had Jason's cat, Red, to protect me in the interim.

From the hallway, through the glass paned front door, I saw two figures step onto the porch. They pressed the bell, and I moved to turn the doorknob. The door swung open and two teen boys dressed in soccer shorts, maybe fifteen, bowed slightly. The taller of the two said, "Hello, Ma'am. My name's Tom Reynolds." He pointed to the boy next to him, "This is my buddy, Joe Mathews. I live in the neighborhood, and we're searching for lawn mowing jobs." He turned and nodded to the front yard, which stood knee high. "Looks like you could use us."

I laughed, "It's a mess all right, but I've already hired a lawn maintenance service. Thanks anyway." I started to close the door.

"Ma'am, we do any kind of work," Tom blurted, apparently the spokesperson for the duo.

Of course they did. Why didn't I think of that? Must be moving fatigue.

He peered around me. "You got yourself a lot of boxes to unpack."

I did need help, but there was no way I was letting two boys I'd never seen before in my house. There were other jobs, though. "What about the garage? You could get that in order." I didn't know how honest they were, but the hammers, screwdrivers, pruning shears and other hardware out there were hardly worth carrying off. It was worth the risk to see how they did.

A broad smile broke out on both their faces, and Tom said, "Just tell us what to do."

I exited the front door and stepped around to the detached garage. "Try your best to unpack the boxes and put everything on the side wall shelves. By the way, my name's June Callaway." We agreed on an hourly wage, and they set to work clearing the mess.

I started toward the house, but heard a voice calling to me. "Yoo, hoo, are you my new neighbor?"

I spotted an elderly woman in a yellow hat, wearing gardening gloves waving at me from the yard next door.

"If you are, I have tomatoes for you." She held up a small brown grocery sack and wagged it at me.

I stepped to the fence and extended my hand. "I'm June Callaway."

She removed a glove, wedged it between the fence slats, and shook my hand. "Bertha Henderson. Pleased to meet you." With the other hand, she extended the sack. "Better Boys."

"Thank you." I took the produce from her. Homegrown tomatoes on my second day in town? A nice turn of events that'd definitely go in my report to Linnea. I noticed my neighbor's garden when I bought the place and hoped for someone with a generous spirit. I'd never shown much expertise in vegetable gardens, but I didn't see how a woman her age managed it, either.

She raised an eyebrow. "You renting or buying?"

"Buying."

She cackled. "Glory be. I haven't had a neighbor on this side stay more than two or three years since Eisenhower." She leaned toward me with the air of someone about to divulge a secret. "Have you seen the basement? I heard from one of the former renters that place is worse than the city dump."

I leaned toward her and whispered, "I've seen it."

"Well, you need a back hoe, but those boys working in the garage might do."

A bit nosy, but she did have a point.

"You have a family?"

"A boy and a girl both in college. My husband died." I didn't say accident, not wanting to get into details.

"My Fred left me, too." She sighed. "And here we are."

"Here we are," I echoed.

"Call me if you need me. I'm in the phone book." She spun around and headed back toward her tomato plants.

I returned to the house to organize the kitchen, so I could at least make a sandwich with my neighborly gift. As I liberated a dinner plate from bubble wrap, I thought about how I'd come to be here. Back in Atlanta before Morris died, every fall we'd relish getting in the car and driving through the mountains to take in the autumn foliage. While on our drives, something about the charm of this area of the Blue Ridge Mountains spoke to us.

I became involved in genealogical research and found in old jury records that my great-great-great-great grandfather, Thomas Jefferson Chesterfield, settled in the Toccoa area for a time just after the Revolutionary War. That did it. Knowing I had family connections made the desire to come here even stronger, so Morris and I began dreaming of retiring here some day.

The memory of all the plans we'd made and the finality of Morris' death washed over me again as I stacked another dinner plate in the cabinet. Oh, how his death had shaken me to the core and exposed my deepest weaknesses.

Almost two years after Morris died—I don't know if I can even explain it—I had this persistent tug toward Toccoa. Maybe I felt I needed to fulfill the dream we had together by coming here, or maybe I just needed a new start. I'd waited and not broken the big grief recovery rule—no big decisions in the first year—but two years and seven months after his death, I followed the moving van here without Morris. How I pressed past all my nagging fears to do it was truly a miracle. Many folks at church had prayed.

As I stacked the last of the dinner plates we'd used as a family for so many years into the cupboard, the old familiar ache of loss continued, but I'd learned you had to keep wading through it. If you didn't, you'd drown, and I should know. I'd come close to going under for good more than once. I only hoped the drowning days were behind me as I hoped to find healing and a simpler life here than the hectic one we'd had just inside the Atlanta perimeter. Isn't a yearning for a less complicated life why everyone moved to small towns? I definitely wouldn't miss gridlock on I-285.

As I closed the cabinet door, laughter from the garage drifted into the house, and I stepped to the bay window to see what was going on. A smile eased across my face to see Tom sporting a Viking helmet Morris used once for a costume party, as he and Joe jousted with a couple of Atlanta Braves foam tomahawks. I thought I'd sent those things to Goodwill. Must've been put in the move pile by mistake.

I opened the back door and like lightning, Tom flung the horned helmet, they both dropped the tomahawks, and together they tore into a box of clay flowerpots. "Hi, Mrs. Callaway." Tom smiled innocently on my approach.

I squinted at them. "You can put the Viking helmet and the tomahawks in a box to give away."

A bit sheepish, Joe at last spoke. "You're getting rid of them?" They exchanged glances "Can we have them?"

I shrugged. "Sure. Feel free." You would've thought I'd bequeathed the crown jewels on them as they dove for the tomahawks and the helmet, each of them grabbing a horn.

Bertha was right. I returned to the house thinking if the boys worked out in the garage, I knew exactly what they could do next.

###

In the basement a few days later, Joe held up a brown plastic box the size of a small suitcase, which trailed a mangled electrical cord. "What's this, Mrs. Callaway?" His blue eyes sparked curiosity; his face smudged from the morning working in my cluttered basement.

I snatched away a cobweb hanging in front of me, lifted the console from his hand, and inspected it. "It's the grandfather of your Xbox. People used to play something called Pac-Man on it."

"No kidding. Wonder if it still works?" Tom took the box from me and he, too, gave it the once over.

"I doubt it." I opened another box. "Even if it did, trust me, you wouldn't be interested. Just toss it."

Tom dumped the console into a crate full of other late twentieth century relics, among them at least a hundred eight track tapes, an old Toccoa High School cheerleader's megaphone, and what might have been the first commercially available cell phone—as large as a lamp base. That didn't even count cartons and cartons of old clothes and shoes.

I held up a mildewed dress. "Looks like a fifties style. What a shame it's ruined." Linnea, into vintage things like me, would have loved this piece had it been in better condition.

"Uh, huh." Tom turned and rolled his eyes at Joe. Did he think I couldn't see? Teenagers! At least I knew what to expect having already survived two of them at my house.

I put what might have once been a bright red print dress back in the box, closed it, and handed it to Joe, who carted it outside along with several other boxes. The closer we came to the back wall of the basement, the further back in time we seemed to be going. I felt as if we were opening a time capsule.

Correct in my earlier suspicions, we uncovered what appeared to be a former rat condominium complex set up in a trunk of old chenille bedspreads. Evidently, someone had called an exterminator, because it seemed to have been vacant for some time.

Nasty, nasty, nasty.

I sighed thinking I'd have to bathe in disinfectant when I finished this job. I studied the last stacks and pointed to a box. "Tom, can you move that one there? I'm sure it's more of what we've already seen, but I feel I have to check it."

Once we cracked open the rat condo, I braced myself before opening every box.

Tom moved the box and behind it, a leg of a table or chest of some kind was barely visible under a dirty drop cloth.

"What's this?" I bent over for a closer look.

"Furniture?" Tom asked.

"Indeed."

About that time, Joe came back into the basement.

"Quick, move these other boxes," I barked, sounding like a drill sergeant.

We shoved the boxes from on top of and around whatever was under the cloth and with every one we moved, my antique-loving heart beat a bit faster. At last, only the drop cloth remained.

I looked at the boys. "Are you ready?"

"Ready!" Whether the boys acted excited for my sake or were sincere in their eagerness, I couldn't tell.

With a flourish, I whisked the drop cloth away and stood speechless at what sat before me.

I stared at the most exquisite piece of furniture I'd ever seen. Motionless for a moment with the ancient dust cloth still in my hand, I dropped it and ran my hand across the aged leather that covered the top. "I can't believe this gold leaf." I traced golden vines, which formed a garland of foliage on the desk apron. The vines climbed around metallic embellishments on the desk corners and encircled the cabriole legs. I was no expert, but the desk appeared to be of French origin.

"How did a piece of furniture like that get down here in this old, moldy basement?" asked Tom, whose allergies had his nose dripping. I'd learned he was a soccer player and I suppose out of habit from being on the field, he wiped his nose on his sleeve.

"Yeah, who would've guessed that rotten sheet had this under it?" Joe echoed.

Recovering from the shock of finding the desk, an inspired thought came: "Hey, guys, let's get this upstairs. I might be able to use it as my writing desk."

"Sure thing, Mrs. Callaway." The lanky young men maneuvered the large piece around the still full boxes on the floor.

As they puffed past me, I added, "Put it in the study."

"Yes, Ma'am."

As they navigated up the basement stairs, grunting and groaning drifted down the stairwell, and I felt moving the desk upstairs might not be such a sure thing, after all.

I followed them up and tried not to supervise as they struggled to get the desk through the study door.

"Why don't you try angling it a bit more?" I couldn't help it—it just slipped out.

They glanced at each other and then at me, as if wondering how many desks I'd tried to move, and finally cleared the door.

"Where'd you like us to put it?" Tom asked as they lowered the desk a moment.

"How about in front of the windows?"

The morning sun streamed in and banked off the gilded desk in a wondrous way as it sat in front of the southeast facing double windows.

"What will I use for a chair?" The only orphan chairs I had were completely out-of-sync with this piece.

"Beats me," Tom offered as he and Joe headed back downstairs.

I grabbed a dust cloth lying near and started to rub away the dirt and dust that had accumulated even under the protection of the sheet. Over all, I found the piece in excellent condition, considering where it'd been for who knows how long. I pulled out a small drawer with an ornate metal fitting, but it was empty except for a few dead bugs and the expected dust. Its keyhole appeared rusted from disuse.

I remembered the secret compartment in the writing desk Laura Ingalls Wilder had, so I dropped to the floor, slipped under the desk and began pulling and pushing on various parts of the desk.

A voice said, "Mrs. Callaway, what are you doing?"

I rose up and hit my head on the bottom of the desk.

"Ouch!" I could see Tom and Joe's feet and wondered why they'd come back upstairs. "I'm searching for a secret compartment."

They immediately tumbled to the floor to crawl around with me, tapping and pushing on the bottom and sides of the desk. In a few minutes, it became clear we weren't going to find anything.

I stood. "Thanks for helping. Did you guys need something?"

Tom's stomach growled as if in answer to the question.

"Right. Wash your hands and I'll get lunch." As they went past me to the bathroom, Red came skidding across the wooden floors of the foyer chasing after a small blue ball.

"It seems you're adjusting to the new place, boy." I stooped a moment to stroke his paunchy belly. He meowed loudly and padded to the desk, sniffed it, and apparently satisfied it was no threat, picked up the ball lying near and eyed me in a pleading way. Jason had taught the cat to play fetch like a dog years earlier, a trick I sometimes found annoying. The cat couldn't get enough of it. "Not now." I tried to avoid eye contact.

On the way to the kitchen, I caught my reflection in a foyer mirror. "Ugh." My head resembled a dandelion with frizzy hair standing on end thanks to humidity, heat, and bending over all morning. Where was a rubber band when I needed it? I moaned.

With the kitchen barely in working order, I washed my hands and pulled out last night's pot roast, mashed potatoes, and green beans from the refrigerator, one of three or four meals that'd kept my family from starving through the years. I heated the food, placed servings of each on plates, as well as a homemade biscuit—my one glory in the kitchen. I wasn't a good cook, but I tried. This was a lot to cook having just moved in, but worth it to have someone to cook for.

As I put the plates on the table, I added tomato aspic garnished with mayonnaise, a dish my grandmother often made. I found the recipe in The Dinner Bell Restaurant cookbook, which I'd bought when I ate at the restaurant the day I first examined the house. The local dining establishment had a fine reputation for southern cuisine, though I hadn't seen tomato aspic on the menu the one time I'd eaten there. It had to be good, though, if they included it in their offerings.

Tom and Joe washed their hands, sprawled in chairs, and Tom pointed at the aspic. "Thank you, ma'am, but what's this?"

"It's tomato aspic. Haven't you ever had it?"

"Not that I can remember," Tom said.

"What's it made of?" Joe studied it as if examining a specimen in a biology lab.

"Gelatin, tomato juice, celery, onion and a little Worcestershire sauce." I wondered how they'd missed what I considered a southern staple.

"Tomato?" Tom appeared to swallow hard.

It seemed once more my culinary attempts would go unrewarded.

###

Later, when the doorbell rang, I opened the front door to find a man sporting a green uniform with a tank on his back and a wand in his hand.

"Ma'am, my name's Jedidiah Turner, but my friends call me Jed. You called, and I'm here to take care of yer yard."

"June Callaway—glad to meet you, Jed."

I stepped out, and he followed me to the side yard.

"I was noticin' when I pulled up, one of yer trees is covered over in kudzu."

I examined the tree in question. "When I first moved in, I couldn't figure out what tree would have the bark of a pine and the leaf of a hardwood until I realized the entire tree was choked with kudzu."

"We can take care of yer trees and yer yard. I always felt weeds was part of the curse of sin. At Jed's Weed and Seed we fight sin from the ground up."

Now that was a new insight on the doctrine of the fall of man.

After Jed took care of the kudzu, I had plans for this sunny spot. "My neighbor, Bertha, told me about a man who used to live over on

Sage Street who was legendary for his dinner plate size dahlias. I'd sure like to plant a few here."

He gestured to the plot in question with the wand he held. "That'd be real purty, ma'am."

I pointed to plants next to the house. "When you spray the weeds, notice the Lenten Roses there; I wouldn't want to lose any of them."

He dropped the wand and held his hand over his heart. "Ma'am, I'll treat yer flowers nice like I would my own mama's. And just so's you know, we're eco friendly at Jed's Weed and Seed."

His sincerity and environmental concern impressed me.

With Jed at work in the yard and the boys still toiling in the basement, I moved back inside. I stopped by the study to take another glance at the desk, climbed the stairs, and plopped down at the makeshift writing station in my bedroom. I turned my computer on and sighed. I had a deadline on an article for a travel magazine. Glad for the work, but…

My gaze fell on a book by author Nan Heron lying nearby. I picked it up and flipped through the well-loved pages. Her fiction had always inspired me, and I'd written her how much her books meant during one of my drowning times. The New York Times bestselling author even responded. I'd always dreamed of writing fiction myself, but no, what was I thinking? A learning curve of gargantuan proportions at my age? I needed to stay focused on the nonfiction I knew how to write. Once more I pushed the dream aside and forced my attention back to the article about Atlanta's Peachtree Street.

However, try as I might to stay focused on Atlanta's iconic thoroughfare, my thoughts kept drifting to the desk. Questions spiraled in my brain—how did such an exquisite piece of French furniture land in my basement, and how long had it been there?

Soon the life-altering answers to these questions would make me feel that I might have been better off not knowing.

Chapter Three

Hidden

"The woods would be very silent if no birds sang
except those who sang the best."
—John James Audubon (1785-1851)

About 4:30, I descended the stairs to pay Tom and Joe for the day's work. They were almost through straightening everything after the big clean out, and I couldn't believe the result.

"You fellows have done a great job. The basement seems so big now." I studied the empty shelves on the walls and the concrete floor swept clean of debris.

Grins filled their sweaty faces. "Thanks for letting us help, Mrs. Callaway." They rested their brooms against the basement wall and each took the cash from me.

Tom put the money in his pocket, pulled out his cell phone and checked the time. "We'd better get to soccer practice." He nudged Joe. "Did you remember my mom can't pick us up? She has to take my brother, Peter, to the orthodontist."

"Yeah, I remember. I hope my mom did and that Becky doesn't have the car this afternoon."

I'd heard Joe talking about his sister and what an amazing ballet dancer she was. Quite a compliment coming from a brother.

Joe reached for Tom's phone. "Let me use your cell. I'd better call her."

###

I'd met Tom's mom, Iris Reynolds, while walking in the neighborhood the day after he and Joe came to my door, but all I knew about Joe's mom, Belle Mathews, is he'd mentioned she worked at the local clock factory.

Outside, while instructing the boys where to put empty boxes, I watched Belle pull in the driveway and exit an old grey Honda. A lovely woman with chestnut hair and posture too stooped for her age, her jeans hung loosely. She had circles under tired eyes and appeared almost as if she'd been crying.

"Are you ready?" she called to the boys who were stacking boxes outside the garage.

"Ready, Mom," Joe replied.

I crossed over and introduced myself. "I appreciate you allowing Joe to help me with my house. He's been a blessing."

"Thank you." Belle's voice sounded worn and her eyes—what were her eyes saying?

"We've finished with the basement, but I'll need help with work upstairs next week if you don't mind him coming back?"

"That'd be nice of you." She half-smiled.

The boys scuttled by, pushing and shoving as they often did when joking around. I heard the word "tomato" drift out of their conversation and watched as they loaded into the car. Joe took the wheel; he'd told me earlier he'd just secured his learner's permit. Belle moved to the passenger side, slipped in, closed the door, and waved to me as they backed out of the driveway.

As I waved back, I wondered about Belle's eyes. I'd seen that look before.

In the mirror.

###

The next morning I made coffee, took a cup out to the patio and settled in a lawn chair. The flowerbeds around me had been largely ignored before I moved in. Evidently, some past renter had a knack for gardening, because there were perennial gladiolas, cannas, and purple coneflowers flourishing even amongst the weeds I'd not had time to pull. The effect was wild, but beautiful. House finches, Carolina chickadees, and titmice competed for birdseed at an old plastic feeder I'd filled a few days before.

As I sat, the world defused a bit and that simpler life I sought seemed a bit closer. A rufous-sided towhee pecked along the ground a few feet in front me searching for seeds that had dropped from the feeder. Made me think of Jason, who was busy at UGA in the Warnell School of Forestry studying to be a wildlife biologist. He had more ornithological knowledge at eight than most adults did at eighty. I missed him.

I breathed deeply and reckoned that from this point forward in my life, missing people I loved would be a hard constant. Sweet Linnea, like her older brother, also had her dreams to pursue. She wanted to be a museum curator. I might be a little prejudiced, but I also thought she was one of the most talented watercolorists I'd ever seen.

I sighed and prayed I'd be able to embrace an uncertain future as the towhee fluttered its wings a time or two and then split the air with flight.

I turned my thoughts to the day. Though more unpacking was in store for me, the big pressure was off, with the boys coming back regularly to help. I'd take my time getting the study in order, but I longed to sit at my newly found desk. I did have a few errands today, though. My deliberate overcooking in order to have leftovers for Tom and Joe had wiped out my cupboard. I needed to stop by the Colonial Store grocery, and I had an appointment later in the afternoon with Roger Wood at The Citizens Bank to discuss moving my banking needs to this area.

Plunk! "Ouch!" I cried. A pecan bounced on the ground beside me and I rubbed a place on my head, looking up. A squirrel chattered high in the oak tree above me. "What are you mad about? I didn't drop a nut on you."

Squirrels! I pulled my hand away from my head, and a drop of blood stained my finger. My back door neighbor's pecan tree branched over into my yard, and though the nuts that dropped this fall would be good for baking, right now the squirrels were still munching on the remains of what had apparently been a bumper crop last year. This squirrel in particular seemed a bit clumsy. Now I had a scratch on my noggin in addition to the bump I received when I hit the desk with my head. Maybe I needed to wear a helmet around the house.

Laughter echoed from the fence. "Hello over there," Bertha called.

I rose and met her by the forsythia.

"Enjoying your early morning time?" She tried to hold back the laughter.

"I was." I shot another look at the squirrel and pulled a tissue from my pocket to wipe the blood off my hand. "Did you get any gardening done?"

"The squirrels carried off all my tulips in the front yard, so I thought I'd try planting a few bulbs back here. Sometimes I wish I had a BB gun, those rodents are such a nuisance," Bertha complained narrowing her eyes at a nest above us.

My heart softened a bit towards the offending nut dropper. "Squirrels have to live, too, Bertha."

Bertha stood erect and pushed her yellow hat back a bit with a gloved hand. She whacked the fence for emphasis with the trowel in her other hand.

"You sound like Melissa. She has a squirrel feeder. Have you ever heard of such a thing?"

I glanced at the yet uninstalled squirrel feeder I'd brought from Atlanta resting against the fence at my feet, and decided to keep quiet and change the subject. "The tomatoes were great. Thanks."

She relaxed a bit. "You're mighty welcome. If it weren't for Jubilee helping everyday with the vegetables, I wouldn't have a garden. He does the work, but..." She paused a moment seeming to make sure she had my attention. "I decide what to put in." She gazed back over her garden. "Yes, he started working for my dear departed Fred when we first moved here. I tell you Jubilee isn't exactly a spring chicken himself. Sure hope he outlasts me."

I'd yet to meet Jubilee but continued to be awestruck at his handiwork. Bertha's yard held six plants laden with juicy tomatoes as well as other vegetables including okra, which by the appearance of things was presently in need of cutting. Keeping the garden going was probably Bertha's way of keeping Fred's memory alive. I understood, because I occasionally cooked liver and onions, which I hated, but were Morris' favorite. Grief does strange things to a person.

I sniffed the air. "I smell sausage."

Bertha's eyes widened. "The garden club's coming over for brunch. I have to take the sausage casseroles out of the oven before they burn. I'll see you later," Bertha turned on her heel and headed to the back door, spry for a woman her age.

"Have a good meeting," I called after her.

###

"Met neighbor and have teen boys helping unpack," I texted Linnea. "Don't worry. Love you." Never could bring myself to use those awful abbreviations when texting.

"Luv U," she texted back.

My report of people who'd streamed across my path in the last few days seemed to satisfy her—a veritable explosion of social interaction. I strolled into the study and stood gazing.

There it was—that marvelous desk. Every time I entered the room, it amazed me. I wouldn't go out and buy it for myself, but I gladly received it. How incredible—made me glad once again to be here. If it hadn't been for that experience in Atlanta at a writer's conference, I don't know if I would've had the courage to make the move to Toccoa.

I could still hear the words the mysterious stranger said to me. While waiting for a session to begin, I felt a tap on my back. I turned around to a handsome man with dark hair. He smiled good-naturedly and said he thought God had given him something to tell me.

"What is it?" I asked thinking him a bit odd.

"Do it afraid," he said.

As I opened my mouth to ask him what he meant, a speaker announced the program was starting, and I shifted towards the podium.

When I turned around again to question the man, he was gone.

I never saw him again, but when I wrestled with whether moving to Toccoa would derail my life even more than it already was, the message gave me courage. When I agonized over whether I'd ever have the kinds of friends I had in Atlanta, or whether Jason and Linnea would want to come to a place where their father never lived, "Do it afraid," helped me press on.

I wanted to be fearless and strong, but I certainly didn't feel that way. Morris had been the brave one.

I shook my head and shifted my thoughts to the matter at hand—books, books, everywhere. I'd tried to sort them in order before I left Atlanta: biographies together, fiction by author, nonfiction by author, series, and then of course reference books, style manuals, dictionaries, concordances, and commentaries. It was easier to unpack them myself than answer a bunch of questions from the boys if they were helping.

As I stood on the step stool shelving George Macdonald and Catherine Marshall, I realized it was almost time for my appointment with Mr. Wood down at the bank. In my haste to get off the step stool, I lost my footing and fell toward the desk behind me. I grabbed hold of the desk in time to avoid falling with my entire weight onto it but managed to bump my funny bone.

I held my elbow for a few seconds waiting for the pain to subside. I'd always been a bit clumsy, but the moving process had multiplied my bruises exponentially. As I pulled myself together, I noticed something on the floor—a key with old tape around it. Had this fallen from the desk? I didn't understand where it could've been since I'd given the desk a thorough going over when I cleaned it. I stooped and lifted the key. Would it fit in the desk keyhole?

Forgetting my appointment at the bank, I reached over and inserted the key into the lock.

At first it didn't move. As I thought earlier, the lock was probably rusted in place, but then I heard a click. A rush of adrenaline shot through me. It fit, but I had a terrible thought—what if the key broke off, and I couldn't get the drawer unlocked again? I thought I might squirt a little oil in it before I tried to turn the key again, but when I started to the kitchen for the oil, I saw a panel had moved on the side of the desk. The thrill of discovery caused my heart to fly like Red after a new ball. I reached over and pulled the panel down.

There exposed like a pearl in an oyster was a yellowed envelope.

I lifted it from the hidden compartment, and as I did, I caught sight of the words inscribed on it.

The thrill from earlier changed to a strange sense of foreboding.

Inscribed in ink faded with time was: "Last Will and Testament of Silas Braham."

Chapter Four

The Lawyer

"The real meaning of eternal life is a life that can face anything it has to face without wavering. If we take this view, life becomes one great romance, a glorious opportunity for seeing marvelous things all the time. God is disciplining us to get us into this central place of power."
—Oswald Chambers (1874-1917)

My mama used to say, "For crying out loud."

I would cry if I thought it would help. In my core, I knew this will could mean a serious complication—maybe even the loss of the desk. The sense of heaviness after I found the will eclipsed the previous joy over the basement discovery. I lifted the flap of the yellow envelope and pulled out a sheet of what might have once been white paper.

Did I need a lawyer to help me sort out the implications of this turn of events? The whole business seemed rather clichéd like something from the detective books I read as a child. No one finds wills in furniture anymore.

Who could've guessed the secret panel in the desk would appear when the drawer was locked rather than unlocked?

I scanned the will in my hand, and in it, a Mr. Silas Braham left all of his earthly possessions, including the desk sitting in my study, to his brother Buford Braham.

I punched Silas Braham into a search on my phone. I was unprepared to see the results. The first result was a photo of him with a group of World War II paratroopers. It appeared that Silas was a war hero who jumped on D-Day—and the desk now sitting in my study once belonged to him. I read a few other results, historical accounts of D-Day which tore at my heart, as so many of the paratroopers died that day. With a heavy heart and a sigh, I clicked off my phone and picked up a photo of Morris sitting on the bookshelves.

What were the odds that I'd find a desk, which belonged to someone who jumped out of airplanes when I was trying to get over the death of someone who jumped out of airplanes?

I had begged Morris to give up skydiving, but he wouldn't. Said it made him feel alive to be up there flying through space after spending hours at a desk. At first, it was just tandem jumps, and then he went solo. The kids and I would often watch and wait for him to land after the jumps, and then one Sunday afternoon something went wrong. So, so wrong. The kids and I weren't there. Jason had been on a scouting trip, Linnea had an art class, and I was against a wall with a hard writing deadline.

I sat down at the desk and put my head down bracing against the memories of that afternoon. We learned later that a brake line broke when Morris opened his main shoot. Though he was in a spiral, he managed to cut away the shoot, but for some reason failed to open the reserve. I shuddered imagining my husband plummeting to his death.

Though, I hadn't been there, the images in my brain seemed as real as if I had. I wanted to erase them, to stop rewinding them over and over.

I lifted my head and tried to drag myself away from the grim thoughts. What should I do now, about this will?

I tried to remember the name of the attorney that closed my real estate loan.

I went into the study, pulled a file folder from a box still on the floor, scanned the documents inside, and found what I was searching for: Theodore Moore. I remember now, because he'd indicated he went by Ted because Theodore sounded like an old man's name. As

I still sat on the floor, I punched the number on the closing statement into the phone.

"James, Harrington, and Moore, may I help you?"

"Yes, my name is June Callaway, and I need to make an appointment to see Mr. Moore."

"Mr. Moore is out of town until next Monday. I can give you three o'clock that day."

"Fine," I replied. "I'll take it."

I'd have to put the matter out of my mind until then. Of course, easier said than done.

###

Toccoa, like many Southern towns established in the late nineteenth century, grew up around the tracks of coal fueled steam trains. The town's name, the Cherokee word for "beautiful," was taken from a nearby waterfall of the same name. In the early years, the vitality of the town rested on its rail connection to points as far north as Washington D. C. and as far to the West and South as New Orleans. Still today, the town straddled the rails, its depot now a flag stop for the Amtrak Crescent passenger train, as well as a thoroughfare for many a freight train.

On Saturday morning, I wheeled down Tugalo Street past the Paul Anderson Memorial Park, turned left on Sage, passed the Courthouse, the Franklin Department Store and then bumped over the railroad tracks on my way to the Dinner Bell for breakfast.

The restaurant's bell shaped sign, striped awning and window boxes full of geraniums lured would be diners in to its homey ambiance. I parked the car anticipating the outstanding food.

I'd just taken a seat in one of their vinyl booths when I spotted Belle come through the door. I waved and motioned for her to join me.

"Are you by yourself?" I asked as she approached.

"I am. I had an appointment downtown today." She checked her watch. "I'm a little early." Belle appeared neat in a khaki skirt and blue blouse, but the weariness I'd seen in her days before persisted making her seem older than her years.

"I have a Dinner Bell cookbook," I said, "but I've not actually eaten here but once for lunch. It's the first time I've tried breakfast."

Belle scanned the menu.

A petite server with a pageboy haircut zipped up to our table. Her Dinner Bell nametag read "Stella."

"Y'all want to hear about the specials?" Without waiting for our answer, she went on. "We got your ham and cheese omelet with spinach and tomatoes today. Now that has your goat cheese rather than your cheddar. We also have cinnamon rolls and biscuits right out of the oven with homemade Muscadine jelly."

"Muscadine?" I didn't think I'd ever had it before.

"Yes, Ma'am. Lucille makes it herself. Since she took over, we ain't served no store bought jelly." Stella swelled a bit as she spoke. "Lucille says the day she has to serve jelly that didn't come out of her kitchen is the day she retires."

I nodded. "Well, I'll definitely have to try it with a biscuit, and bring me the omelet special as well."

Stella moved her yellow pencil across a note pad, andthen turned to Belle. "What about you Ma'am?"

"Just coffee. I don't' really have time to eat."

"Suit yourself," Stella said. "But them cinnamon rolls is real good."

"Maybe another time." Belle closed the menu.

Stella took our menus and almost ran back to the kitchen. No way of knowing how many calories she burned every day.

I turned to Belle. "Joe's been such a help."

"I'm glad he could do it. He was trying to find a way to make a little extra money and still go to his soccer practices."

We discussed the weather, the benefits of living in Toccoa, and our children, but all the while Belle kept checking her watch.

Stella burst through the kitchen doors and careened over with a tray.

"Don't this smell good?" she asked as she placed my omelet on the table.

Heavenly.

She cradled a tiny bowl in her hands as if it contained liquid gold. "And you ain't never tasted nothing this good before in your whole life." She placed the bowl on the table, its purple contents glistening in the fluorescent light.

I spooned a bit of jelly onto a biscuit half and decided she was right as the slightly tart jelly slid across my palate. I nodded at Stella. She beamed, grabbed her tray, and flew back to the kitchen leaving a plume of coffee scent in her wake.

"You have to try this." I offered Belle the other half of my biscuit.

She shook her head as she checked her watch. "I'd better get going. Can't be late for my appointment at the bank." She had a few dollars in her hand and reached for the bill.

I put my hand on top of hers. "The least I can do is buy your coffee for letting me borrow your son."

She nodded, "Thank you," and put the money back in her purse.

She left the restaurant and drove off in her shabby Honda. An appointment at the bank was probably not a good omen. I 'd noticed that Joe never mentioned his dad and had discreetly asked Iris about it. She hesitated a moment, but said I probably needed to know that Joe's dad left without a trace ten years earlier. The family hadn't seen a cent of child support in all that time.

Poor Belle.

###

I handed a copy of the will to Ted Moore and felt a slight flush in my cheeks as I had noticed the man had dimples when he smiled. I'd met him when he closed the loan on my house, but couldn't remember if he had dimples then. He couldn't have just developed them, could he?

"Mrs. Callaway? Mrs. Callaway?"

"Yes, yes I'm sorry. What did you say?" Why was I stammering?

"I was asking you where you found this will."

I went through the whole story about finding the desk, the key, the secret compartment with the will inside, and learning that Silas Braham had jumped on D-Day. "My question is what responsibility do I have in this matter?"

He picked up the phone and asked his administrative assistant to bring in my closing documents. When the assistant, Louise, with lovely grey hair handed them to him, he appeared to search the papers.

"It seems there've only been two other owners of the house, the Jones family, and the DeVilles, from whose estate you purchased the house."

"Are you looking for something in particular?" I asked.

"I was trying to see if we did a bill of sale that conveyed all items of personal property remaining in the house to you. Yes, here it is. We don't normally do this, but I believe I remember the house had been in rental for years."

"Because the landlords lived out of town, and the property wasn't managed well, junk had accumulated from occupants who left things behind."

"Since we knew that, we took the precaution of preparing this bill of sale which makes you a bona fide purchaser for value. In laymen's terms you own everything that came in the house and have no legal obligation to pursue this any further," declared Ted.

"Good to know my actual legal obligations. I love this desk and don't want to part with it, but . . . . "

"But?" he questioned.

"But I'd like to find out more about Silas Braham. I didn't find anything more recent than the World War II information for him and nothing about his brother Buford."

He stared at me a moment before answering.

"We might check the probate records to see if there's a record of his death. Obituaries from decades ago often don't appear on line. Let me see what I can do."

I thanked him, and he smiled at me in a way that brought a flush to my cheeks again. I almost ran out the door to breathe fresh air.

How embarrassing.

I stood for a moment on the front porch of the Victorian home, which James, Harrington, and Moore had tastefully renovated for offices. Rockers filled the wraparound porch, and yellow marigolds bloomed in terra cotta pots.

I breathed deeply, shook my head to clear it, and headed down the steps to my car.

Chapter Five

Heroes

"Lord, purge our eyes to see within the seed a tree
Within the glowing egg a bird
Within the shroud a butterfly
Till, taught by such we see
Beyond all creatures, thee."
—Christina Rossetti (1830-1894)

I drove up Tugalo street to find a truck parked in front of my house with the lettering "Jed's Weed and Seed" on the side and "We fight sin from the ground up" stenciled on the tailgate.

I pulled in and met Jed in the driveway. "Yer yard's as dead as a doornail, Ma'am."

I'd noticed the increasing brown in my lawn and wondered what Jed had in mind.

"Only green left out here after we killed the crab grass and the dandelions is a little Bermuda. I can't stand Bermuda." A scowl formed on his face. "Gets in the flowerbeds and all. This lawn's been a mess for so long before you came; the only thing to do is start over."

"What do you suggest?"

"Well, fall is just a couple of months away, so I believe we ought to put in fescue. You'll have to water but that's the way it is."

"And how much will this cost?"

The amount of money it'd take to keep my front yard from becoming one large deposit of Georgia red clay stunned me."I guess I don't have any choice. Do what you need to do."

"Thanks, Miz Callaway. We'll get right to it. If you got a minute, I ain't showed you my missus yet." He waved toward the truck.

I thought I'd seen a figure in Jed's vehicle when I pulled in. A petite woman also in a green jumpsuit emerged from the passenger side. As she came closer, I could read "Jed's Weed and Seed" and the name "Ethel" embroidered in loopy script on the left shoulder.

"Miz Callaway, this here's my wife." Jed beamed as he introduced her.

"Pleased to meet you."

"Good to meet you, too, Mrs. Callaway."

"Ethel helps me in the business. It's a family company. She helps with the seed plantin' and sendin' the bills. I don't do nothin' with computers. Jed's Weed 'n Seed wouldn't be here without her. She keeps it goin.'"

I caught the smile on Ethel's face during Jed's praise.

"We'll get started," Jed said.

I watched as Jed went to the truck, pulled out a tiller, and helped Ethel get out a bag of seed. The two appeared quite the couple in their matching green jumpsuits.

###

The next morning while shelving books and unpacking the S's, I found a volume out of place in the box—a Zane Grey—Morris' book. He loved western books, western movies and always wore a pair of cowboy boots whenever he watched one of his John Wayne films—an eccentricity linked to his childhood. Holding the book in my hands brought back the piercing pain of loss again. Morris, the investment banker with the calm demeanor, passionately pursued his interests and hobbies outside of work.

The ringing phone interrupted my thoughts.

"Mrs. Callaway," said the voice on the line.

"Yes."

"This is Louise, Ted Moore's administrative assistant; there's something he thinks you might find of interest. Could you possibly meet him on the courthouse lawn at say, four, this afternoon?"

I checked my watch, "I can. What's this about?"

"He thinks you'll find it worth your time to come. Good-bye."

###

I parked in front of the courthouse as the clock in the tower began to sound four o'clock. The chiming of the hour was one of the wonders of living in Toccoa. How had I lived so many years without this hourly touch point? I put money in the parking meter and trekked up the steps to the courthouse lawn. I found Ted Moore standing in front of a large granite marker.

He turned to me, and gave me one of his dimpled smiles. "I thought you might want to see this." He pointed to the marker, on which I read aloud an inscription:

"This marker erected to commemorate the heroes of the 506th Parachute Infantry Regiment, The Currahees, who along with their comrades in the 101st Airborne Division bravely parachuted behind enemy lines at Normandy France on D-Day, June 6, 1944, and who also defended and held the city of Bastogne, Belgium against German aggressors for more than a month under extreme conditions. Thank you. We will never forget you."

Ted gestured to one of the names on the marker.

There it was—Silas Braham.

Ted nodded toward a concrete bench. "Let's sit down over there"

As he steered me to the bench, I pulled a small water bottle out of my handbag and took a sip.

We eased down on the bench, and Ted seemed to study me a moment before continuing. "I've attended several D-Day celebrations, and each year they read aloud the names of area men who served that day. I thought you might want to see the marker."

I nodded and wasn't sure I wanted to know the answer to the question that burned in my brain. "Do we know if he's still alive?"

"We'll know more tomorrow. I sent a clerk to the probate court this afternoon to see what she can find."

Robins feeding a short distance away flapped into the air. "'The Currahees have an interesting history, don't they?'" I asked.

"I had an appointment cancel and spent a little time brushing up on history to refresh my own memory."

A squirrel darted up a magnolia, and I hoped he wasn't as evil intentioned at the one at my house.

Ted continued."The 506th Parachute Infantry Regiment formed on the first of July in 1942, and activated at a camp a few miles from here later that month."

I'd read that, too. "That's the camp near the mountain."

"Right. These men took as their motto "The Currahees" because of the legend that the Cherokee meaning of the word, which is as you probably already know, 'stands alone.'"

"I'd heard the mountain's name resulted from the peak standing a distance away from the closest range." I turned to see if I could see the mountain from the courthouse lawn, but only the very top was visible as much of it was obscured by buildings and trees. I wondered if it might be more visible in the winter after the trees dropped their foliage.

"The paratroopers became well known for their bravery. They even wore a silhouette of the mountain on their insignia. The Currahees were and still are a remarkable group, though there's so few of them left."

"I'd be interested in reading more of that history myself. There might be a more thorough account at the library than the one I found online."

"No need. Walk back to my office with me, and you can borrow one of my books," Ted offered. "I'm sure you've heard of the Currahee Military Museum at the train depot. You can learn a lot there, too."

I'd read about the museum and definitely had it on my to-do list. We stood and set off across the courthouse lawn. "I also wish I knew more about the origin and style of the desk. You wouldn't happen to know anyone with that kind of expertise would you?"

"I know an appraiser who owns an antique store up in Highlands. He's over this way fairly often. I'll give him a call and ask him to get in touch with me the next time he's in town."

As we strolled to Ted' office, I noticed how comfortable it was to be around him. What was going on? How could I feel this way? What was wrong with me?

###

Later that afternoon, the phone rang in the study and I moved to answer it.

"Mrs. Callaway, Louise again, would you hold for Ted Moore?"

A moment later, "Mrs. Callaway, we found there's no record of Silas Braham's death in this county. And of course, he never owned the house you live in."

"Thanks, anyway." I rubbed the leather top of the desk.

"Just enjoy. You have a nice bit of provenance about the desk belonging to a war hero."

"I'll get the history book back to you in a couple of days."

"No hurry, take your time," Ted said.

I hung up, took a deep breath, and collapsed into a dining room chair I'd pulled in behind the desk.

I opened the desk drawer and studied its emptiness. What had Silas Braham kept in this drawer? Did it once hold his personal notepaper, his ink pen? Perhaps a service medal?

As a person looking for healing and simplicity, why did I sense a snarl making its way toward me—one which might be worse than any I-285 traffic—even worse than the notoriously congested interchange of spaghetti junction at five o'clock. I stroked the top of the desk again. Silas Braham, whatever happened to you?

I'd seen *Band of Brothers* years ago.

Some of those men who plunged from the C-47's died before they hit the ground. Others were seriously injured or died later in battle. It took a special kind of courage to do what those men did on D-Day. I couldn't even imagine it. Our country as well as people around the world owed a huge debt to these heroes.

I took a deep breath and exhaled slowly. I rose from the desk and gazed out the windows behind me towards the direction of the mountain. Though, I couldn't see it because of the tree canopy, I knew it was there: strong, steady, enduring.

I'd sought counseling for the shock of Morris' death and was better now, but I didn't want to stumble back down the dark road from which I'd just emerged by digging up the past. I didn't want to have the nightmares and flashbacks again. What if I stirred all this up and caused distress not only for myself but for Silas' family members as well. Drowning days for sure.

But still, after all Silas Braham had done, didn't I at least need to try and follow through on his last wishes?

Didn't I owe a real hero like him that much?

Could I somehow push my fear of sliding backwards aside to pursue this? Could I "do it afraid"?

A new resolve came over me.

I'd try. I would.

Since my online research had not turned up very much, perhaps someone in town might know of the Brahams.

I knew just the person I'd ask about it.

Chapter Six

A Learning Curve and a Big Surprise

"It's never too late to be what you might have been."
—George *Eliot (1819-1880)*

On Saturday morning, a droning lawnmower sounded from the yard next door, and I glimpsed Bertha's daughter, Melissa, whizzing by. Bertha told me that Melissa held a doctorate in education, and was an administrator in the local school system but insisted on doing Bertha's lawn each week.

The jobs at Bertha's seemed to be clearly divided—Melissa did the lawn, Bertha did the flowers, and Jubilee did the vegetable garden.

A terror on a tractor, Melissa circled the magnolia in Bertha's yard at warp speed on her John Deere. A squirrel in her path ran for his life, and I could only hope it was the one who dropped the nut on my head. Would serve him right.

I stepped out the back door, heard rustling next to the fence, and found Bertha on her hands and knees.

"Planting, Bertha?"

She peered up at me. "Vinca Major was taking over in the daffodil bed. You can't trust that stuff to stay in one place. The sun wasn't even up when I started chopping and pulling—can't stand the heat—bad on my heart."

I thought about Jed Turner and wondered what opinion he might have of Vinca. He'd probably lump it in the "sin" category.

"You've lived here your whole life. Have you ever heard of a Braham family?"

"Braham? That name does seem familiar, but I can't place them right now. Why do you need to know?" Bertha suspiciously raised one eyebrow.

I'd learned she liked to keep her finger on the pulse of goings on in Toccoa, but I didn't want anyone to know about the will yet. I might have Braham imposters coming out of the woodwork. I avoided her question, "Doing a little research."

Bertha narrowed her eyes. "Research, huh?"

I checked my watch. "Better get going. See you later," and took off before she had a chance to say anything else.

###

I leaned forward to study the game from my place on the metal bleachers, but the shouts around me at my first ever soccer game were confusing. I had no idea what was going on.

"Settle the ball," a man behind me shouted.

"Shoot," a teen girl in front of me yelled.

Tom's mother, Iris, stood and cried, "Header."

At least I could figure it out when another mother screamed,"Handball." I'd seen the ball hit a player's hand, but I didn't know why that was a problem.

Tom and Joe had invited me to their season opener but what was "off-sides"? It didn't look anything like when they used to call off-sides in Jason's high school football games.

Alas, I felt myself headed around a learning curve. The only familiar thing was the smell of fresh cut grass.

"What's going on?" I asked Iris about a hundred times. I hated to be annoying, but I couldn't stand not knowing what was happening.

"Corner kick." Now that was easy—they took the ball to the corner and kicked it, but why? The woman to my left appeared to understand the game as well as Iris.

"Do you have a boy out there?"

"Number 14. His name is Jonah. Played with the team two years."

I extended my hand. "I moved to town a few weeks ago, June Callaway."

She took my hand. "Babs Lawson. Nice to meet you June."

"Do you work outside the home?"

"First grade teacher at Big A Elementary for twenty five years."

"How'd you learn so much about soccer?"

She handed me a book lying on the bench beside her—*Soccer for Blockheads*.

I thumbed through it.

"I ordered it on line." She turned in my direction. "It's all that's stood between me and yelling something like, 'Touchdown.'"

I nodded, handed it back to her, and wondered how much express shipping would cost.

Babs' eyes widened, and she yelled, "Kick it."

The crowd screamed, and I turned in time to see Tom shoot a ball into the net. I stood with the rest of the crowd to cheer for the Toccoa Shooters. At least I knew one truth about soccer—goals were good.

###

I entered the doors of Emmanuel Church on Sunday, where a lovely dark haired woman with a nametag, which read "Betty," greeted me, and handed me a bulletin. I took a seat near the back and spotted the Reynolds family a few seats over. Iris and I exchanged smiles.

Later, Pastor Grady stood and asked the congregants to turn to Acts 2:17:

"In the last days, God says, I will pour out my Spirit on all people. Your sons and daughters will prophesy, your young men will see visions, your old men will dream dreams."

He recited the scripture "by heart" as my mother would've said, and his sermon on "Visionaries and Dreamers" stirred me. The flickering hope I'd had for the future seemed to grow a bit brighter.

After the last, "Amen," I gathered my things to leave and an announcement on the back of the bulletin caught my attention.

"CHOIR MEMBERS NEEDED!"

I grimaced. How awful it would be to have to go through an audition to sing in a choir. The liturgist had announced that morning that the choir would be returning in a few weeks after their summer hiatus.

I read, "NO AUDITION REQUIRED."

No audition required?

I hadn't sung in a choir since high school, but I'd missed being involved in music. Maybe, I'd call the choir director later in the week.

###

On Wednesday, I stood in the hallway next to a door signed, "Choir Room," as conversation and laughter drifted out from the practice room.

I'd spent the whole afternoon tracking down Brahams I'd found online, but none of them brought any clarity to the desk situation. With military records only noting Silas Braham's World War II service, and nothing more, I really didn't know where else to turn. Discouraged, I didn't need any more hurdles tonight.

Thankfully, this situation seemed non-threatening enough. I peeked through a crack in the door and could see folks seated in three rows of chairs set up in semi-circles. An attractive woman with brown hair in the second row spotted me. "Come on in. I hope you sing alto."

"I don't know exactly what I sing, it's been so long." I stepped through the door.

"Well, sit beside me. We need altos. My name's Debbie Benton."

"I'm June Callaway, pleased to meet you Debbie." Others introduced themselves, as well.

After someone handed me a folder of music, a blonde-haired woman dressed in a tangerine pants suit wearing stiletto heels entered. Her make-up seemed a little over-done. She stopped just inside the door.

"Y'all can start now. I'm here," the woman announced.

Laughter rippled through the room.

"We weren't about to start without you Rhonda Kay," a man from the back said chuckling.

"I know `cause I'm such an asset." She paused a moment and noticeably exhaled. "I've felt like I had the vapors all day, I been so worn out. Anybody seen my music? It ain't in my car. I turned it upside down before I came in here—I guess I could've left it at home—but I don't think so. I believe I'd seen it. I'll get me some more." Rhonda Kay pranced over to a bookcase, picked up the top copy off several stacks, and plopped in a seat.

I didn't know what to make of her.

A woman who I supposed was the person I'd spoken with on the phone, Laura Goodhay, came into the room, and stopped at the director's stand. She smiled when she saw me. "I see we have a new face—you must be June. Have you all introduced yourselves?" she asked. Learning they had, she announced the first piece, and then became distracted.

"Rhonda Kay Smith, is that new music in your lap?"

"Shore is, I done lost mine again."

"Did you check your car trunk? That's where you found it last time."

"I forgot." Rhonda Kay looked sheepish. "I'll investigate first off after I leave tonight."

Laura turned to me, "June, I know you haven't practiced this piece, but this is the one we've been preparing for our first Sunday. We'll hit it head on after we warm up a little. If you need me to stay and go over parts with you afterwards, I'll be glad to."

I nodded and fought the fear. I'd need more than a few moments warming up to get my voice in shape. After a few exercises, Laura began the count, the pianist started the introduction, and from the first note, I was amazed at the sound that came from such a small group. The sopranos especially had an incredible blend. Laura bowed her head to one of them, I couldn't see who, but a brilliant full voice sang the solo part.

I almost fell out of my seat. It was Rhonda Kay. It threw me so much that I lost my place in the music and had to ask Debbie where we were. After the last measure, Laura nodded to Rhonda Kay, "Beautifully done."

When choir was over, I hurried over to Rhonda Kay, "You have an amazing voice."

"Thank you, ma'am. People tell me all the time they don't know how my singin' voice, and my talkin' voice ever got put in the same body. I don't know neither. It surprises me as much as everybody else. I try to work on it, go to singin' lessons and all. Maybe I ought to be goin' to talkin' lessons, too," she said with a laugh.

I liked Rhonda Kay. We strolled to the parking lot together where Rhonda Kay popped the trunk lid of a pale blue Cadillac. She reached inside and held up a black folder. "I'll be the mother of a tadpole if it ain't my music."

Chapter Seven

More Surprises

"Make your work in keeping with your purpose."
—Leonardo da Vinci (1452-1519)

Sitting in front of the computer, I toyed once more with the idea—this whole dream to write fiction.

Here I was facing another fear hurdle.

Could I do this afraid, too?

I'd read a couple of books on fiction writing and had at least a rudimentary knowledge of the craft.

I picked up a book lying near, and flipped it over.

"What should I write about?" I asked the lovely face on the back cover.

No response.

Talking to book covers now.

Who did I think I was to write fiction?

For the next two hours, I stared at the computer screen typing and deleting, not having any idea where I was going.

Maybe there hadn't been enough time since Morris' death for me to take on such a big project. I couldn't seem to put meat on the bones of the few ideas I had. Plus, I had the distractibility factor.

As I traced the embellishment on the apron of the desk with my finger, my thoughts shifted to its mysterious origins.

Would I ever find any answers about the will and the Braham family? Bertha had been no help, and there didn't seem to be any answers in the phone book or online. I didn't know what else to do. Every road seemed to lead nowhere.

I closed the computer screen, swiveled in my chair and through the window, caught sight of Bertha falling flat on her back.

###

"I was going to water the mandevillas at the mailbox because of how dry it's been, and stumbled on a crack in the driveway," Bertha said weakly while lying in bed at the Stephens County Hospital. An intravenous line ran to her left hand. Abrasions criss-crossed her right arm.

"Bertha, I'm sorry," I said, "but you came through the surgery well. The doctor reported your hip's as good as new."

"Doesn't feel like it," Bertha moaned.

A nurse who'd come into the room to check the monitors slipped out and closed the door behind her.

Melissa placed her hand on my arm. "I'm glad you were there when it happened. Mom could have been out there for a long time." She tucked a crisp white sheet under Bertha's chin.

Bertha's long time friend, Eunice, had just arrived, and still held a potted peace lily in her hands. She placed it on the windowsill. "That's right. That Atlanta paper man is in such a hurry every afternoon, he'd have flung out the paper and beaned Bertha right in the head without so much as a glance. You probably saved her from a concussion, too, June."

Bertha's brow furrowed. "Jubilee's coming over in the morning to work in the cabbage patch. He'll be worried if I'm not there."

I stepped to the head of her bed. "I'll meet him as soon as he gets out of the car, and tell him what's going on. Concentrate on getting better. You'll be up walking in no time."

###

I heard the phone ringing as I came in the door from the hospital.

"Yes, I'll hold for Ted Moore." I thought my business with the lawyer had concluded.

"Mrs. Callaway, I didn't know if you were still interested in talking to someone about your desk?'

"Yes, yes, I am." I put my purse down on the desk.

"The appraiser Robert Giles was in town today from Highlands on other business, and I asked him if he would have time to stop by your place. He said he could."

"I'll be at home the rest of the day."

###

"Bureau plat, eighteenth century," declared Robert Giles, a distinguished African American man with an *Antiques Roadshow* air about him. "This is a museum piece. Where did you find it?" He adjusted his silver-rimmed glasses.

"In my basement under a sheet," I said almost apologetically.

"In the basement? Who would put such a treasure in the basement?" He glared at me accusingly as if it'd somehow been my fault.

"I've asked that very question myself." I cautiously took a step back.

He gazed on the desk with adoration. "I rarely get to see such an exquisite example of eighteenth century French furniture. I want to check one other detail." He dropped to his knees and craned his head under the desk. "Yes, it's there."

"What, Mr. Giles?"

As he stood, he said, "The stamp that was added to guild produced furniture in France in the eighteenth century: the maker's name, which in this case is Antoine Joubert and the JME stamp for *jurande des menuisiers-ebenistes,* which meant the guild members approved the quality."

I remembered seeing writing on the underside of the desk when I examined it for a secret compartment. "Should I have it insured? Is it terribly valuable?" I'd hate to have to put a rider on what I considered an already exorbitant insurance policy.

"This is strictly an unofficial estimate as a favor to Ted, but with the gilt-bronze mounts, I would say this piece of furniture, if properly offered, would bring close to a half million dollars."

###

I closed the front door after Robert Giles, leaned against it, and sank to the floor. As I rested my head against it, I thought nobody should have a desk worth more than their entire house. But I did.

What now?

The phone rang—Ted Moore, the caller ID read. I clicked it on.

"What did Robert say about the desk?"

I filled him in on the details.

"I see. Well, it seems you have a pretty valuable place to keep your pencils."

He was so casual about it, as if every other day someone in Toccoa uncovered a museum quality antique in her basement.

"Just wondering, would you be interested in going with me to the library benefit Friday night? Several regional authors will be reading. As a writer yourself, I thought you'd like it."

I'd hardly had time to regroup from the desk shock before Ted hit me with the benefit invitation. "I'd love to go," I heard myself say.

"I'll pick you up at seven," Ted replied

Wait, what just happened?

Chapter Eight

Local Color

"Lord, how Thy wonders are displayed where'er I turn my eye:
If I survey the ground I tread, or gaze upon the sky?
While all that borrows life from Thee is ever in Thy care,
And everywhere that man can be, Thou God, are present there."
—Isacc Watts (1674-1748)

I rose early the next morning to wait on Bertha's patio for Jubilee Johnson. While I stood watching a yellow-bellied sapsucker plunge his beak into a cake of suet, I had to wonder what came over me the night before. Was I going on a date? I didn't even know if that's what people called it anymore.

The sapsucker cruised off, and two chickadees followed him into the bright blue sky. I checked my watch, and after about twenty minutes, I called Melissa to make sure I'd understood correctly that Jubilee was supposed to come this morning. I thought maybe with the fall, Bertha had been confused.

"She told me before she fell he was coming today. He doesn't have a phone, so they always work out their plans while he's there. A couple of times I've had to go to his house to tell him something for Mom, but he's never failed to show up—must be a problem," Melissa concluded.

I definitely wasn't in Kansas anymore. I hadn't known anyone who didn't have a phone since I couldn't remember when. Surely, he at least had a burner.

"You say he doesn't have a phone?"

"Says he hasn't needed one for the past seventy years, and he didn't need one now. Says the U.S. Mail is good enough for him."

Wow. "If you'll tell me how to get there, I'll check on him." If I was going to be the one to report to Bertha that her cabbages weren't weeded, I needed to know why.

It turned out that Jubilee's house was further out of town than I'd anticipated. As my car bumped over the last bit of pavement onto the winding dirt road, I couldn't help but feel I was entering a time warp. Decades separated me from the last dirt road I'd traveled. According to Melissa's instructions, Jubilee's house sat about a half mile down the road after the pavement ended. I turned slightly to the left under a giant magnolia, caught my first sight of his place as I hit the brakes, and tried to catch my breath.

Never seen anything like it.

Reflectors and bottle caps covered his fence and mailbox. I exited the car and in front of a replica Capitol building fashioned as a birdhouse, whirligigs resembling several well-known political figures greeted me as I entered the front gate.

I followed a concrete pathway to the front door, and determined it might've been poured by Jubilee himself because of its uneven surface and irregular sides. A veritable crowd of whirling cultural icons lined either side including one of Elvis plunked in the ground just before I ascended the steps.

A group of wooden flamingos I recognized as various country music singers posited on the porch.

A man with tanned leathery skin and unruly grey hair opened the door and through the screen, I saw below his plaid sleeve, his left arm was in a cast.

"Jubilee?" I asked.

He nodded and gave me a toothy grin.

"I'm Bertha's next door neighbor, June Callaway."

"Yes, Ma'am. She told me about you. Sorry I couldn't get over to Bertha's today. Yesterday, I was on a ladder puttin' up a new weather vane. That thing got to rockin' and first I knew I fell slam over in the petunia bed. I knew something was broke right off. I managed to pull myself up and get in the Buick." He looped a finger on his right hand under his overalls strap.

I checked out the enormous vintage blue automobile sitting in his driveway.

Jubilee went on, "Mighty good I can drive with one hand." He unlooped his finger and held up his right hand, splaying his fingers.

Thank God for the invention of power steering, too.

"They treated me right well at the hospital—hurtin' pretty bad today, though. Bruised you know."

"You'll never believe it, but Bertha had a fall yesterday, too." Since it happened, the fall had played in slow motion in my brain. It could've been so much worse. Strange how life can change in a fraction of a second. I knew that well enough.

"Ah, shaw?" Jubilee asked.

"Had to have surgery for a broken hip and will be in the hospital a few more days. She was concerned you'd come over, not find her at home, and worry."

I dreaded breaking the news to her about Jubilee's accident, but I knew what I had to do. "Don't bother about the cabbage patch. Melissa and I can handle it until you start feeling well enough to come."

I turned around and gestured to the yard exhibits. "This is quite a display you have here!"

"Yes ma'am. I been workin' on it for years. If ever I start feelin' low, I get out there in the woodshop and make me a new whirligig, a bench or something and in not too long, I'm feelin' like my old self. That's why I gotta get over this broke arm quick. I been studyin' on a new whirligig."

"There's a woman over in Athens who's writing a book on primitive artists and yard art. I know she'd love to come up and speak with you, maybe take some pictures. I met her at a writer's conference a few months ago—Sally Phillips. Would you mind if I gave her directions to your house?"

"Tell her to come on. I love to have company. Ever once in a while, somebody from town drives out here to see my place. It tickles me when folks like my work."

"I need to go, but can I do anything for you? Medicine or food?"

"Mercy, no, got plenty of food, and my daughter bought my medicine on the way back from the hospital, but that's awful kind of you."

As I left, I noticed an East wind caught one well-known congressman's hand and sent him into a flurry of activity.

###

To use my mother's verbiage, the events of the week had left my head "swimming." Bertha had been quite upset when I told her about Jubilee's accident.

"Is he in the hospital? I'll go down and see him," she said trying to get out of bed.

"No, Bertha, he's at home. Doing fine." I helped her get back under the cover. "You'll be home soon. I'll pick him up, and you two can visit."

"What about..."

"Melissa and I will take care of the garden." I was about as good in a garden as I was in the kitchen, but desperate times required desperate measures.

###

Later at home, I studied the three outfits I'd laid on the bed, but couldn't decide which one to wear. Tonight was the night I'd agreed to go with Ted Moore to the library benefit.

Maybe I'd wear my bathrobe. I didn't feel quite up for this "dating" business. For fleeting moments, I still entertained the idea that Morris was just off on a long trip, and would be coming back. Other times, the finality of it all almost choked me.

Plus, I had this new twist in my life—the desk. What was I going to do with it? I was almost afraid to use it now. It legally belonged to me, yet there was a heaviness in my spirit that I couldn't explain every time I looked at it, almost as if I had something that belonged to someone else. Who did it belong to? I was beginning to understand why someone might have put it in the basement to begin with,

I was thinking of doing the same—sending it back to the basement. Out of sight, out of mind.

###

Ted picked me up in a vintage Ford Mustang. Bright yellow. "What a car," I said awestruck as he held the door open for me.

He grinned. "Thanks. It's a 1967 model. I love seeing something broken restored to beauty."

"Must take patience." I eyed the immaculate interior.

He shrugged. "I enjoy working with my hands after sitting at a desk all day."

A lot safer hobby than jumping out of airplanes, too, I thought. "Have you restored many cars?"

"More than half a dozen, I guess." He closed the door after I'd taken a seat.

Later at the library benefit, as Ted and I listened to a string quartet, the music soothed me. Earlier in the evening, there'd been a reading by the poet laureate of Georgia, a professor at a college further north, which had folks lined up in droves for her book signing. Still to come was a nature writer who promised to read a short story from his most recent collection. When I still lived in Atlanta, I'd read accolades about him in a New York Times review, never dreaming I'd get to hear him read in person someday.

Ted was right. This was an event a writer liked. I looked at him, grateful he'd thought to ask me. In the end, I hadn't worn my bathrobe after all, instead I chose a purple sweater and grey slacks with a piece of handmade sterling and glass jewelry I'd found at a local arts festival.

I caught Ted's eye, and he flashed that million-dollar smile at me.

There was the flush again. Would this never end?

Afraid he'd seen the color in my cheeks, I turned quickly and headed over to examine a display of North Georgia nature books. I chose one indiscriminately and began to read.

Ted followed, and as he picked up a book from the shelf he asked, "Would you like to drop by the Dinner Bell on the way home and have coffee? Their carrot cake is out of this world."

###

Stella magically appeared just after we took our seats in a booth. Ted ordered the carrot cake.

"We ain't got no carrot cake tonight," Stella said.

I thought Ted might cry.

"But," she smiled sly, "we do have your German chocolate. Lucille says you don't have no business baking a cake if you ain't gonna use fresh ingredients, so she uses coconut so fresh you'd think it just fell off the tree." She licked the end of her pencil. "Would that be one piece or two?"

She leaned over toward me. "If I was you, I'd get my own piece. He ain't much for sharing." She pointed toward Ted. "Why we're lucky to get the plate back with this one."

I stifled a laugh.

"Make it two pieces," Ted said dryly with a twinkle in his eye. "And coffee would be nice, too."

Stella sped off to retrieve our orders. "How long have you lived in Toccoa?" I settled back in my seat.

"I came here fresh out of law school, because of the kindness of an old friend of my father. Mr. James of what was then James and Harrington agreed to give me a chance in his firm. I began to do more and more of their real estate work and in a few years, Mr. James made me a partner."

Ted paused for a moment rotating his coffee cup clockwise studying the whirl inside it. "He died a couple of years ago." He diverted his eyes to the car lights entering the parking lot. "I miss him. I'd lost my dad young, and Mr. James was like a second father to me—had the ability to walk into a room and bring order to any situation."

Stella flew up and deposited our desserts on the table. "Y'all need anything else?"

We shook our heads, and she almost lifted off the floor, she split in such a hurry.

"Does she run?" I asked Ted.

"I don't know, but I've always thought she'd be a great contender in a 3K." He let go a laugh as he forked a piece of German chocolate cake. "Mr. James used to keep a box of candy behind the sofa in his office. Every client's child in Toccoa knew that box was there. They'd come running in the law firm looking for Mr. James, because he always had a treat for them. "

"He sounds incredible." I placed a bite of cake in my mouth and almost fainted from delight. "This is good."

Ted nodded and put the forkful in his mouth, chewed and swallowed. "The best. Anyway, you can understand why I never wanted to move. Of course, I had friends from law school who became partners in big firms in Atlanta, and though they pulled in big bucks, that life never held any appeal for me. Toccoa has been a wonderful place to live."

I swallowed hard before I asked the next question. Ted didn't have on a wedding ring, but I needed to know.

"Have you always lived alone?"

He hesitated a moment. "No, my wife, she died a few years back. Four years and two months ago to be exact." He pushed the coffee cup away and spread his hands on the table.

I instantly regretted the question. "I'm sorry."

He shoved his hands in his pockets. "No, perfectly all right. It still hurts, but it's a hurt I can live with now."

I wondered how that ever happened.

"What brought you to Toccoa?" He leaned toward me.

"Well..." I paused wondering if Ted was ready to hear the story, so I told him the abridged version. "My husband, Morris, and I had planned on retiring here, but he died. I needed a change after that, so I moved." Succinct. To the point. Just not all the details. I really didn't want to talk about Morris' accident.

Stella slid up to the table and filled our coffee cups. "You folks still doing okay?" she asked as she whisked away our empty plates.

"The cake was outstanding tonight." Ted leaned back in his seat with satisfaction.

"We aim to please, especially since you're one of our best customers."

"You bet I am," he said. "If it weren't for the Dinner Bell, I don't know what I'd have done these last few years."

Stella smiled and shot back to the kitchen.

Ted turned to me, "So it was a big move?"

"The biggest."

"What are you looking for here?"

"A less complicated day to day life." I hesitated a moment. "I guess I'm hoping for a breakthrough in my writing, too."

"How so?"

"I've had a dream to write fiction—not going so well right now."

"Maybe, it'll just take time," Ted said.

I was pretty sure it was going to take more than time when it came to my attempt to write fiction.

I cupped my hands around my coffee, held it up, and inhaled the wonderful aroma. "And…"

"And?" Ted asked.

"Well, this isn't anything I planned on doing when I came here, but I feel I have to find the owner of this desk—to see if he or any of his relatives are alive. It almost feels like a moral obligation, somehow."

"I'm at your service," He bowed his head slightly.

I laughed. "Thank you, kind sir." I returned the bow.

As we returned to the Mustang later, I noticed a sticker on the rear bumper. Over a silhouette of Currahee Mountain read the words Currahee Climbers. "What's that?" I asked pointing to the sticker.

"Member of a local hiking club," he said. "You should join us sometime."

"Sometime," I said not meaning it.

###

The days seemed to have flown since I moved, a waft of fall temperatures blew in over Toccoa making it a bit chilly to sit outside. I perched at the kitchen table sipping from the coffee cup in my hands as a female cardinal glided onto the feeder, and whisked away a sunflower seed. Red lay in a sunlit stupor on the window seat. He blinked his eyes at the flutter of wings, but lapsed back into drowsy slumber.

Through the kitchen window, the rising sun shed its glow on the maple between my house and Bertha's. A slight breeze ruffled the tree making leaves shimmer in the bath of light. When I lived in Atlanta, I'd always had to drive a couple of hours to get the early impact of autumn in Georgia, but I'd driven just a few miles out Highway 123 toward the mountain yesterday and found the peak glorious with maples leaning to orange and reddening oaks all on a background of shortleaf pine.

I thought about Linnea's watercolor paints. Though, I was no artist, I'd bought enough watercolors for Linnea over the years, and the colors I'd pick to paint Currahee would be alizarin crimson, cadmium yellow, burnt umber, sap green and a color Linnea reported that she rarely reached for—thalo green. She said one dot of thalo green might cover an eight by ten room, but I thought the strength of that color would be essential to paint the mountain.

I don't know what it was about Currahee. It was almost as if the deep green of the pine spires pointed me toward heaven. When I looked at it, I felt as if I received an infusion of strength.

An infusion right now would be great. Too bad I couldn't see the mountain from the kitchen.

I sighed, still stuck with no more information about the desk. It was mine and yet, it wasn't.

I went into the study, settled into a chair at the desk, and stared at the blank screen on the computer.

Once more, gridlock set in. I typed a few words. Deleted them all.

Technical writing and articles were easier—I was given a topic, did the research and wrote the piece. I liked being assigned topics; writing a novel required imagination.

Couldn't someone assign me a topic for the book?

I typed a few more words. Deleted those, too.

I wondered if I had an imagination. Surely, I had one somewhere.

This was misery.

Where was that breakthrough?

I shut the computer, and headed out the back door actually looking forward to weeding Bertha's cabbages.

###

I exited my car for Wednesday night choir practice about the same time Rhonda Kay arrived.

"How you likin' the Christmas music we been practicin'?" she asked as she approached me.

"Delightful." I hated to admit how much I struggled with the parts, but I'd listened to some recordings on YouTube and that seemed to help a bit. "It helps you to get in the Christmas spirit, don't you think?"

She stopped short studying me as if I'd grown an extra nose or something. "I don't need no help gettin' in the Christmas spirit. I put my tree up before Thanksgivin' and leave it up 'til after New Year's. My husband, Cletus, has already got the lights up on the house—just waiting to pull the switch. We're big on Christmas."

She smoothed down a tiny wisp of hair that the hair lacquer she was so fond of had escaped. "One thing's for sure, though, Jesus is right out front in the manger. When all them folks line up to see my lights, I want them to see Jesus first."

I studied Rhonda Kay with her chandelier earrings, lime green pantsuit, and signature stiletto heels. It seemed God was making sure I realized you can't judge what's in a person's heart by their appearance.

Chapter Nine

Getting Up a Crowd

"Those who trust in the Lord are like Mount Zion,
which cannot be shaken but endures forever.
As the mountains surround Jerusalem, so the Lord
surrounds his people both now and forevermore."
—Psalm 125: 1-2

Bertha came home with a bang.

"Pull into *The Quik Biscuit*," she'd told Melissa on the drive home from the hospital. "I'm starving."

Before they left the fast food restaurant though, Bertha determined they'd been overcharged twenty-five cents for the bacon, egg, with cheese biscuit and coffee she'd wanted. "Go back in and get your money. It's not right they get a quarter tip for nothing," she demanded of Melissa.

She was so relentless; Melissa went in and asked for the money back.

Next, they stopped to pick up Bertha's medicine at the drug store. "I'll be back in a minute." Melissa started to open the car door.

"I'm going in." Bertha grabbed her purse. "I have to talk to the druggist myself."

It was a major ordeal with the walker being new, the surgery being recent, and the back of the store where the druggist was being so far.

Bertha threw her purse up on the counter when she reached the back of the store. "I need a refill on my blood pressure medicine," she commanded the druggist. "Call the doctor's office and get one."

Melissa couldn't believe it. "Is that all you wanted? I could've told the pharmacist about the prescription."

Bertha stared at her in an imperious way. "Why don't you get a box of Epsom salts for me."

"Mom, you already have enough Epsom salts to cleanse the systems of half of Toccoa."

Bertha pursed her lips. "Fine then, I'll get them myself."

"It must be the drugs," Melissa told me in the kitchen after Bertha finally settled in her bedroom at home. "I've never seen her be so cantankerous." Melissa collapsed wearily into a kitchen chair.

"Well, she's been through a lot. She probably has a right to be a little cantankerous. You have to be exhausted yourself. I can stay until the lady you hired to be with her comes," I offered.

Eunice, who was sipping coffee at the breakfast table, broke in. "Ah, both of you need to go home. I'll stay with Bertha. I can handle her. She used to try to sass me on the playground when we were little, and I set her straight right off. She knows she can't pull that stuff on me. I won't stand for it, broken hip or not."

At that, Melissa and I gladly left leaving Eunice in command.

###

Sitting at the kitchen table, I tried to work, but Red twirled in my lap kneading my bathrobe. He nipped and pawed at my fingers while I typed. For a woman who lived alone, I sure struggled with distractions.

With Thanksgiving and Christmas around the corner, I'd have to put the whole matter of the desk on the back burner. It didn't seem there was much option anyway with hardly any leads. Jason and Linnea would be coming home, and though I dreaded the holidays without Morris, my children's presence brought something of a healing balm to the wound of not having him around.

I rose, reached for the coffee pot, and poured myself another cup. I'd already begun my Christmas shopping while frequenting the mountain arts and crafts festivals this fall. I was happy with the lizard sculpture made from salvaged tin that I'd bought for Jason. Maybe he could put it on his desk when he graduated and found a job as a wildlife biologist. For Linnea, I'd purchased a wool scarf that was spun, dyed, and knit on a local sheep farm. I felt proud of having already made a little dent in my to-do list. Maybe my early shopping would make for a more relaxed season.

It would be only the three of us like last year. I'd buy a turkey breast for Thanksgiving dinner instead of a whole turkey, and that'd be plenty for my small brood.

I thought it all settled when a thought came to me. I fought it hard but in my heart, I heard, "Do it afraid."

###

I took out a Toccoa phone book and punched a few numbers into my cell phone.

"Bertha, it's your neighbor. I wondered since you're still in recovery mode if you and Melissa would like to come over for Thanksgiving dinner."

"I've spent every Thanksgiving for forty years in this house but I'm about ready for a change. I'd love to come, and I'll check with Melissa to see how she feels, but I can guess she's ready for a change, too, since she's been cooped up with me for the past few weeks."

I said good-bye and punched the button on my cell. Three became five.

###

Iris Reynolds called and told me Tom and Joe had a soccer tournament the week before Thanksgiving at the local fields. Could I come? Of course, I could. I'd been studying my copy of *Soccer for Blockheads* and hoped to have at least a working knowledge of the game at this point. I'd also watched the soccer channel, but the games were so fast moving, I needed my own personal commentator to keep up with the action. I was glad Tom and Joe's matches moved at a slower pace.

I arrived to see more cars than I ever imagined could fit in the soccer field parking lots. Thankfully, traffic directors helped folks find spaces. I had no idea the Toccoa Cup was such a large tournament. Iris told me they'd be playing on field D. I felt like a real soccer mom with my folding chair in a zippered case hanging from one shoulder. I missed all those football and basketball games I used to attend when Jason was in school, as well as all the art events I attended for Linnea. Being here now was somewhat consoling. I found the Reynolds and squeezed my chair in beside Iris. Tom and Joe strode to the center of the field.

"They're captains for this game," Iris explained.

I felt a certain sense of pride in these boys that someone else besides me had seen their fine qualities.

As the game started, two players came flying after the ball right in front of me and almost knocked me out of my chair. They stopped short when the ball went out of bounds.

"Why does this game seem to be moving so fast?' I asked Iris.

"This team is playing in a higher division than the Shooters. They'll force us to play faster. It's good for the Shooters to play teams better than they are."

The words were hardly out of Iris' mouth when the other team scored. I didn't like the looks of this. The Shooters tried to take the ball down to the opponent's goal but once more, the other team took control of the ball and moved it to the Shooter's goal. Whoosh!

The score ended ten to three.

"I don't think I can stand two more games in the tournament like this," Tom moaned as he plodded to the sidelines after the game. He turned to me. "Thanks for coming Ms. Callaway. I'm sorry you had to see us get beat like that, though."

"You played a good game—nothing to be sorry for."

"That's right," Tom's younger brother, Peter, agreed. Admiration for his brother sparked in Peter's eyes.

"June, join us for a picnic. We have plenty. It's too hard to leave the tournament for lunch, so we find a patch of grass and spread our food," Iris said.

"I'd love to."

"Peter, why don't you help me with this cooler?" Tom's dad, Sam, asked.

We found a spot under a few trees to shade us from the unseasonably warm sun, spread a big quilt Iris had brought, and then out came stuffed eggs, turkey sandwiches, chips, and of course sweet tea. I'd just taken a big bite of my sandwich when I noticed Belle and Joe walking a few feet away.

"Belle, hello," I tried to say but with my mouth full it came out "Bellow."

Belle spun around and saw us.

"Come join us," Iris called.

As Belle and Joe collapsed on the quilt with their lunches, Joe's face said he, too, was taking the loss hard. Jason used to have the same problem when he lost a football game.

I tried to think of something to talk about that didn't involve soccer. I turned to Belle. "So you work at the clock factory?"

I noticed a glimmer in her eye, I hadn't seen before. "I have for years, but I just quit a couple of weeks ago to work as a paraprofessional with Babs Lawson."

"Paraprofessional?" I had no idea what that was.

"A teacher's assistant. I work under Babs' supervision."

"I met her." I was glad to be able to say I knew someone here. "At the soccer game. She has a son that plays on the team." I pulled my copy of *Soccer for Blockheads* out of my purse and held it up. "She's the one who told me about this."

The whole crowd erupted when they saw it. Even Tom and Joe seemed to forget their disappointment as they showed no restraint in their bursts of laughter and fell back on the ground cackling.

"It really helped," I said defensively.

"That Babs is a fountain of information." Iris tried to pull herself together.

Belle took a paper plate from Iris. "She just happened to mention at one of the games that her assistant had to move to take care of an aging parent. Even though I can't take the training until the spring, the school system hired me, anyway. Do you know Babs was teacher of the year for the whole county a couple of years ago? She really knows what she's doing. I get to read to the children and help them with their writing, and today we made little turkeys out of pinecones and colored feathers to decorate the room for Thanksgiving."

"I didn't know you wanted to be a teacher," Iris commented.

"Always, just never finished my degree. I was a junior when I quit school to marry Harold. I never had a chance to go back. It's too late, now, I guess." Her face hardened a bit.

"So, you maybe have a year and a half of course work. Have you checked to see what it would take to finish?" I asked putting a chip in my mouth.

Belle took a sip of tea. "I didn't see the point."

"Maybe, you should." Iris passed around a pitcher of tea.

"I mean, what do you have to lose?" I asked the question like it was so easy. I knew how she felt, though, as long as you don't try, there's the fortress of not risking failure. As I'd learned with trying to write fiction, starting something new was hard, hard, hard.

Belle appeared doubtful. "Maybe, I will."

"It's about time for the next game," Tom announced as he and Joe got up and headed for the field.

I collected plates and dumped them in a nearby trashcan as Iris gathered the picnic food and placed it back in a cooler.

"What are you folks doing for Thanksgiving?" I asked as we worked.

"We're going to go to my mom's in Lavonia. All my brothers and sisters get together on that day." Iris snapped a lid on the plastic container of stuffed eggs.

"My folks are gone, it'll just be us." Belle brushed grass from her jeans.

I tried to ignore the impulse pushing to the front of my brain, but the impulse had already sent the message to my mouth, as I simultaneously heard my heart say, "Do it afraid."

"Why don't you join me and my children for Thanksgiving?" were the words the impulse created.

"Are you sure?" Belle asked.

"Quite," I replied.

She checked her watch. "Oh my goodness, I have to run. My shift at Mall Market starts in twenty minutes.

"Mall Market?" I asked confused.

"The paraprofessional job didn't pay as much as my other job, so I have to work a second one at Mall Market.

"That sounds hard," I said.

"It's all right. I enjoy it really, and of course, the kids try to help. Becky wants to dance professionally, and all she talks about now is perfecting her triple pirouettes, but she still manages to work at the drug store to pay for her lessons. I don't want her to wind up like me seeing her dream slip away, and I don't have to tell you what a hard worker Joe is."

I turned to see Joe dribble a ball across the field during warm-ups.

Belle smiled and did seem genuinely happier than she was before, but how did she manage with two jobs and two kids?

Speaking of managing, my Thanksgiving guest list had grown significantly.

Five became eight.

Eight!

Forget the turkey breast. We were talking full-fledged gobbler. How many pounds? Morris had always taken care of buying and smoking the turkey. It'd been years since I'd cooked a big bird. I'd have to find one with instructions. I didn't even know if I had a pan big enough, having given away a lot of my cookware when I moved thinking I wouldn't need it for myself and occasional visits from my kids.

Culinary terror threatened.

Cleansing breath.

I could do this.

My children would arrive on Tuesday. That gave me until Monday to solve the pan and turkey problem. I thought how my earlier dreams about the days ahead being more relaxing were ludicrous. I had to get the extra leaf out for the dining room table, and make sure the linens were pressed. I needed more side dishes. I'd better sift the Dinner Bell cookbook to see what I could find.

I was definitely having tomato aspic. It would add a pop of color to the table.

A referee blew his whistle, and I turned to see the game lurch into action.

###

On Monday evening while searching for a turkey, I found Ted milling around in the frozen food aisle of Colonial Store.

"Hello, June. Shopping for Thanksgiving?" he asked closing the door on the Lean Cuisines.

"Have you seen the turkeys?"

"In the end freezer. I didn't look closely. I'll be eating my turkey in an aluminum tray. I usually eat dinner with some of my hiking friends, but they're out of town this year, and The Dinner Bell's closed that day."

I thought Ted should be ashamed for dropping such an obvious hint.

"Would you like to join us for Thanksgiving?"

"I thought you'd never ask," he replied dimples shining.

Nine.

The twenty-pound turkey I bought hardly fit in the refrigerator. I hoped it would thaw by Wednesday. My head spun. I'd never cooked for this many people without help. I hoped my barely adequate cooking skills would see me through this. Do it afraid, again.

###

Tuesday morning before Thanksgiving found me in the backyard gathering pecans to use in a German chocolate pie. I hoped the nut-dropping squirrel was otherwise occupied this morning, but I heard rustling next-door. "Bertha? Jubilee?" I called as I crossed to the fence.

"It's me, Ma'am. I'm over here coverin' up the beds for winter."

I leaned over the fence to see Jubilee scattering pine straw with his good arm. "How are you doing?"

"Pretty fine. I got my cast off which was the Lord's blessin'. Good to get back out in my shop. Made me some fine new yard ornaments."

The irrepressible impulse again. "Jubilee, what are you doing for Thanksgiving?"

"I usually spend it with my daughter, but she's goin' to spend the day with her husband's aunt in Atlanta. The aunt's real sick, and they got to thinkin' they ought to go since it's the last of his folks. I'll be stayin' around home."

"I have a twenty pound turkey in the refrigerator. Several others are coming. We'd love to have you."

"Well, I believe I will Ma'am. When I come, I can tell you about that lady you sent over to my place that's writin' the book. She's real nice—asked a lot of questions and took a good many pictures. I ain't never had nobody so excited about my work before."

"Glad to hear it. We'll be expecting you on Thursday around noon."

Ten.

###

I studied the menu I'd written down as I sat at the kitchen table. Bertha had called to say Melissa was bringing sweet potato casserole and broccoli. Belle was bringing coconut cake and corn. I told Ted not to bring anything, but he insisted on bringing rolls. Said it was the least he could do. Jubilee evidently made fried apple pies from apples he'd dried himself and promised to bring an abundance of them on Thursday.

This was not going to be hard after all. Well, not too hard. Okay, it was going to be hard, but it was something I knew I had to do, kind of the same way I felt about the desk, how I knew I had to track down Silas Braham. Still no idea how, though.

I checked the to-do list lying beside the menu. I had to cook the turkey, make the dressing, the German chocolate pie, and of course the tomato aspic.

Tired already.

Chapter Ten

Thanksgiving

"Give thanks in all circumstances . . ."
—I Thessalonians 5:18

Loud bangs on the front door.

Had to be one of the children, because no child of mine ever remembered to have their house key with them. I opened the door to Linnea who threw her arms around me. "Mom, I've missed you."

I held my second-born close, and then pulled away, and gazed at her. Her naturally curly blond hair hung long and loose as always, but her face seemed slimmer. "You've lost weight. You're not eating right."

"A couple of pounds. Big deal. I've been busy with school, that's all."

"Looks like more than a couple of pounds, but not to worry, based on the menu for Thursday, I think you'll have ample opportunity to gain it back. You won't believe who's coming for Thanksgiving."

Linnea dropped her backpack and suitcase in the hallway and studied the piles of linens and silver on the dining room table.

Skipping over who I was inviting, she asked, "How many?"

"Ten."

She regarded me with obvious skepticism. "Ten? Are you sure? You've never cooked for this many before. Really?"

Good to know I had her vote of confidence. "I know, it sounds like a lot, and my culinary expertise is not exactly out the roof, but it'll be okay." I didn't know who I was trying to convince—her or me.

"What can I do?" she asked.

I held up the turkey directions still in my hand. "Help me understand these instructions. It says to baste every thirty minutes with turkey stock. Where do I get turkey stock? It didn't come with the turkey." Instead of helping me, however, Linnea began meandering around. She'd not had a chance to see what I'd done to the house, as she and Jason hadn't been home since I moved in. When she entered the study, she cried out, "Mom, where did you get this desk?"

I hadn't told my kids about the desk, because, well, I didn't know why. Just seemed like another complication in their already complicated lives. "I don't know if you're ready for this or not, but in the basement."

"The basement?" Linnea's mouth gaped open. "I had a course last semester that covered European furniture of the eighteenth and nineteenth centuries. This looks like a French piece."

"It is a piece made in France." I proceeded to tell her the whole story.

###

Jason arrived early in the evening with much the same fanfare as Linnea—loud banging on the front door. I heard Red's paws hit the hardwood floors upstairs as he bounded from his sleeping spot as if he knew exactly who it was.

I found it no surprise Jason was majoring in wildlife science. Since a toddler he'd been fascinated by animals. His cat Red missed him since he went away having slept with him every night before he left for college. I opened the front door.

"How you doing, Mom?" Jason questioned with a big grin, barely making it inside before he dropped his backpack and duffel bag.

"Better, now that you're finally here." I stepped forward and gave him a big hug.

"I was late leaving, and then I got hung up in traffic. It's good to be home," He moved into the foyer, and as Red skidded toward him,

Jason scooped him up and threw him over his shoulder, stroking his head and back. "Good to see you, boy. Wow, am I tired, and that sofa's calling." He started into the study but stopped a few feet inside and exclaimed, "Where'd you get that desk?"

###

It took all three of us, but by 11:30 on Thanksgiving morning, I thought we had the meal under control. I'd need to turn the oven up to warm the rolls Ted brought, but I at last breathed a sigh of relief.

Cooking made me nervous. An endless array of possible catastrophes presented themselves when I was in the kitchen.

The doorbell rang. I reached over and turned one of the oven dials, and moved to the front door.

Jubilee was the first to arrive with a basket in one hand and a whirligig in the other. I stared at it. It couldn't be. "You like it?" Jubilee asked.

"I, I don't know what to say." I stammered trying to think of a response.

"I worked on it way into the night tryin' to get it right. I hoped you'd be tickled."

'Why, I've never been more tickled over anything in my life. I took in the crinkly hair, the nose with a slight hump on the bridge, the brown eyes. It's me, isn't it, Jubilee?"

"I reckon it is, Ma'am. I studied on it for quite a while. I put a pen in one of your hands and a notepad in the other cause I heard you was a writer. I think it turned out right nice if I do say so myself."

I took the hand with the pen in it, lifted it, and watched it fall loosely at the figure's side. I'd never imagined my likeness would be featured in a yard ornament, but I had to admit the idea was growing on me. Where would I put this? That would take more time for consideration than I had right now.

As if reading my thoughts, Jubilee said, "I believe it'll stand mighty fine in your backyard."

"Thank you, Jubilee. I'm honored."

Jubilee placed the ornament into my hands and bowed slightly. "You're welcome Miz Callaway. Thank you for havin' me over. Where can I put my fried apple pies?"

"On the sideboard in the dining room will be fine. Come in and make yourself at home."

The fragrance of the pies hit me as Jubilee passed by, and an avalanche of childhood memories came back of being at my grandmother's house at apple drying time. Every fall, old screen doors on sawhorses were loaded with apples to dry in the sun.

My grandmother's fried apple pies, the most treasured of delicacies, were kept in a pie safe in the dining area. I knew when I visited in the fall, there'd be a few for my enjoyment along with sweet potato custard pies stacked five or six high.

As Christmas drew near that same pie safe always held my grandmother's unique peppermint cake. That was a taste I hadn't had in years.

Ted, Bertha, Melissa, Belle, Becky, and Joe were shortly behind Jubilee. As they came in, I introduced them all to Linnea and Jason. I took in the scene in my dining room, and was almost moved to tears at the sight of so many sharing their lives with us this Thanksgiving.

Soon, a scent other than Jubilee's apple pies infiltrated my nostrils, an all too familiar smell. The grey mist that always accompanied that odor filled the room.

###

The whole crowd stood in my kitchen staring at the very big, very black bird in my oven. I'd been sure I'd moved the knob to bake, but instead I'd moved it to broil, and I forgot to take the warming turkey out before I switched the knob. We'd opened the doors and windows, but the smell of burned bird hung over us like a shroud.

"I like my meat well done," Jubilee offered.

"Me, too," Bertha graciously interjected. "I can't stand juicy poultry."

My throat tightened. I gave up having perfect dinners long ago, but I was hoping for more than this.

Jason came to my rescue. He opened a drawer in the kitchen, pulled out a carving knife, and held it up. "Mom, I'll see what I can do." Blessedly Morris had passed on his carving skills. "It's such a big turkey, I bet I can cut away the burned parts and still have plenty of meat for all of us."

"Cheer up, June." Ted gently patted my back.

For quite a while, Jason whittled, sliced, shaved, and somehow carved enough turkey off the charred bird, so that each of us would have a taste of it, and we took our places around the dining table.

Jason volunteered to return thanks.

"Lord, thanks for all this great food—even the burnt turkey."

A few giggles around the table. I peeked at him just as he opened his eyes and winked at me.

"We have so much. Help us to remember where it comes from. Thank you for this bunch of new friends that are helping my mama feel at home here. Thanks for Jesus. Amen."

I forgot all about the charred bird. We passed the food and raved about the dishes, and, as predicted, all was fine, even the blackened poultry. When I gathered the plates, I noticed that on all plates except two, tomato aspic remained. Only one other person besides me had finished it. I remembered Joe and Tom's reaction. Did no one in Toccoa like tomato aspic? Why was it in the Dinner Bell Cookbook then? Who else ate the aspic? I certainly couldn't ask.

###

"We have German chocolate pecan pie, coconut cake, and fried apple pies for dessert. What would you folks like?"

"I want everything I'm supposed to have," said Ted.

"Does that mean a little of everything," I asked.

"It sure does," declared Ted.

"Ditto." Joe held up his fork to punctuate his words.

Bertha mimicked Joe with the fork. "And me, too."

Before I could serve dessert, I heard the unmistakable sound of Red bouncing his ball on the stairs in the foyer. When he felt ignored, he'd often drop his ball on the top step and race to retrieve it at the base of the stairs. This must be one of those times.

Melissa looked awestruck. "Would you look at that cat."

"Ain't never seen nothin' like it," Jubilee agreed.

Jason rose from the table to show Red's full capabilities. He bounced the ball and Red jumped four feet into the air to grab it. Next, he threw it down the hallway and Red caught it and brought it back to Jason.

"Acts like a Labrador." Bertha rose from the table trying to get a better view.

"Do you have any videos of him doing that?" Melissa asked also standing.

"We don't, but we've always thought we should film him. I don't think too many cats are able to retrieve like he does." I studied the orange tabby.

"I've bought a brand new digital camcorder. Could I try it out by filming Red?" Melissa offered.

Jason smiled broadly. "Sure."

"Fine," I agreed.

"I'll come over this week," Melissa said.

I asked everybody to move to the study where I served the dessert and coffee. Bertha slowly maneuvered her walker into the room. This was a big surgery to come back from, but if anybody could do it, Bertha could. As she moved by the desk, she stopped and gave it the once over. I could see the question coming. "Where'd you get that desk?"

Knowing Bertha, she'd probably watched the movers unload every piece of furniture I had, so she knew I didn't bring the desk from Atlanta. I hadn't thought of what I'd say if anyone asked about it. I shot a glance at Ted and then at Linnea and Jason. I didn't want anyone else to know I had a museum piece worth hundreds of thousands of dollars. This complicated the matter greatly of finding anyone knowing the Brahams. I'd have people coming from miles around to lay claim to it. I wanted to solve the mystery of the desk quietly. "I, uh, just came upon it."

"Found it in her basement," offered Joe. "When Tom and I told the guys at soccer practice about it, they couldn't believe we found something that nice buried in all that crummy stuff, either."

Oops. I'd forgotten about Joe being there when the desk was found. How many people did they tell?

"That desk was down in that old musty basement? It's a wonder it's still in one piece. I wonder who left it down there—seems to be a pretty fine antique. I guess it'd be hard to find out since there have been so many renters through. Sure glad you bought the place, June. It's nice to have neighbors who plan on sticking around for a change," declared Bertha as she moved on toward a study chair. "Well, if anybody deserves this nice desk, you do. You ought to get a little something for all the work you've done to bring this place back to life."

I exhaled in relief. "Thanks, Bertha." I quickly turned to Jubilee trying to change the subject, "Now, Jubilee, why don't you start at the beginning, and tell us about your visit with my friend Sally who came to see your yard art?"

###

Ted lingered until everyone else was gone and helped me to load the dishwasher. He knew about my desire to keep all things desk related close to the vest. "That was a close call."

I rinsed a mixing bowl and handed it to him. "The turkey or the desk?"

He laughed. "The desk."

"I don't know what I was thinking—inviting everyone over here without considering they'd notice such an extraordinary piece of furniture. It's not like I have anything else even close to it in my house. But I don't suppose any harm was done. I hope Bertha doesn't go home and start thinking about it too much, though."

I rinsed several pieces of cutlery and passed them to Ted who dropped them in the dishwasher tray. "I can't answer any questions, because I don't have any answers. For the time being I want to forget I found the desk. I'll start searching again after Christmas. After all this time, another month won't make a difference. I have other things to think about for now. I want to enjoy my family."

"Sounds like a good plan." He closed the dishwasher door and faced me. "Thanks for inviting me. I know you could see through the pathetic hint I gave you at the Colonial Store. I hate to be alone during the holidays. I was perusing the frozen food entrees dreading Thanksgiving when you happened by."

I put my hand on his arm. "Actually, I was glad I ran into you. One of the hardest things about moving to a new place is when you go to the grocery store, you don't see anyone you know. It's kind of a lonely thing to do. But, there you were almost like you were waiting on me. I can't imagine having to face the loss of a spouse alone during the holidays. I've had Linnea and Jason with me. Plus I owe you, because you've helped me so much where the desk is concerned. At least I know a little about the original owner and how much the desk is worth."

He checked his watch. "I guess I'd better get going." He pivoted towards the hallway, and I followed him to the front door.

"How about dinner next Friday night? We can eat downtown at a little Italian place I like."

"Italian is good." I dreaded the decision of what I'd wear.

"I'll pick you up at 6:30." He started patting his pockets. "Oops, I forgot my cell phone or I'd put it in my calendar right now. I need to get that thing sewed into my coat pocket. Can't ever remember to take it with me. I'll remember, though." Ted gave me a parting smile and shut the door on his way out.

As he opened the door of the Mustang parked on the street, got in, and pulled away, I watched with tugs of conflicting emotions. Why couldn't anything be simple?

Chapter Eleven

Eliza Doolittle, Addie, A Sad Tale, Touching Heaven, and Oh, No

"God does not give us overcoming life;
He gives us life as we overcome."
—Oswald Chambers (1874-1917)

Jed stood on my front porch extending a magnificent wreath toward me.

"How wonderful." I inhaled the poignant spruce as I took it from him.

"It's our little way of sayin' thank you," Jed beamed. "We want our customers to know we appreciate them."

I inspected the evergreen wreath—perfect for my front door.

"Just went up to North Carolina and brought back a load of trees. You won't find none fresher. Come by my place, take a gander, and we'll make you a good price. I'm headin' over there in just a minute."

"I will, and thanks for the wreath," I said.

As I shut the door, Jason traipsed down the stairs. "Who was that?'

"We're going to get a Christmas tree."

###

"Is these your young'uns?" Jed asked pointing to Jason and Linnea.

"They are, and I'm awfully glad to have them home. Jason, Linnea, this is Jed Turner."

After the introductions Jed said, "Y'all have a look around. When you find yourselves a nice tree, call me, and I'll come trim it up for you."

I turned around and Linnea had vanished. Jason and I navigated past the first row of trees, and I noticed her slipping behind a magnificent Alberta Spruce. When we finally caught up with her, she was staring at a shorter tree, which leaned decidedly to the left. It had a big hole on one side, and the top had a crook in it as if it couldn't decide which way to grow.

"This is it," she declared.

Jason and I exchanged glances.

How could we have forgotten that taking Linnea to pick out a Christmas tree means bringing home the ugliest tree on the lot. Linnea felt sorry for trees as if they were mangy puppies and wanted to buy the one she thought nobody else would take. She wandered Christmas tree lots scouting out Eliza Doolittles she could transform.

"Don't you want to shop around a bit more," I offered lamely, knowing it was futile to fight her on these things.

"No, this is definitely the one." She appeared firm in her conviction.

"I'll get Jed." Jason shuffled off with resignation.

In a moment when they returned, Jed's eyes widened as he took in the tree. "Ma'am, surely you don't want this here tree. I can't even tell you how it got on my truck. Must've been a mistake. This tree's got problems."

He pointed to the base. "Look here, if I take off these branches so you can get it in a tree stand, you're gonna have a tree that's almost bare of limbs on one side. That ain't even takin' into account the crooked top, and it leanin' to the left."

"This is the one we want, Jed. Do the best you can." I sighed and turned back to the car to get my checkbook.

"Well, I can't charge you full price," he called after me sounding disappointed.

Later, when we reached home and set the tree in a stand, it appeared as if it had weathered a hurricane with its missing branches, and limbs grown at a strange angle because of the leaning center trunk. Still, it had its own appeal in a homely sort of way.

Linnea opened a box and handed me a small replica of a riverboat—an ornament we'd picked up in New Orleans.

I found since Morris' death that hanging the ornaments was a bittersweet experience. Everywhere we traveled, we'd bought an ornament to remind us of our trips—Yellowstone Park, the St. Louis Arch, Louisa Mae Alcott's house in Concord, Massachusetts, Paul Revere's house in Boston. This part of Christmas was like re-visiting our travels and opening the door to all the memories with Morris. I hung the riverboat on the tree. If it weren't for Jason and Linnea, I didn't know how I'd manage to stay afloat.

We worked into the evening until the tree lights shimmered in a hazy glow and ornaments hung from every bough.

We stood back to get the whole effect. We had to tilt our heads slightly to the left, but it did seem the leaning, crooked, holey tree had been transformed into a conifer of beauty. Yes, Eliza Doolittle had become a fair lady.

"Mom, isn't it beautiful?" Linnea asked her eyes shining.

I caught an eye roll from Jason.

"Have you ever seen a Christmas tree you didn't think was beautiful?' he asked.

###

On Sunday afternoon, Jason and Linnea both prepared to return to school. Somehow, I fought back the tears as the old fear and lonely grief threatened to seep back in. Was it C.S. Lewis that talked about how similar deep sorrow felt to anxiety?

"Mom, we love you." Linnea wrapped her arms around me. "You're going to be fine."

I found myself wondering exactly when my daughter started sounding so motherly.

"Yeah, mom. We'll call you," Jason said.

How I hated good-byes. I kissed both of them, and handed them the baskets of food I'd packed for them to take back to school—sans the blackened turkey. And the tomato aspic.

###

"What happened to your Christmas tree?" Ted asked when he came to pick me up for dinner Friday night. "Did Red try to climb it?"

"No, Red did not try to climb it. We bought it that way." I'd found through the years, that others had trouble understanding why our trees always appeared as if we'd pulled them from a roadside leaf and limb collection pile.

"You bought a crooked tree on purpose?" Ted appeared unbelieving.

"Yes, we bought it that way on purpose. Linnea goes for the ugly trees because they appear forgotten. We've always had weird looking Christmas trees."

Ted glanced back over at the tree, squinted a moment as if trying to picture it a bit differently and shrugged. He gave me that smile of his. "Ready?"

"Ready." He helped me with my wrap. I'd been close to wearing my bathrobe again when I remembered I had a red blouse I wore at Christmas that'd be perfect with my black pants. The wool shawl I'd bought on a trip to New York worked nicely with the blouse. This dating stuff required too much thought.

###

Downtown Toccoa glowed with thousands of twinkling lights strung from one end of Main Street to the other. City workers had logged overtime hours weaving lights around lampposts, creating a winter wonderland for downtown evening visitors. Being just such visitors, after parking our car, we leisurely strolled the street enjoying the night air, which had just enough chill in it to make us glad we'd dressed warmly.

Store windows bright with Christmas displays included two at the Franklin department store, which featured hundreds of dolls wearing elaborate hand sewn garments. The dresses for these dolls, made by the women of Toccoa, (as well as a couple of men whose names I spotted among the creators) were judged for the best dressed awards, and then distributed through The Salvation Army to needy families. I stood for a few minutes mesmerized by the intricacy of the lovingly sewn garments. Among my favorites were a red wool coat and hat with a fur muff, a pink party dress with a tulle skirt trimmed with gold sequins, and a purple velveteen dress. Each dressmaker's name was displayed beside their doll along with their award. I read Grace McCurley, Most Elaborate; Nell Dooley, Best Over-All. I caught my breath as I read the name under the purple dress: Addie Braham, Neatest Stitching.

###

I slumped into the booth at Sherrino's. "Ted, I checked the phone book. No Brahams were listed in the Toccoa phone book or in any of the communities around here. I searched the Internet for Brahams, and called the few who came up. They were all dead ends. How can this be? Where does she live?"

"June, I don't know, but when the store opens in the morning, I think you should call and see if they can tell you how to get in touch with Addie Braham. Surely, they have to have entry blanks filled out with each doll." Ted settled back in his seat.

The waitress brought our water. I sighed, rested against the back of my own chair, and took in the surroundings of Sherrino's restaurant that I'd previously been too pre-occupied to even notice. The scents of Italian spices, fresh baked bread, and coffee floated in the air. Original paintings graced the walls, some oil, some watercolor, but all of Toccoa landmarks and vistas. The old Prather's Bridge that used to stand outside of town, the higher-than-Niagara Toccoa Falls, landscapes of the local countryside, and of course, Currahee Mountain, were all represented. The candles on the table glimmered in the evening light, and the urgency of the desk faded as my anxiety level lowered. My eyes met Ted's. He gazed at me with such intensity, I almost felt uncomfortable.

"What is it?" I asked.

"Nothing." He diverted his eyes.

But the tugs inside me declared there was definitely something.

###

I gathered all my courage and entered the gathering room of the Mountain Gardens Assisted Care Facility. I had no idea what I was about to get into. As I came through the door, in the corner of my eye, I glimpsed a cat jumping off a chair and what might have been a dog tail disappear in one of the doors in the hallway ahead. I went to the information window and asked for Addie Braham.

The young woman scanned the gathering room behind me. "Yes, Miss Braham. She's usually not in her room. She likes to sit out front here in the gathering room." The receptionist pointed to an elderly woman with a cat in her lap seated by a large bank of windows. "There she is."

As I approached the woman the receptionist had directed me to, I noticed she had an almost queenly air, as if she were used to presiding over something or someone. I had the urge to curtsy when I drew near her.

"Miss Braham?"

"Yes, I'm Addie Braham."

"You can't imagine what a joy it is for me to meet you."

She nodded her head of lovely grey hair twirled into a bun. "Pleased to meet you, too. Who are you?"

"Oh, sorry. My name's June Callaway and I've been trying to contact someone in your family for quite a while. I found you through the lovely dress you made for the doll contest."

"The doll dress? Oh, yes. I sure did enjoy making it. Why don't you have a seat?" She gestured toward a dark red chair beside her, and I situated myself in it.

Addie continued. "I hadn't sewn in a long time, but when they put the notice up on the bulletin board about the contest I remembered the scraps I had in my sewing basket and decided I'd try it. I had it in my mind to make that dress like one my mama made for me when I was a little girl."

"I loved it. It was one of my favorites, so that's why I noticed your name. I scanned the phone book for Braham's, but none were listed."

"No need to have a phone. No one to call. When you're as old as I am, you've outlived everybody you ever knew. It's just Misty and me now." She stroked the cat in her lap.

I reached over to pet the grey cat, too, and asked tentatively, "Did you ever know Silas Braham?"

Addie's faced brightened with surprised. "Lord, yes. He's my nephew."

I stopped petting Misty. The ages of these two people didn't compute in my mind. Not another dead end. "Oh, I'm sorry. The man I'm hunting for would've been your age or older than you."

Addie laughed. "That's right. I was born an aunt. Mama was forty-four years old when she had me, and there was twenty-four years between me and my oldest sibling. I had brothers and sisters with kids older than me when I was born. People had children young in those days. I used to get such a kick out of telling my schoolmates that big old Silas and his brother Buford were my nephews. They were always at least a foot taller than me."

"So you did know Silas?"

"Know him? Why, we were inseparable growing up. I was pretty adventurous when I was young, and I loved to tag along with Silas and Buford. We walked to school together, and after we finished our chores, we set out for the woods to see what we could find. Sometimes, we'd go fishing. Those were fine times—makes me smile to think about them."

I knew I had to ask the next question though I was sure that the answer could dredge up things maybe best forgotten. "Addie, what happened to Silas and Buford?"

Misty looked up and mewed. Addie's eyes grew distant.

"Silas joined up with the army when the war started. He was one of the men who made the jump behind enemy lines on D-Day, an army paratrooper."

"I've seen the marker on the courthouse lawn. He was sure brave."

"I've always been mighty proud of him. Silas once wrote to me about that day in 1944. Said he was scared."

"Understandable." I watched as Misty jumped from Addie's lap.

"I don't think being brave has anything to do with not being scared. Being brave is going ahead and doing a thing even when you're scared out of your mind. That's what Silas did. My brave nephew helped liberate a country and stop a madman. He's a real hero, don't you know?"

I nodded and braced myself for what Addie might say next, hoping against painful memories.

Addie paused as the front door opened and a couple came in and went to the information desk.

She caught her breath and went on. "He met a girl in England when he was stationed there—a French girl sent there by her parents to escape any possible occupation. Of course, the Germans did occupy France, and she wasn't able to get back for a long time."

A French girl. Maybe he'd lived in France all these years.

Addie paused again. "Her name was Anne Marie. How Silas loved that girl. They married, and she was going to meet him in the states after she made contact with her parents. She found her family, and they wrote each other during that time. Silas had much on his mind after the war, I guess from all the horrible things he saw while he was over there. His one joy was knowing Anne Marie was coming."

"So, he's lived here since the war?"

Addie shook her head.

What a winding story.

Addie paused another moment, and I knew sadness was coming. Misty jumped back into her lap and gazed up at Addie in an almost compassionate way. Addie stroked her, sighed, and continued.

"Finally, the day came. He went out to meet the ship and found out," Addie paused and tears came to her eyes, "Anne Marie died on the way over. They never knew exactly what happened." Addie wiped her eyes with a lace-trimmed handkerchief she took from her pocket.

I touched Addie's arm. "I'm sorry to have stirred up all of this. I only wanted to find Silas." I remembered the sense of impending difficulty I'd had earlier. This was exactly what I'd dreaded would happen.

Addie shook her head. "You didn't stir it up." Her eyes turned toward the window. She seemed to draw up her courage. "Now, let me tell you the rest, or at least the rest of the story that I know. Anne Marie brought her dowry from France—personal belongings, a piece of family furniture. Silas was so devastated; he couldn't even look at what she'd brought. Buford came, took her belongings, and stored them. I know several times Buford tried to get them back to Silas, but he said he never wanted to see them again. As I remember, Buford told me she brought a lovely desk with her. Buford even wrote the family in France to see if they wanted her things back, but he never heard from them. Anyway, Silas was so broken hearted he enlisted for another tour of duty, and then another. Became a career military man. I guess he never did meet anyone to compare with that French girl."

Addie grew silent, and I saw the grief in her eyes when she spoke again. "Silas has been lost to us for many years now. Buford told me he'd heard Silas had moved to England to be near the place where he first met Anne Marie. It seems after she died, Silas closed the door to a future with anyone else, and he closed his life off to us as well. I imagine he's gone now." Addie wiped her eyes again.

Addie's sense of loss resonated deeply in me. "I'm so sorry. I know you miss Silas."

"Miss him?" Addie cleared her throat. "There's hardly a day goes by that I don't think about those wonderful times we spent together in Toccoa. It broke my heart for Silas that he didn't get to spend his life with Anne Marie. He was such a kind man and would've done anything for her. It was tragic."

I searched for a bit of good news. "What about Buford, is he still living?"

"He passed. Buford moved to California after the war. Strange, how we all scattered to the four winds after being so close when we were growing up. I visited him once when he lived in San Diego. He married a girl from out there and had a pretty little daughter named Doris. Buford died in 1973, and I've lost touch with the family. Doris married a man named Robert, but I don't remember his last name, and I don't know where they moved to after she left home."

It seemed all roads concerning this desk led to dead ends. I sighed and studied the woman in front of me. So much sorrow, yet about her still hung that queenly air. "Addie, what about you. Would you tell me your story?"

"There's not much to tell. I taught school for forty-three years in the state of Virginia."

Her stately presence must have come from years of presiding over a classroom.

"I went to the University of Virginia, and while there, my parents died. I didn't know what to do. There was nothing for me to come home to. Several of my friends were staying in the area after they graduated, so I decided to stay on, too."

The front door opened and closed again as an elderly man with a cane entered and strode down the hall as purposefully as one could who used a cane. Somehow, he managed to hold a small bouquet of flowers in one hand. Addie smiled. "I had suitors, but none of them seemed to be the one for me. Since I never married, my students became my family. I stayed in touch with many of them, but a few years ago I started wanting to come home."

She turned to the window, where the foothills of the Blue Ridge rolled out in front of us, their signature color evident even through the mist that hung over them this morning. "When the doctor told me I would have to find an assisted living facility, I made up my mind I was coming back to Toccoa to spend the last years of my life."

Addie turned and steadied her gaze directly at me. "I'm glad I came. I don't have family here anymore, but still, it's home. I have this beautiful room to spend time in." She pointed toward the window. "And just a glimpse of the mountain."

Through the window, the evergreen peak of Currahee rose majestically above the tree line in the distance.

"I get mail now and then from my students. Of course, I have my friend Misty here." Addie rubbed Misty's head and studied me a moment. "Now, I'd like to ask you a question. Why are you so curious about my family?"

###

"What is the address of the house you live in?" Addie asked later.

"5210 Tugalo."

"I can't seem to think of any reason the desk would wind up there. I wish I could be of more help. If I could just remember the name of the man Doris married or where they might have moved. If you're trying to find a beneficiary, that's the direction the desk needs to go. If you'll give me time to think, maybe something will jog my memory. Will you come back and visit?"

I didn't even hesitate to answer. "What about next week? Is there anything I can bring you?"

"Anytime is fine with me, and no, I don't need a thing, but I'm going to ask Jesus to help me remember."

"I see they allow pets in this facility. Did I see a dog a few minutes ago?"

"Yes, that's been one of the big blessings here. I was able to keep my cat Misty. The dog actually is facility owned, but he visits with everyone. We even have a pot bellied pig that makes me laugh every time I see it."

"A pot bellied pig makes me laugh, too." Just before I left, I leaned over, gave Addie a hug, and Misty a pat on the head. Though heavy in my heart with the information I'd learned, still, maybe this dead end had an upside.

###

The Christmas Musical Celebration at Emmanuel Church was only a week away, and I struggled. Singing alto was not as easy as I remembered it being in high school. I didn't know if I made any discernible contribution to the sound of the choir, but I had fun trying. The choir was having a dress rehearsal tonight in the sanctuary. I took my place next to Debbie.

"Are you ok?" Debbie asked seeing my hands shaking.

"A little nervous." I wasn't very coordinated, and I'd given considerable thought to how I was going to balance my music, keep my reading glasses on my nose, sing, and smile all at the same time.

"You'll be fine." Debbie patted my arm.

Laura brought everyone to attention. "Tonight we have a special guest who's rehearsing with us. He's singing a duet with Rhonda Kay. Please welcome Joseph Mitchell." Everyone clapped as a young man in his late teens or early twenties stood. "We're going to let Joseph and Rhonda Kay sing their duet first, so as not to hold Joseph here longer than necessary."

The two stood, and the pianist began to play the introduction to a piece I'd heard on one of my favorite classical music CDs. Very ambitious, I thought, especially with the Italian lyrics.

Rhonda Kay began in English, and then Joseph echoed her in Italian. As their voices soared and intertwined, it was exquisite, and I would've paid any asking price to hear these two sing. I couldn't believe I was able to hear them just because I volunteered to sing in the church choir. I along with others around me scrambled for tissues.

When Joseph and Rhonda Kay finished, the place went silent for a few seconds. But in a moment, everyone in the choir stood, and clapped. When Rhonda Kay turned around, her eyes were glassy, too. Somehow, that evening the doors to heaven seemed to crack open a bit.

"Ah, cut it out." Rhonda Kay waved her hand. We all laughed, wiped our eyes, and opened our music.

###

I'd left my Christmas tree lights burning while at choir rehearsal, and when I came home, their cheery glow greeted me through the window, though the ambience of the lights could not add anything to the warmth I already felt in my heart.

I fumbled for my house key on the front steps and put it in the antiquated lock. I'd meant to change the locks after I moved in, but I hated to give them up as they appeared original to the house. Besides, Toccoa was such a small town compared to Atlanta. Still, I had no way of knowing how many keys were floating around with all the renters there'd been through the years.

When I stepped in the house, I had the odd sense something was wrong. I flipped the light on in the foyer and then turned to walk into the study to put my choir music on the desk.

The desk was gone.

Chapter Twelve

Fog

"God moves in a mysterious way His wonders to perform.
He plants His footsteps in the sea, and rides upon the storm."
—William Cowper (1731-1800)

I awoke to the sound of rain coursing through the downspouts. Still dark outside, I rolled out of bed, grabbed my robe, and went downstairs to turn on the coffee pot. A small amount of light came through the bay window in the kitchen, but it was still nothing like daylight. Haze hung just above the treetops and shrouded my whole world this morning. I wondered if the mountain itself might be completely obscured from view by fog, as if it had never existed.

I poured myself a cup of coffee, and slumped in a kitchen chair to sip its consoling warmth. The police were in and out of the house for nearly two hours before they had everything they needed the evening before.

"Why in the world would anyone steal a desk and leave the computer, television and even the Christmas presents? That don't make a lick of sense." Police Detective William Rust had said. He peered at me curiously.

How should I know? How could someone else find out about the desk's worth? I'd only told Ted and my children. Of course, there was Robert Giles, but Ted assured me he had an outstanding reputation as an appraiser, in fact he was nationally known.

Detective Rust went on."There ain't no sign of forced entry. That means whoever did this had a key."

My concerns about multiple keys floating around were valid. Someone did have a key and last night, they used it. I felt a sense of violation. A person I didn't know had touched my things, had been in my house.

"What's the value of the desk?" Detective Rust asked with a pen poised in his hand above a notepad.

"I've been told it's quite valuable but I don't have an official estimate, and it's not insured as an antique. I imagine the most I'll get on my insurance is five hundred dollars." I regretted not paying the money to get an official estimate on the desk, so I could have it insured. I kept thinking I'd find the heir and let them take care of it.

"What did you pay for the desk?" he asked.

"I didn't pay anything. I found it in my basement when I moved in."

"Found it in your basement?" He clicked the pen and then wrote something. "We'll go with five hundred dollars as the value."

Detective Rust surveyed the study around him. "That about wraps it up. You gonna be all right, Miz Callaway?"

All right? I didn't know if I would be or not. I thought when I moved to Toccoa, I would somehow escape the kinds of things that happened routinely in the big city I left behind, and here I was dealing with a break-in less than six months after moving in.

"There ain't much else going on tonight. I could have an officer cruise by during the night."

"That'd be fine," I said grateful.

He called to an officer standing near. "Cletus, why don't you ride by Miz Callaway's house about every hour tonight?"

That name was familiar. "Are you the Cletus that's married to Rhonda Kay?" I asked.

"One and the same," he responded as he took a step toward me.

"We sing together in the choir. She's such a joy."

"They surely did break the mold when they made her." Cletus replied smiling. "Don't you worry, Miz Callaway. We're gonna be looking after you tonight."

"Thank you," I had responded my voice quavering a bit.

The locksmith was coming this afternoon. I knew I should've had him here earlier.

I emptied the dark roasted brew from my cup, thankful this was the first morning I was to volunteer at the public library. I'd signed up to be on the library guild the night Ted and I had gone to the Library Benefit.

The thought of staying at home alone on this grey day with all this desk business in my mind was not appealing. So, I went upstairs, dressed, and grabbed my umbrella as I headed out the door.

Set in the downtown area, the mid-century modern architecture of the library provided a foil to the nineteenth century buildings around it and contributed to the winsome eclectic appeal of Toccoa.

I introduced myself to the head librarian, Cynthia Green and her assistant, Carolyn Appleby. I'd volunteered for many years at the library in the suburb where I lived in Atlanta, but every library had its own way of doing things, so Carolyn covered the checkout procedure, their method of preparing magazines for the shelf, and the layout of the library.

With Carolyn's careful explanations, I felt confident to face the job, and set out to do what all volunteers do—I shelved books. The Dewey Decimal System and I were long time friends. In my very first assignment of shelving fiction F through He, I was holding a couple of Nan Heron's books in my hand, when I couldn't help but overhear a whispered conversation coming from the seating area to the right. I tried to tune it out and concentrate on my work, but I couldn't.

"This is a terrible situation. I feel like I'm being pulled from pillar to post. My head is swimming tryin' to figure out what to do. I've done lost sleep three nights in a row. I almost fell asleep at the wheel drivin' over here."

"Well, we don't know certain it's happenin'," another voice said.

"I heard somebody say on one of my soap operas yesterday that denial's not a river in Egypt. That big truck's been over there a lot."

"Yeah, but our own kin. How can we call the police on our kin?"

Obviously, they didn't know I could hear them as I was obscured by a row of magazine racks. Frozen in place, I didn't know what to do. Over the top of the books, I spied a woman with a copy of

Country Gal magazine get up and put it back on the rack. As I peeped through the books, another woman joined her. They went to the circulation desk, checked out a stack of children's books, and then exited.

After they left, I slid over to the circulation desk, and while I pulled more returned books from the drop box, I scanned the name on the computer screen left from the last books checked out—the patron's name was Gladys Pickens.

###

When my shift was over, I checked the library volunteer schedule for the next week, told Cynthia and Carolyn good-bye, picked up my umbrella and headed to the car.

Who knew that while shelving the He's, I would became privy to suspicions about someone I'd never met. When they mentioned the truck I wondered if they could've been talking about a theft ring? Might even have to do with my desk. Life in Toccoa seemed to be taking a definite sinister turn. I needed to talk to Ted.

###

Just as I began to understand a few basics about soccer, the season was over. I placed *Soccer for Blockheads* on my bookshelf in the study confident I'd need it again.

My cell phone rang, and I plucked it from my pocket. "I heard about the desk theft. I'm so sorry." I recognized Iris' voice.

"I am, too."

Iris continued, " Tom and Joe are playing basketball now. Could you possibly take them to the game this Friday? Belle's busy, and Sam and I have to make a trip to Atlanta on Friday evening and won't be back until late. Peter will be with us."

Thankfully, I had a bit more understanding where basketball was concerned. "I'll be glad to." I sat in the dining room chair I'd pulled into the study, but with the desk gone, I guessed I'd move it back to the dining room.

Since I needed advice concerning my unfortunate experience at the library, I hatched a plan, and made a call. No answer. Probably forgot his cell phone again, so I called the law firm and asked for Ted Moore.

"Ted, Iris asked me to take Tom and Joe to their basketball game this Friday. Would you like to come along and help cheer them on?"

"I have a meeting that lasts until around six, but I think it'll be over in time. Maybe we could take the boys and go to Sherrino's for pizza afterwards. I want to talk more about your desk theft, as well. Any news?"

"Not yet." And maybe not ever, I thought.

"Sure must've been scary."

"It was, but Detective Rust has an officer cruising by regularly." A small town benefit that definitely wouldn't have happened in the big city. "By the way, I called your cell, and you didn't answer."

"Forgot it again," he said.

So much for living in the twenty-first century.

###

After finding the old Toccoa High School cheerleader's megaphone in my basement, I was surprised to learn from Bertha that the school no longer existed. Evidently, back in the seventies, the city and county schools had combined to form the Stephens County High School. This weekend, Tom and Joe would be playing for the Stephens County basketball team as they took on one of their archrivals, Baxter County.

Ted and I dropped off the boys, parked, and then headed inside ourselves. As we entered the gym, the all too familiar gym smell of leather balls, stale popcorn, and sweat greeted us. Jason had played rec basketball every year until he entered high school when he decided to play football exclusively. I knew my way around a gym after having warmed many a metal bleacher seat.

Ted and I took a seat on the home side, and watched the warm-up. In no time, the buzzer sounded, and the game burst into a furious pace with both teams vying closely for the lead. The beginning of half time found Baxter edging ahead with an eight-point advantage and exhausted players from both sides fleeing to the locker rooms.

"I think I'll get some popcorn." Ted looked in the direction of the concession stand. "Would you like some?"

I declined. While he was gone, the Stephens County High School pep band played a rousing rendition of "Hey, Baby," which I greatly enjoyed.

When Ted returned, I thought it might be a good time to talk to him about the stolen desk, my conversation with Addie, and my day at the library. I'd only spoken with him a few minutes the night the desk was stolen, but we didn't have much time with the police needing me to help with the investigation.

He offered me popcorn, and I shook my head. He crammed a handful into his mouth and crunched.

"Just when I thought I was getting somewhere by finding Addie, the desk disappears. There hardly seems any point now in pursuing the ownership of the desk with it missing and Addie not knowing anything." I did enjoy talking with Addie, though.

Ted swallowed and his eyes filled with concern. "I'm sure sorry about the desk being taken. Are you sure you feel safe?"

"I'm okay. Rhonda Kay's husband, Cletus, is the one Detective Rust has looking out for me. But I still feel violated."

"Understandable." Ted shook his head. "The story of the desk is sure a sad one." He smiled that engaging smile of his. "But maybe something good will come of it, yet." Ted seemed to be good at finding the positive.

I filled him in on what I overheard at the library." What do you think?"

He slid his hand into the popcorn sack to ferret out the last of its contents. "About?"

"About all that suspicious talk. It might have to do with the desk."

"Just talk. Might have nothing to do with it." He turned to me and gave me a bit of a long-suffering look, like this line of discussion was beneath his pay grade. He put the last of the popcorn in his mouth, chomped a few times, swallowed, and then flashed that melting smile again just as players streamed back onto the court. After a few minutes of warm up, the buzzer sounded, and the action ramped up again in the third quarter, with Baxter holding on to their lead.

At the beginning of the fourth quarter, Joe went up for a rebound, grabbed the ball, dribbled outside the lane, turned, and sank a three pointer. The crowd roared.

A Baxter player fouled one of Tom and Joe's teammates, and for that offense, after the free throws, the gap narrowed to 3 points.

For the next few minutes, we watched one of the most intense games of basketball I'd ever seen. Ted and I along with everyone else in the stands screamed and cheered until I felt a bit hoarse. With the home team one point behind, Tom grabbed the rebound after a missed Baxter shot. He took it down the court, and waited for Joe to get open under the basket. He passed it to Joe with 10 seconds left on the clock. Joe went up, shot and . . . it was good. Baxter inbounded, and took a wild shot at their basket, but it was too late. The buzzer sounded.

Stephens County won by one point.

The crowd went wild as the players jumped up and down in celebration. Ted and I clapped, shouted, and joined in the spirit of the whole event. Before we knew it, we'd put our arms around each other, and hugged.

What was I doing? The tugs within threatened to split me in two pieces. I pulled away, and dared to meet Ted's eyes. It seemed he knew what I was thinking.

"June, it's okay. It's okay."

I fought back tears and turned to gather my things.

Okay? I didn't know when anything would actually be okay, again. I gulped air and tried to keep my head above water.

###

All of Toccoa was at Sherrino's, apparently not caring how long they had to wait to be seated or to receive their orders. Most of the would-be diners seemed to spend their time rehearsing the game and celebrating the victory.

My sense of jubilation from earlier had evaporated a bit, and I found it challenging to be in the company of so many revelers. For the boys' sake, I tried to conceal my struggle.

Joe had gotten an elbow to the eye during the game and was beginning to swell considerably, but he seemed unconcerned. I had the waiter bring him a baggie of ice to hold on the injury. In his excitement, he only managed to keep it on for about thirty seconds.

"I know your mom would've loved to see you get that winning basket, Joe." I tried placing the ice back on his eye.

"She's trying to work to make up for the difference she was paid at the clock factory. We don't get to see her much." Joe winced as I applied a small amount of pressure.

"She didn't feel well this morning and said she was getting a cold. Didn't look so hot, either."

I wondered how long Belle could keep up the pace of two jobs. I wished I could do something to help.

###

As we strolled back to the car after dinner, I noticed a big sign in one of the windows of the Franklin Department store, "Follow the Footprints of Santa."

Beside the sign, on the floor of the entryway, were two huge red footprints that were the first of a many I could see through glass doors. The tracks continued in a straight line and around a corner out of sight. Something about that sight resonated with the child in me, and I found myself wanting to take off after those stenciled shapes. If the store hadn't been closed, I would have.

Maybe later.

As I lay in bed that night, my thoughts kept returning to the embrace Ted and I had found ourselves in. Scary. Strange.

For some reason, my thoughts then shifted to something Addie mentioned—that Silas closed the door on his future with anyone else because of his broken heart.

How sad.

Chapter Thirteen

Praying About It

"The peace of God in a man's heart does more
to hold him steady than anything else can do."
—R.G. Letourneau (1888-1969)

I balanced the pink poinsettia in my left hand, as I pulled open the door to the Mountain Gardens Assisted Care Facility with my right hand. It was such a large plant, I could hardly see over it as I came through the door. I looked around for Addie, but not seeing her, I stopped at the information desk and asked where she might be.

The receptionist checked the clock on the wall. "They're having art activities right now." She pointed down the corridor. "Walk that way, and turn left at the dining hall."

I followed the instructions, and found myself peering through the windows of a large room where residents of the facility worked on ceramic pieces at three large tables. The room also held birdcages, gigantic plants, and at least two dogs. I spotted Addie, meticulously painting a ceramic plate. Surprised at how well she controlled the brush, I slipped through the door and stood behind her.

I shifted the plant obscuring my vision, and studied the plate with a floral design. "Beautiful. They're dogwoods aren't they?"

She rotated in her chair. "Why there you are. I knew you'd be back." She returned to her work. "The Dogwood blossom is my favorite flower. I always think of Toccoa when I see them." She pivoted back to me and pointed, "What's that shrub in your hand?"

I pulled a branch down, and peeked through the leaves. "I didn't quite understand how big it was until I started to carry it out of the store. I hope you have space for it."

"No worries about space. We'll put it in the gathering room, so everyone can enjoy it. That's where I spend most of my time anyway. What a lovely color." Her eyes sparkled with interest.

I inspected the plant in my hand with the unusual pink, slightly variegated leaves. "The folks at the florist called this variety 'Pink Peppermint.' I thought you might enjoy something a little different."

"I'm partial to pink." Addie regarded her creative endeavor again. "I can work on this later. Let me give you a tour of the place." She handed her brush to one of the staff and reached for her cane resting on the table next to her.

###

"I'm sorry I haven't been able to think of anything to help you find Silas' heirs this week," Addie said as we neared the gathering room after the tour. We had seen her room, the dining hall, and a lovely garden where the residents grew roses and vegetables in the spring and summer. I placed the poinsettia beside a green chair near the front door, and we took seats.

"I rummaged through a few old letters to see if anything might jog my memory, but so far I've drawn a blank." Misty leaped into her lap as soon as she was seated.

I leaned over and stroked the cat's head lamenting the loss of the desk. "It may be a mute point because the desk was stolen out of my house last week."

"Stolen? How unthinkable!"

"It's a puzzle. Whoever it was had a key, because there was no sign of forced entry. Maybe one of the former renters. I don't know."

It was strange. The desk had been in the house who knows how long with people passing in and out, but no one took the time to clean up the basement and find it. If the person who stole it was a former renter, it had been under their nose the whole time they lived in the house.

"You're the only one that wasn't too lazy to tackle that bad job." Addie's ire seemed to rise. "I'll be talking to the Almighty about this. If you don't want the desk, it ought to go to Buford's descendents. It's not right someone else should have it." She struck the floor with her cane for emphasis.

"I agree." I could definitely see the teacher in her emerge.

Addie glanced toward the wall. "What time does that clock say?" she asked.

"5:30," I answered.

"How would you like to eat with me tonight? We're having salmon croquettes. You won't have to go home and make supper," Addie asked persuasively.

I only had to think for a minute. "I'd love to." I remembered one of my aunts used to prepare them.

"You're about to have the best I've ever tasted except for my mama's. Buford and Silas used to manage to get an invitation to stay for dinner when we were having salmon croquettes. They loved them."

On our way to the dining hall, Addie turned to me, "I've told you all about my life, now I want to hear about yours."

I took a deep breath, and began.

###

When I returned home from Mountain Gardens that evening, I found a message on the answering machine from Detective Rust.

I pressed play. "Afternoon, Mrs. Callaway. We didn't find one fingerprint at your place from the burglary—must've used gloves. Pretty slick. Don't seem like any of the neighbors saw anything either. We'll put the word out for antique dealers to be on the watch for your desk, but I can't imagine anyone trying to sell it around here—that'd be way too risky. I'll call if we hear anything. Don't you worry none. Cletus will be cruising by again tonight."

###

Laura Goodhay took her place behind the director's stand and leaned forward. "I want to thank everyone for the superb job you did last Sunday night. I've had nothing but glowing comments about the music. All of you must know what an incredible ministry you have here at Emmanuel. Thank you for the time you give."

Rhonda Kay stood, "Laura, I ain't much on speeches but we can't thank you enough for puttin' up with us all this time. Why, if it weren't for you, I'd have never known I could sing worth a toot. I know there's more folks besides me that feels the way I do. You're about the best thing that's happened to this choir."

Rhonda Kay pulled a package from underneath her chair and handed it to Laura. She opened it to find a framed portrait of the choir during their Christmas presentation with notes of gratitude to her written on the mat by each one of our choir members.

"Thank you all." Laura wiped a tear from her cheek.

Chapter Fourteen

Memories

"Happy, happy Christmas, that can . . . recall to the
old man the pleasures of his youth, and transport the
traveler back to his own fireside and quiet home!"
—Charles Dickens (1812-1870)

Trying to get the stolen desk out of my mind, I went back to follow the footprints of Santa at Franklin's Department Store and found they led in a circuitous route similar to one I'd seen Billy in the *Family Circus* cartoon take.

The store had grown larger through the years by taking over spaces vacated by other establishments. The Franklins simply knocked out walls and added steps to join the spaces. The footprints tracked through many of these additions, up and down steps, around and around. I couldn't help but form an analogy to the twists and turns my life had seen in recent years—a roller coaster of unforeseen developments.

I stopped a couple of times to pretend I was shopping for something so as not to give away that as an adult, I was indeed following the footprints of Santa. I paused once to examine a wool scarf in a deep purple which I really did like and once to study a stack of turkey roasters in which I had zero interest, but they were the only things near when I detected a sales person peering at me with curiosity. Finally, after the clerk returned to straightening a stack of dish towels, I resumed my journey and followed the stenciled shapes down a long flight of stairs to a basement full of toys—set up as Santa's workshop.

A sign hung by an elaborate chair indicated that Santa was out and would be back at three o'clock. I surveyed tables brimming with dolls, remote control cars, dollhouses, action figures, and other temptations for children.

For just a moment, I was a kid again myself leafing through the Sears and Roebuck catalog.

I stood before a dollhouse and studied the intricate designs of a tiny sofa covered in red velvet. I would've loved this when I was a child, but considered extravagant for our family, I would never have even thought to ask for one.

"May I help you, ma'am?" a young sales clerk asked.

"Just taking a trip down memory lane."

A twinge of homesickness came over me as I gave the house one last glance, and left the store following a more direct route than the footprints afforded, stopping once more to look at the dressed dolls in the exterior windows.

###

Because Melissa had to make an out of town trip, Bertha's friend, Eunice, and I took Bertha back for a check-up to the doctor who did her surgery.

"Why do I have to get undressed again?" Bertha asked the nurse who escorted us into the examining room.

"Because Dr. Goodman has gone to Colorado skiing," the nurse tried to explain as she took Bertha's blood pressure and removed the cuff. The nurse grew quiet as she checked Bertha's pulse. When she finished, she said, "Dr. Tanner is substituting and he hasn't seen you before. He needs to make sure everything's OK." She jotted down a few numbers on a chart lying nearby on a counter.

"Why can't he read about me on that chart you people are always carrying around?" Bertha asked pointing to the folder. "I get tired of doctors looking at all my sags and bags."

The nurse opened a drawer, pulled out a blue print hospital gown and extended it to Bertha. "Mrs. Henderson, would you please put this on, so Dr. Tanner can examine you?" The nurse sighed as she exited and closed the door.

After quite a while, a knock sounded. Bertha sat on the examining table in her gown. "You might as well come in."

The young Dr. Tanner entered and smiled broadly. "Well, hello Mrs. Henderson."

Bertha immediately lit in to him, complaining about having to get undressed, about him seeing her "sags and bags," and about the whole situation in general.

"Mrs. Henderson, do you know what Dr. Goodman has written on your chart?"

"I have no idea," Bertha said defensively.

Dr. Tanner studied her a moment. "C-H-A-R-A-C-T-E-R, in big block letters."

###

"Can you believe that?" Bertha fumed as we left the office. "When Dr. Goodman gets back I'm going to give him a piece of my mind. We've been friends since we were in high school. The very idea of him writing notes about me like that. He hasn't heard the last of this."

"Truth is truth." Eunice opened the car door for Bertha.

"You be quiet," Bertha shot back as she sank into the car seat and slammed the door.

###

Two days before Jason and Linnea were due to come home for Christmas, I picked up the red and white candy striped box I'd wrapped for Linnea and adjusted the ribbon.

A scary thought came to me—that I should try making my grandmother's peppermint cake.

I put the box back under the tree.

No way.

I was about the worst baker I knew, and the turkey fiasco hadn't helped my confidence either.

I didn't even have a recipe and would have to invent the cake from scratch. All I remembered about it was seeing my grandmother melt peppermint candy in a saucepan when she made it.

Julia Childs I was not.

###

"There." I stood back and studied the cake on the stand with fluffy seven minute icing. Starlight mints encircled the base interspersed with sprigs of fresh green mint from Colonial Store.

At least it looked good.

Now, after two days of experimenting, here's hoping it would taste good. I'd made the kitchen one giant Velcro spot with all the melted peppermint and sugar I'd gone through.

Every time I took a step, my shoes stuck to the floor. Even Red seemed to have trouble getting across the tar pit in the kitchen, as there were several blobs of red fur also adhered to the hardwoods. From experience, I knew this would be a challenge to clean because when water was added to sugar, it would make a glaze that spread across the floor.

Oh, the joys of baking.

As for the cake, I supposed nobody would know how it was meant to taste since no one here had ever had my grandmother's peppermint cake. Only I knew how high the bar was set.

I'd see what Jason and Linnea thought when they arrived home tonight. They'd texted that they'd be home before dinner.

I went into the study, settled in a club chair, and opened my computer. I'd finished another article earlier in the day—a travel feature on Jarrett Manor, a historical site near Toccoa with ties to Revolutionary times.

With that finished, I pecked around a bit toward my less-than-inspired work of fiction.

Nothing.

###

"June, I've been thinking about that desk," Bertha said when I clicked on my ringing cell phone later in the day.

Oh, no. Just what I'd hoped to avoid—Bertha getting involved in all the desk business. I held the phone between my ear and my shoulder, closed the computer in my lap, and placed it on a shelf in the study.

"I've been wondering which one of the people that lived in that house could've had a fine desk like that. I don't remember anybody lately who appeared they could've had the money to own it. Quite a puzzle."

How could I redirect Bertha's interests? I went into the kitchen and through the bay window, I could see Bertha's house. Less than fifty feet away, she was in her kitchen stewing over my desk. "Don't worry yourself over it, Bertha. The desk is gone, and I don't know if I'll ever get it back."

"I'm still double locking all the doors at night because of your robbery, with it being right next door and all. It's such a mystery, though."

Bertha was right, but I'd about turned my brain inside out trying to solve it. I tried to change the subject. "You received a great report at the doctor's yesterday."

"I did, but I'm not letting that Dr. Goodman off the hook."

I'd hoped her aggravation had subsided, but I guessed not. "Well, the good news is that Dr. Tanner reported your hip is healing amazingly. How's Jubilee?"

"Doing right well. We're both going to be in fine condition when spring planting time comes along. The seed catalogs arrive next month, and Jubilee and I are planting extra special things this year. He's busy right now trying to get his own yard in tip top shape for the photographer that friend of yours is sending over."

"It sounds like she's definitely going to include him in her book."

"I'll say. She calls on him often to see how he's doing. She doesn't want him to change very much. She says she likes his yard the way it is," Bertha explained.

"It's definitely a wonder." I spotted my own Jubilee creation standing right now beside my patio in the back yard. Its moving arm seemed to be writing at a feverish pace.

If only I could sense that kind of inspiration in my own fiction endeavor.

###

The phone rang on Christmas Eve morning.

"June."

The urgency in the way Iris spoke my name shook me.

"It's Belle, they've had to take her to the hospital in an ambulance. The kids are over there with her in the emergency room right now. I thought you would want to know."

"I'm on the way." I reached for my purse.

"See you there," Iris responded.

###

Iris and I stood from the chairs where we'd been waiting when we saw Joe and Becky enter from the examining area. Joe blinked back the moisture in his eyes as he spoke, "She has pneumonia and can't go home—has to stay here until she's better, because she waited too long to get help. She kept saying it was only a cold."

"She was doing this for us." Becky wiped her face.

"You can't blame yourselves," Iris declared as we hugged them both. "Belle knew when she took the job at the school she was faced with extra work. It's what she wanted to do."

"We've tried to help when we could." Becky said her voice tinged with despair.

"Right now, all that's important is that she gets better. We'll deal with some of these things later," Iris declared.

I agreed. "What can we do for you right now?"

Christmas in the hospital. There had to be a way to cheer this family.

And then it came to me.

###

Around 2:00 on a windy Christmas Day, Linnea, Jason and I arrived at the Stephens County Hospital with arms loaded.

I braved the blustery weather holding a peppermint cake on a stand, and carried it through the hospital like an Olympic torch. Linnea had the plates, napkins, forks, and cups. Jason bore a gallon of sweet tea. I found great pleasure in the fact I might be able to cheer someone with my cooking.

Unbelievably, my attempt at the peppermint cake had been deemed successful by my children, even though I thought it paled in comparison to the original version. Even so, I made another one after Linnea and Jason went to bed on Christmas Eve.

As we passed through the hospital corridors, heads turned to see the white fluffy cake loaded with peppermint candy. We knocked quietly on the door of Belles' room and heard a "Come in."

When we entered, Joe and Becky's faces lit up. Even Belle managed a faint smile.

"We bring Christmas cheer," I announced with drama.

"It's beautiful," Belle whispered. But the expression on her face told me that it didn't matter what the cake tasted like. It was just that we were there. "I've never seen a cake like that before. What is it?"

"It's an attempt at a cake like my grandmother made when I was a little girl. I had to make up the recipe, but Jason and Linnea insist it's edible. We wanted to share it with you."

I detected a bit of reservation in Joe's eyes, probably first put there by the aspic episode.

I placed the cake on a ledge by the window and began cutting slices for everyone. Linnea passed them around while Joe poured tea. I couldn't help but think of how happy my grandmother would've been to witness this scene.

The room grew quiet for a few moments. I waited for a verdict.

Joe chewed and swallowed. "Never had it before, but this stuff is good."

Belle and Becky added their approval as well, and I breathed a sigh of relief. In a few moments, everyone except Belle had tossed his or her plates in the trash. Belle had only picked at her cake.

I asked, "Why don't all you kids go for a walk and get a breath of fresh air. I'll stay with your mom." Joe and Becky exchanged glances and nodded.

Jason and Linnea joined them as they exited the room, and I settled into a chair beside Belle's bed. "How are you? Really?"

She coughed hoarsely. "Disappointed we have to spend Christmas here." She shook her head. "I've created such a mess. My medical bills will eat up all the money I've earned working the second job plus more besides." Belle sighed, pulled an insulated cup from the bedside table, and took a sip. She coughed again, and I could see her fighting back tears.

I recognized a drowning time when I saw one.

I hardly knew what to say, so I just placed my hand on her arm and said the words so many had spoken to me. "I'm sorry this happened, but I'm sure God has a way for you." I'd always tried to believe this, but had come up short more than a few times.

"I'm not sure I get mail from God anymore." Bitterness laced her words as Belle placed the cup back on the table. She tried to take a deep breath, but fell into a coughing fit. At last, she could catch her breath. "God is somebody very far off for me. I feel alone." She turned and looked me in the eye. The wind rattled the window beside us. "If God cared about me, why would He let this happen?"

Aw, the age old question. One I'd turned over repeatedly in my own mind.

A chill came over me, and I pulled the coat I'd taken off earlier back up around my shoulders. "I don't know if anyone has the answer to that question. I sure don't."

I remember the kinds of explanations I'd heard about living in a fallen world and that bad things happen even to good people. Those things didn't seem to help much when it felt like you were breathing through a straw.

I'd read the *Problem of Pain*, but I was no C.S. Lewis and probably the least likely person on earth to help someone else cope with such a huge question. I pointed to a drawer beside the bed. "Could I peek in there a moment?" I asked.

Belle nodded, and I pulled out the drawer, reached in and moved mouthwash, soap, and a tissue box until I spotted a Gideon Bible. I lifted it from its place and opened it to a few familiar lines in Romans.

I tapped the words with my finger. "These words kept me from sinking to the bottom of despair," and I read, "And we know that in all things God works for the good of those who love him, who have been called according to His purpose."

I closed the book, and put it back in the drawer. At first, Belle's expression was unreadable to me, and then she leaned forward and uncharacteristically spit out the words, "I don't see how that applies. God has never called me, and I don't have any idea how He would use this for good."

How often over the past two years, I'd thought and said exactly the same thing. There really didn't seem to be any easy answers. I breathed a prayer for help.

"All I know is that for me, I have to keep trusting Him with the circumstances in my life—all of them—good or bad. It's a continuing challenge. I couldn't face it at all until nearly a year and a half after Morris died. It took that long for the anger to subside. Still—it wasn't easy. Trust has often been a slippery slope for me. Trusting one day, doubting the next."

Belle stared beyond me out the window. "But, I've tried to be a good person."

I wasn't much of a theologian, but I tried to think of a way to explain what I wanted to communicate, and remembered something I'd heard Pastor Grady say only a few weeks back. "It's like Christmas when we receive gifts. Think how awful if we refused the gifts our loved ones tried to give us. God wants to give us gifts too, of love, forgiveness and life, but we have to accept them. We can't earn them or they wouldn't be gifts."

Belle seemed thoughtful. "I guess I thought the more good things I did the more God would like me. But what you're saying is that doing stuff has nothing to do with Him accepting me."

I nodded. "I think it has more to do with you accepting Him."

Just then, the kids blew in. "It's cold outside." Becky rubbed her arms covered only by a thin sweater, "We had to come back in where it's warm."

"You mean *you* had to come back in where it's warm." Joe grinned mischievously at his sister. "I was fine."

"Oh, be quiet," Becky shot back jabbing him in the ribs.

Siblings.

"We'll see you all later. I hope you're out of here soon, Belle." I patted the keys in my pocket.

"Me, too," Belle glanced at the crumbling remains of the cake. "Thanks. We'll get the stand back to you soon."

"No hurry," I said. "Merry Christmas."

We gathered our things, but strangely, as we went out into the parking lot, the wind picked up again, and it seemed the words I'd spoken to Belle boomeranged piercing my own heart. But wasn't I trusting? Wasn't I surrendering?

Chapter Fifteen

Gifts of Many Kinds

"You can give without loving,
but you can never love without giving."
—Les Miserables, Victor Hugo (1802-1885)

Our next stop was the Mountain Gardens Assisted Care Facility. We pushed past the wreath bedecked exterior doors and entered the gathering room where a tall Leyland Cyprus almost touched the ceiling. Addie, seated at her usual post by the window with Misty in her lap, brightened when she saw us and extended her hands.

I took the softly creased fingers in mine. "Merry Christmas, Addie!"

"Merry Christmas, to you! Who do you have with you today?" Addie asked releasing my hands and studying my children.

"This is my son, Jason, and daughter, Linnea."

"I'm pleased to meet you. Enjoyed getting to know your mama, and this, "she stroked the grey tabby's head, "is Misty."

"Pleased to meet you, ma'am. Your cat's a real beauty." Jason leaned over to pet Misty.

"He's a big cat fan," I said.

"I know we'll hit it off, then." Addie beamed at him.

"We brought you a piece of cake and a little gift." Linnea extended a paper plate wrapped in aluminum foil and a glossy red box tied with green satin ribbon.

"Mercy, what a beautiful present, and this cake looks delicious. What is it?" she asked as she peeked under the foil.

I explained about the cake.

"A special cake. I can't wait to take a bite, but I'll wait until after you folks have gone."

"Go ahead and open your present, Addie." I perched in a chair opposite her.

With slightly trembling hands, Addie peeled away wrapping paper from the box. When she opened the lid, she laughed. "I'll be the hit of Mountain Gardens with these on." She held up slippers that I'd found online designed to resemble a grey tabby cat with big yellow eyes. "I hope Misty doesn't get jealous of my feet. Every time I wear these, I'll think of the wonderful friends God sent to me. Thank you." Her eyes twinkled as she spoke.

I nodded as Jason picked up Misty and held her.

Addie placed the slippers on the table next to her and stood. "Now, I want all of you to see the Christmas tree in the dining room. It's a beauty—decorated with all kinds of birds. We had quite a time in there today. There's also a crèche the Women's Group at Emmanuel Church made for us—so lovely."

I took Addie's arm, and with Jason and Linnea following, we made our way down the hall toward the dining room.

About half way there, we caught a glimpse of an escaped potbellied pig with a big red bow tied around its neck running directly in front of the cafeteria followed by more than one Mountain Gardens worker calling, "Virgil, here Virgil!"

###

I invited Ted over for dinner on Christmas night. Jason and Linnea wanted to watch a movie in the den, so we had our peppermint cake and coffee by the fire in the study.

We'd hardly taken our seats before Ted rose again. "I asked Henrietta, one of the ladies in your choir who works at Franklin's to tell me if she'd seen you in the store and whether you were looking at anything special."

I remembered the purple scarf. It'd go perfectly with a black sweater I had, but I didn't know which department Henrietta worked in. Thoughtful of him.

"She noticed you because you were following the footprints of Santa. They're not many adults who do that, you know. Anyway, she'd heard from one of the other employees that you were looking at something in particular."

So much for flying under the radar.

I couldn't believe the sweet thing he'd done, though. I didn't know whether we were exchanging gifts or not, but just in case I'd asked Linnea to do a small watercolor of the mountain from a photograph I'd sent her at school.

Ted went to the foyer, and came back with a giant box. I studied it a moment wondering if he'd tricked me with the wrapping and nestled the scarf deep inside. "It's huge."

"For you." He extended the box to me.

A rich red ribbon encircled the box before me, beautifully wrapped in silver paper. I hesitated a moment, but then took the package, and was surprised by its weight. I untied the bow, and pulled back the paper. Emblazoned on the side of the box were the words, "Stainless roasting pan with rack and turkey forks."

My festive spirit slid into my socks.

"A turkey pan," Ted declared as if he'd given me pearl earrings. He smiled his dimpled smile, but its appeal for me had dimmed. "I thought you'd love it. It's supposed to be fool-proof."

He was a lawyer, supposedly trained in the art of rhetoric.

I hated appliance or kitchen gifts. I particularly hated them on the cusp of just having had a cooking disaster. Even the near success of the peppermint cake hadn't erased the memory of blackened bird.

Morris would've never given me something like this.

Foolproof, huh.

"Thank you," I said perfunctorily. What was he thinking?

I set the pan aside knowing it'd be the first item I'd put down in my newly cleaned basement. I reached behind the sofa, pulled out the watercolor and extended it to him. "For you."

He ripped the paper from the package and studied the painting. "I love it."

"I had Linnea do it," I wondered why I'd gone to so much trouble when I could've just gone to the hardware store and bought him a screwdriver.

"Thank you. Merry Christmas," he beamed.

"Merry Christmas, to you." I tried to remember it was the thought that counts, but as I glanced at the big box and read again, "Stainless roasting pan with rack and turkey forks," I had to wonder what the thought actually was.

###

An arctic cold settled over Toccoa in early January with three straight days of high temperatures that barely broke out of the teens. I rolled out of bed, dug out my thermal underwear and put them on under my fleece. On top of that, I wore a bathrobe and twined a wool scarf around my neck.

I'd planned to write, but I couldn't imagine sitting at the computer all day, because even with wearing gloves, my digits felt like ice. I went downstairs to the kitchen and looked out toward Bertha's house feeling miserable. It's then that I noticed one of my peace lilies on the window seat had ice on it. I pulled out my cell phone and called Bertha. "Are you all right? I can't get warm over here."

"Warm as toast. I'm having my second cup of coffee as I'm writing out my order from the seed catalog. Did you leave your water dripping? Your old house doesn't have much insulation, and the pipes will freeze."

"I forgot. I'll do that right now, but I wonder if something is wrong with my heat."

"Nothing is wrong with your heat except it's old. The heat over there never has worked too well. Fred bought an all-new system and had insulation blown in the walls here before he died. I don't even have a sweater on."

I didn't need to hear all of that. I hung up.

Shivering, I moved to the sink and turned the faucet on—nothing came out. Strange.

I moved to the bathroom. Ditto.

Upstairs bathroom. Dry, again.

Oh, no. Nothing to do but call a plumber. I went back to the kitchen, opened the Toccoa Yellow Pages and ran my finger down the listings. One, Pickens Plumbing, offered complimentary flower seeds with every house call. That sounded friendly, so I called them.

"Wait for the thaw, and hope for the best?" The plumber had not been very encouraging.

I called Bertha again. "It's too late, I'm already frozen."

"Well, bring jugs with you for water when you come over to take a shower this evening."

"Thanks, Bertha."

A piece of ice broke off from the peace lily and dropped to the window seat with a "plunk."

My relationship with Ted had been a bit frozen, too, since Christmas. I'd spoken with him a few times on the phone, but that was about it. I needed time to think about what I might be getting myself into. The tugs within had started to twist.

Over the next twenty-four hours, temperatures began to climb. Standing in the kitchen the next day, I could hear dripping. I followed it to the basement and found the culprit—one of the pipes under the kitchen dripped water onto the concrete floor. I was sure glad we'd moved the mess out of there last summer. We would have had an even worse disaster if all that stuff had gotten soaked. I called the plumber back.

A couple of hours later the doorbell rang, and I opened the door to see two men, one of which was Jed Turner.

"Jed, what are you doing here?" I asked surprised to see him.

"Well, this here's Ethel's brother, Elmer Pickens."

Elmer tipped his hat to me.

Jed continued. "He owns Pickens Plumbin'. I help him durin' my slow season, which is usually his busy season. Elmer's the best plumber anywhere around these parts."

Jed extended a sandwich bag with seeds in it to me. "Here's your free gift. Just throw these out in the garden, and you'll have a show come spring."

As I took the seeds with a computer printed label, which read, "Cleome." I thanked him for the free gift and had to wonder at this odd turn of events. I led Elmer and Jed down to the basement.

Elmer looked up at the pipes under the kitchen. "Busted all right. I'm gonna need a ladder to reach these pipes. I gotta go back to the truck."

I was in the kitchen making a sandwich as Elmer came through the front door with the ladder. I heard him rumbling down the basement stairs, and then voices, and then quiet. A few minutes later, Jed yelled up the basement stairs, "Miz Callaway?"

"I'm in the kitchen." I braced myself for a plumbing disaster story as Jed and Elmer tromped up the stairs into the kitchen.

Jed spoke first. "Elmer was gettin' up the ladder to try and fix the pipe when he saw somthin' layin' on the top of the sewer pipe runnin' from the kitchen. He reached over and picked up an ole rotten handkerchief. You won't believe what we found inside. I think you better have a seat."

As I positioned myself in a nearby kitchen chair, Jed handed me a large maroon plaid handkerchief with a lump in it. I unfolded it and found several bundled packages of one hundred dollar bills. On the top of one of the Federal Reserve Straps were the words, "For my beloved, with all my heart." I glanced up at Jed, and then took a closer look at the bills. To the right of the portrait on the front the date, 1934, was stamped.

"This is very old money," I observed.

"Yeah, we was thinking you robbed a bank or somthin' 'til we saw the date." Jed laughed.

I wondered what the end would be to the surprises in my basement. I flipped the bills. Five packs of ten, which meant I had $5,000 in my hand.

"Reckon how the money got down in that old basement?" Jed asked. "Who'd a put that much money on a sewer pipe, less they was tryin' to hide it from somebody?"

I had no idea, but I was impressed with Jed and Elmer's honesty. "Thanks for giving this to me. I'd appreciate you folks not spreading this around town, though. People might think there are all kinds of treasure in the basement."

"Yes ma'am. Elmer and me, we don't discuss nothin' that goes on when we're on the job. We're professionals."

I nodded in appreciation.

"Well, we got work to do. We'd best be gettin' back down the stairs," said Jed.

After they left, I leaned over and collapsed face first on the kitchen table.

###

"It's coming back to me now. I don't know how I could have forgotten that part of the story. Mercy, what's happened to my memory?" Addie put the book she was reading on the table beside her chair.

The front doors of Mountain Gardens Assisted Living swung open and a couple of toddlers skipped in followed by what must have been their mom. They continued down the hallway seeming to know exactly where they were going. Addie paused a moment to watch them.

I grew a little impatient to find out how so much money wound up in my basement. "So, what's the story, Addie?"

"As I remember, Silas knew Anne Marie was bringing that fine desk and some other things with her when she came. He didn't want to meet the boat empty handed. So, he withdrew all of his money he'd been saving. Now, Silas was a big saver. He probably had every penny he'd ever made and then some. He was going to meet Anne Marie at the boat, show her the money, and tell her that was their nest egg for a house."

That explained the inscription on the Federal Reserve band, "For my beloved with all my heart." Such a sad story, this one about Silas and Anne Marie.

Misty lumbered across the floor in front of us and flipped over on her side. Addie continued, "That much money would have bought a mighty fine little house in those days. When he found out she'd died, he gave the money to Buford like the rest of her things—said he didn't have any use for that money anymore. I guess maybe Buford thought he'd change his mind, or that he'd meet someone else and want the money back. I suppose he hid the money as he did the desk. I don't know why he didn't put it in the bank. I guess he didn't want Uncle Sam to think it was his."

I needed to know what I was dealing with here. "Addie, can you think of anything else that might be in my basement?"

"June, the minute you asked me that question, I remembered something else. There is this one other thing."

Chapter Sixteen

Complications

". . . and there is a Catskill eagle in some souls that can alike dive down into the blackest gorges, and soar out of them again and become invisible in the sunny spaces. And even if he forever flies within the gorge, that gorge is in the mountains; so that even in his lowest swoop the mountain eagle is still higher than the other birds upon the plain, even though they soar."
—Herman Melville (1819-1891)

When the caller ID on my cell phone flashed Ted's name later in the evening, I almost didn't pick up. I'd already had a somewhat disconcerting day, but I collapsed in a chair in the study and pressed a button.

"We need to talk," he said.

"Okay," is all I could get out.

"I was so desperate, I asked Iris what was going on," he stated.

I wasn't sure I liked him going behind my back. I kicked off my shoes and leaned back accidentally knocking a devotional book I'd used that morning off the table onto the floor. The writing had been on forgiveness.

Ted went on. "She wouldn't discuss it, and all she said was the turkey roaster I gave you might've sent a message I didn't intend. I started thinking about it and realized it could've been an insult to you."

Could have? I didn't know what to say to him.

"I never meant to do that."

I heard the sincerity in his voice. Maybe I had overreacted. It was probably a result of the conflicting tugs in my heart, pushing away, pulling close.

I felt my resolve starting to crack and knew deep down inside that I needed to forgive him even if he didn't fully understand what he'd done. Really, comparing him to Morris wasn't fair. I seemed to remember Morris giving me a fondue set the first Christmas we were married. It didn't go over very well, either.

I glanced at the devotional book in my lap. I needed to let this go. "Let's just forget about it."

An audible exhale on the other end of the phone. "So, what's new?" he asked.

I told him about the money Jed and Elmer found in the basement and shared about my conversation with Addie.

"Ted, we might never find what Addie told me about, plus, we don't know if someone's already found it, and it's long gone. We could have thrown it out when we hauled all of that junk out of the basement." I thought about the mounds of debris Tom and Joe helped me clear from down there.

"If you're supposed to find it, you will," Ted said in a pragmatic way.

That was a sobering thought. I struggled to reconcile myself to it.

"I have a suggestion—call Roger Wood. He's something of a numismatist . . ."

"Numismatist?"

"You know, someone who studies currency and coins. He might advise you on how to handle this money. Since it's old, it could be worth more than face value. But, I have a bit of bad news—you're going to have to pay tax on the value of the money next year."

"You're kidding."

"If the desk hadn't been stolen, you'd be paying income tax on its value this year. Since you didn't have it itemized on your insurance, all you have to pay is the tax on the five hundred dollars you received from the insurance claim which is a big tax difference from the tax on the half million actual value of the desk."

I placed the book in my lap on the table and pondered Ted's words. It seemed he had a real gift for wringing a positive out of a negative.

###

I found choir practice a welcome respite from the many questions begging answers on a cold January evening. I could lose myself in the music, and of course, I always enjoyed the social interaction. I'd often wondered why Rhonda Kay didn't have her own talk show. She was one of the funniest women I'd ever known.

She was no disappointment this evening, either.

Before Laura came in the room, Rhonda Kay turned in her seat to speak to those sitting behind her. "I almost didn't get here tonight. Them chocolate covered cherries Cletus gave me for Christmas have done hit their mark. I didn't have nothin' I could wear. I finally dug these out." She patted the waistband of a very tight pair of black pants. "I don't like to wear black, reminds me of a funeral parlor. No sir, I want color."

She turned back around and faced the front but we could still hear her, "I'll tell you this—I'm gonna be hitting Jenna's Gym every day starting tomorrow. This lard is coming off," she declared triumphantly.

The whole place dissolved into laughter as Laura came in. She stopped before she reached her stand.

"Rhonda Kay?" she asked.

"Rhonda Kay," a voice from the back answered.

Rhonda Kay turned around and winked at the choir members making everyone erupt in laughter once more.

Laura began to hand out music. "Rhonda Kay, would you search your car trunk again to see if you have any extra music. I'm missing several copies of each of these anthems."

"Why, I never," Rhonda Kay said defensively.

###

Roger Wood was more than a little interested in my questions about the hundred dollar bills.

"Well, of course they're worth more than face value, and their value only increases if they are sequentially numbered. How did you come to have them?" he asked over the phone.

I sure didn't want to go into that saga as I pushed the grocery cart through the produce aisle at Colonial store. "Long story. I didn't check to see if they are sequentially numbered or not." Why hadn't I thought to look at the numbering?

"Well, let me know, and I'll do a little research and get back to you."

###

I hoped volunteering in the library might also provide a welcome break from the disturbances of the last few days. At least, if I didn't overhear any more conversations. On the way there, I caught a glimpse of the mountain now wearing its winter finery of thalo green, the evergreens more distinct than ever. However, I still anticipated the coming of spring. Bertha told me that hyacinth bulbs were planted next to my patio. I couldn't wait to see what color they were.

On arrival, I went about my usual job of shelving books, which today consisted of the P's. I finished my cart and went back to the circulation desk to retrieve more volumes. When I did, I caught a glimpse of the same women I'd seen in the library the last time I worked, one of whom was Gladys Pickens. It's then I remembered Jed's brother in law was named Pickens. Were Elmer and Gladys related? Out of the corner of my eye, I saw the older of the two women go to the magazine rack and pick up the latest issue of *Country Gal* while the younger woman headed off for the children's books. I made it my business to be at the circulation desk when they checked out. The younger one was whispering to the older, "He was over there again last week."

"Shh, I know it," came the reply.

I scanned *Runaway Bunny*, tried to pretend I was not listening, and smiled. "Have a wonderful day."

"Same to you," the older woman said.

###

That evening as I loaded a soup bowl in the dishwasher, I stewed on what I'd heard at the library earlier in the day. Maybe, what I overheard didn't relate to my desk at all, however, the conversation did seem sinister.

Wow! Had I taken a page out of Bertha Henderson's book? Nosing around in other people's business. I'd have to watch that. I closed the dishwasher door and pulled my cell phone from my pocket. I needed to call Belle who was now at home recuperating.

"I'm better, thank you," she said, her voice bright. "I'm trying not to worry so much. By the way, that Preacher Grady of yours has called several times."

"I hope you don't mind that I told him about your situation. I thought he might encourage you. I know what you mean about the worrying." I pressed the start button on the dishwasher and eased into a kitchen chair. "I have that same struggle, but I keep reminding myself of what Jesus says in Matthew 6 '...give no thought for the morrow.' I wish I could say I've always done that. My biggest struggle has been giving thought for the morrow."

Belle managed a laugh. "Me, too. I'm hoping to go back to work next week. The doctor indicated I could if I feel strong enough. I'll have to work part time the first week or so, and then hopefully I can ease back into full time."

For a woman who'd had pneumonia, Belle sounded stronger than she ever had before. What was going on?

###

I perched on the side of the bed still in my bathrobe. "At least twice the face value?" I whined into the phone early the next morning. "That means, instead of five, I have at least ten thousand?" I couldn't believe the bills being sequentially numbered made such a difference in the price.

"Don't sound so discouraged Mrs. Callaway. This may come as a surprise to you, but most people are excited to know their money is worth more than face value," said Roger Wood.

"Yes, of course. I appreciate your hard work. Thank you for all you've done." I hung up the phone, and sank back on a pillow.

Rats, I thought, something else that needed to go to Silas and Buford's heirs. How would I ever find them?

Chapter Seventeen

A New Perspective

"Lord, make me see thy glory in every place."
—Michelangelo (1475-1564)

In early February, I met Ted one evening at the Dinner Bell after choir practice. The heat was acting up in my car and I had forgotten my gloves. I could hardly wait to get inside the warm restaurant as temperatures were beginning to slide down into the twenties. We took our seats, ordered, and I started warming my hands around a cup of coffee.

Stella careened over with two giant slices of carrot cake.

As she placed them on the table, the scent of cinnamon wafted up from the five layer slices. "How does Lucille manage to cook so many different kinds of wonderful offerings?" I asked.

Stella smiled with a proprietary air. "Lucille don't give away her trade secrets. Now, can I get you folks anything else?"

We shook our heads; she topped off our coffee, and raced back to the kitchen.

Ted directed his gaze toward me as he lifted a forkful of cake. "So, do you want to come with my hiking group to climb Currahee in a couple of weeks?"

I nearly spilled the cream he'd just passed me and set the pitcher down with a plunk.

"What are you talking about?"

He pointed to his right in an exaggerated way. "You know that big mountain over there. My hiking group's climbing it."

Very funny.

I shrugged. "I have this thing about heights." Morris' death had done that for me. It was all I could do to get in an airplane these days, but no need to go into all that.

"So do you want to come or not?"

Climbing Currahee had not been on my to-do list. I was content to observe it from an altitude closer to sea level. I lifted my coffee cup and let the liquid warm me against the thought of trudging up the side of a cold mountain. I gripped the mug as I lowered it to the table. "I'll get in the way, slow everyone else down."

"No, you won't. We take things pretty slowly. We'll give you plenty of time to rest."

Right.

###

I absolutely couldn't believe my scheduled scripture reading the next day:

"It is God who arms me with strength and makes my way perfect. He makes my feet like the feet of a deer; he enables me to stand on heights," from Psalm 18:32-33.

Okay, Lord. I'll do it, but I can't do it alone. I need you every step of the way.

"Do it afraid," is the next thing I heard.

###

I strolled with Rhonda Kay to our cars after choir practice the next Wednesday night and told her about Ted's invitation.

"Climb the mountain? Are you crazy?" she blurted out. "You'll mess up your hair, and you'll perspire. What are you thinking? Why, if you want to exercise, come on over to Jenna's Gym. You can wear a cute outfit and all."

"I feel like maybe God is leading me to do this." I shared the Psalms scripture God had given me.

She slapped her leg. "Well, why didn't you say so to begin with? I thought you was doing this on your own. If the Lord has done told you to go, you gotta go, messed up hair or not."

With that affirmation, Rhonda Kay clicked her door lock and took a seat in her baby blue Cadillac. Just as she closed the door, I saw a leopard skin stiletto pump being pulled into the car.

###

"Are you alive over there?" Bertha asked over the phone.

"I am. What about you?" I dropped frozen chicken breasts in a pot so I could make a casserole for tonight's supper with Ted.

"Fine and dandy, now, but I have to tell you what happened to me today. Jubilee and I went to the next town over to my old bank to cash out some certificates of deposit, because I found I could get a higher interest rate at the Citizens Bank.

When I got to my old bank, they didn't want to give me my money. They sent one of the officers out to try to make me change my mind. He came out saying stuff like, 'My, don't you look pretty today, Mrs. Henderson,' and 'Isn't that a nice suit you have on.'"

I turned the heat up on the burner for the chicken. Obviously, the officer had no idea who he was dealing with.

"He said Fred wouldn't want me to take the CDs out. Can you believe that? I told him to leave Fred out of it, that I could get one percent higher elsewhere. I asked him if he was going to give me my money or not. He fumed, but he sent one of the tellers to write the check. She stayed and stayed. I didn't think they were ever going to give it to me. When she came out and handed it to the officer, who said real patronizingly, 'Now, Mrs. Henderson, where are you going to get this extra percent?'"

The pot began to boil as I anticipated what I knew was going to be a great answer.

"I grabbed my check, started walking away, and said, 'You can call around like I did and see who has the highest rates.' Jubilee had the motor running, so I hit the door, got in the car, and drove straight to the Citizens Bank where that kind Mr. Wood treated me as if I had brains instead of oatmeal between my ears. Imagine trying to take advantage of a widow like that other bank did."

One thing Bertha was not and that was a victim. The chicken breasts bobbed furiously in the boiling water.

"Bertha, you're an inspiration for women everywhere. Proud of you. What did Melissa say when she heard this story?" I asked.

"She said, 'You go, girl!"

"Well put!"

###

I clicked the mouse on my novel folder early one morning and tried to work on the book again in earnest. Outside, the grey skies hung just above the treetops, and the wind rattled the short leafed pines. Perfect writing weather. I eventually sent a couple of articles off to various magazines, but didn't get any further with the book.

Here it was months and months down the road, and I was no closer than I'd been when I started—I'd deleted volumes.

I turned the computer off and put my head in my hands.

Lord, if this is what You want me to do I sure need to hear from You.

###

The Currahee climb was scheduled for February 10. I thought I felt a little cold coming on a couple of days before, so I called Ted.

I blew my nose loudly into the phone. "I'm sniffly. I don't want to hold everyone back."

"Bring tissues. You don't want to miss this, June," Ted replied.

Help me Lord.

###

Laura had just taken her place at the music stand when seemingly out of nowhere we watched as a bundle of music launched into the air and landed at her feet—a couple of dozen anthems that splattered in every direction as they landed.

"Whooeee," said Rhonda Kay. "Where in the world did all that music come from?"

Laura rolled her eyes at Rhonda Kay," Well, on first guess I'd say it came from the trunk of your car."

Rhonda Kay held her right hand to her heart feigning being taken aback."Now, I have to tell you, you are only partly right. I did find some in the trunk of my car, but I found a piece in the magazine stand by the recliner, one in my exercise bag, a piece up under my car seat, and Lord, I don't know how it got there, but I found a copy of 'Hallelujah, Thine the Glory' in my big make-up bag."

"Not surprised." Laura stooped to pick up the music, and her eyes immediately brightened. "Wow, there are four pieces of that one we've been working on for Easter. I thought I was going to have to order more. Thanks, Rhonda Kay."

"You're mighty welcome." Rhonda Kay smiled looking proud of herself.

###

When Ted came to pick me up for the Currahee climb, the dimples faded from his face. "You have too much on; we're not climbing Mt. Everest."

I wore a down parka, a fleece jacket, a sweater, a turtleneck, and thermal underwear. On my head, I sported earmuffs, and a stocking cap. Under an old pair of hiking boots that used to belong to Jason, I'd put on three pairs of socks. Of course, I had cozy down mitts on my hands. "I can't stand to be cold."

"You're going to die of heat prostration in all that stuff," he said, "You must take some of it off."

"I've never climbed a mountain before, and I sure don't want to get up there and freeze to death. I bet the wind blows at the top."

"I'm telling you June; you're going to get hot once we start."

"No." Family members had told me that my stubbornness had come down to me from my dad's side of the family.

Seeing my determination, Ted sighed, went to the door and opened it. "After you."

I could feel his eyes boring holes in me as I passed him.

When we arrived at the mountain, we parked next to a little white building, joined the other members of the club that were to hike that day, and began our ascent up Currahee.

Pleased with my clothing choices, I felt snug and warm in the February chill. The initial approach on the five-mile trail did not have much of an incline, but it was not long before it became abundantly clear we were ascending the slope. Tiny beads formed on my forehead under my stocking cap. A small rivulet of perspiration inched down my neck.

Getting warm.

I tried to slip out of the down jacket without anyone noticing, but finally had to stop to get it off. I put my mitts in my mouth and tied the coat around my waist, which was hard, because the sleeves were so bulky. After tying the sleeves, I took off the stocking cap and put it in one of the pockets of the coat. I was out of breath when I caught up with the others, and still had to blow my nose.

Ted studied me. I could see him choking down, "I told you, so" but thankfully, he didn't say it. Maybe he'd learned something after the turkey pan debacle.

Fifteen minutes later up the trail, I took off the fleece jacket and tied it on top of the down jacket. I swigged a few sips of my water bottle. Thankfully, the others were stopping as well. I stuffed my mitts and earmuffs in the fleece jacket pockets. "How much longer?" I feared if it was much farther, the path upward might start to look like the Oregon Trail if I began flinging all these garments to the side. Instead of the family silver, those that followed would find vestiges from the pages of L.L. Bean and Orvis catalogs.

"We're about halfway there," Ted answered as he glanced up the trail.

I craned my head toward the summit and realized it wasn't going to get any easier from here. Someone could have made a twin bedspread from the fabric I had wrapped around my waist. Heavy.

Ted couldn't even look at me without shaking his head.

I patted down my forehead, blew my nose, and joined the others on the trail. I was sorry I'd been so pre-occupied with my heat wave that I hadn't had a chance to spot any wildlife or take note of the trees, which is one of the main reasons for making the climb.

The slope was steeper, now.

Hot, and out of breath.

"I have to stop."

Ted turned around to see me sitting on a fallen tree. I peered up at him with eyes that said, "Please don't say anything." He didn't.

My feet were aching and sweaty in their multi-layers, and I could feel a blister forming on the top of my right foot.

"It's a little bit farther. You can make it. Here, give me one of those coats. I think I can stuff it in my backpack." He graciously took my fleece jacket, which he rolled up and punched down into the zippered compartment in his pack. He pointed up the trail.

My feet declared I couldn't stand, but I stood anyway.

At last, Ted and I reached the summit. The others had already been there a few minutes, and by the expression on their faces, this was the first time they'd noticed my sweaty face and clothing evidently sufficient for an arctic expedition.

"June, won't you come and have a look off the ledge here," one of the female hikers asked kindly.

I didn't want to. I didn't like high places. All I wanted to do was lie down, strip to my thermal underwear, and wait for the others to go back down. I'd expected it to be windy at the summit. It wasn't. At midday, the sun beat down from a cloudless sky.

Extra hot.

Why hadn't I listened to Ted?

"June, come on, take a look," another hiker said.

I blew my nose again, dropped all the extra clothing and edged slowly over to the rock cliff. When I neared the rim, my breath caught.

Not since the lower falls of the Yellowstone had beauty made me forget my fear of heights. But here before me was my world—the world that was mine because I'd faced my fear and dared to have a new life. I lowered myself to the ground and spotted the steeple of Emmanuel Church, the library, and the Colonial Store. I couldn't see my house for the trees, but I guessed its approximate location. The road leading out of town toward Jubilee's house was clearly visible, as well as the courthouse, and the Dinner Bell.

"Breathtaking?' I heard Ted ask.

"And to think I almost let fear cheat me out of seeing all of this."

"But you didn't."

We both sat down and reposed in silence, stilled by the panorama before us.

And then, the idea came to me. Why hadn't I thought of it before? I grabbed Ted's arm. "I've got it! I've got it!"

Fear rose in his eyes. "June, are you having a seizure from all those hot clothes? You've got what?"

"I know what I'm supposed to write. I know what the book is about." I jumped up and clapped my hands. "Finally, I know. It's been with me all along, and I couldn't see it."

Ted stood up and grabbed me by the shoulders, "You have to get hold of yourself. I don't want you falling off this mountain. Let's move a little further away from the edge."

By this time, hot tears rolled down my face adding new streaks to the make-up undone by perspiration.

"After all of this time! How incredible. I'm so thankful I came."

"I am too." He studied me in that way of his that I didn't quite understand.

Someone called, "Time to go down."

Ted helped me gather all my castaway clothes, which by now included a down coat, a fleece jacket, a sweater, and a pair of socks I'd stripped off when we arrived at the top.

"I could always put all of this back on and roll down the mountain," I said.

"Not a bad plan," Ted responded.

Chapter Eighteen

Inspiration

"Learn to associate ideas worthy of God with all that happens in Nature—the sunrises and the sunsets, the sun and the stars, the changing seasons, and your imagination will never be at the mercy of your impulses, but will always be at the service of God."
—Oswald Chambers (1874-1917)

The next morning I awoke realizing that at the top of the mountain, the beauty had struck a chord in my imagination.

I prayed my imagination would be totally given over to God.

I anchored myself at the computer still wearing my pajamas, and the words flowed like the Niagara River. For days, I couldn't type fast enough or long enough to get everything that poured out of my head.

The laundry piled up.

Dishes overflowed the sink.

I didn't answer the phone, and the answering machine light blinked numbers into the double digits.

I hadn't been to Colonial Store in days and was reduced to tuna and crackers. Red was on his last can of cat food.

"June, you have to take a break," Ted told me one night on the telephone.

"I might need a few things from the grocery store." I opened the refrigerator door, studied the empty shelves, and shut it again. "You don't know anyone who helps with housework, do you?"

"Only the lady who helps me. I'll see if she can come over one day," he said.

"That'd be a blessing." I hung up the phone and crunched down on a stale cracker.

###

The doorbell rang, and as I went down the stairs, I noticed the clock in the study read 10:00. I'd been up since 5:00. I couldn't believe my eyes when I opened the front door.

"Hello, my name is Gladys Pickens. Ted sent me over here to help you with yer housework."

"You're the lady he sent?"

"Yes ma'am. Mr. Moore called you didn't he, 'cause I don't mean to be intrudin' on you?" Gladys asked.

"Oh, yes he told me he was sending over the lady that helps him in the house." I had no idea it would be Gladys Pickens. I guess I'd never mentioned her name when I told him about the woman at the library, and he'd never mentioned the name of his help. Ted had passed over my comments, so I hadn't given him any more information.

"Thank you for coming. I'm behind because of some writing I'm doing and need a little help catching up." Gladys still stood on the front porch. I motioned for her to enter. "Come in, come in." As she came through the door and deposited her purse on the foyer table, I took her coat and thought of my plumber. "Gladys, I had a plumber over here a few weeks back with the last name of Pickens—Elmer Pickens. Do you know him?"

"Why, uh, well, I, uh, why do you ask?" Gladys stammered.

"Curious, is all."

"Ain't I seen you somewhere before?" Gladys asked peering at me suspiciously.

"I'm fairly new in town—the grocery store, or downtown. I do volunteer at the library. Maybe you saw me there." I knew exactly where Gladys had seen me.

"The library. Been over there with my niece a few times of late. She has little ones that just love to have you read to 'em."

"You can never read too much to your children." I hoped my face didn't betray what I was thinking. "Gladys, let me show you what I need done."

After giving her instructions, I returned upstairs, and phoned Ted.

"You don't say?" was his reply when I connected the dots for him as to Gladys' identity.

"She never actually gave me an answer about whether she's related to Elmer or not." Curious. "I don't know why she avoided the question. If you ask me, Elmer has to be a fine fellow, because he and Jed didn't have to give the money they found in my basement to me. I would've never known about it unless Addie had suddenly remembered. I really believe he's on the up and up. In any event, thanks for sharing her with me."

"Glad to be of service," he replied.

###

Later that day, while getting some fresh air, I noticed at long last the hyacinths that lined the patio were coming up, and the buds appeared to be purple, my favorite. I strolled around the side of the house and encountered a camellia with the largest pink blossoms I'd ever seen.

When I'd first moved in, I'd taken note of the plant, but had no idea exactly when it would bloom, and Bertha couldn't remember either when I'd asked her about it. I stood for a while mesmerized by the size of the flowers, and then ran back in the house to get a pair of clippers, so I could cut a bouquet. I had a Waterford vase Linnea had given me for my birthday that'd be the perfect size for them. I might even float a blossom in a crystal bowl.

After clipping camellias, I strode around to the front yard to snip Lenten roses, which had already been blooming for a week or so. I loved Lenten Roses. They said spring even when snow was on the ground. I'd cut the blossoms with their droopy little heads and put them in tiny vases in the kitchen. They'd helped my spirits on many a cold February morning. I shivered in my fleece jacket, but held on to the hope that spring was near with so much in bloom.

Even with the chill, I took my basket of blooms and decided to sit for a few minutes on the patio before I went back inside. My thoughts drifted to my relationship with Ted.

Something about those dimples both delighted and terrified me.

We'd settled into a friendly companionship that I was comfortable with, but I was beginning to sense Ted wanted more—marriage, even.

I grew tense against it. I hadn't even told Ted how Morris died. Just couldn't bring myself to do it. Ted had to be curious.

Lord, when will I ever be able to let Morris go?

I breathed deeply the North Georgia air, and smiled at my Jubilee crafted whirligig. As the breeze caught the flying pen, I shook off the heavy thoughts and was inspired to return once more to my desk.

###

On and on I forged, and then came to a wall that was impenetrable. I knew why, and would have to be patient. But I had to keep writing something, so I returned to my magazine work.

After so much intense writing, I'd fallen behind on several things. It was mid-March, and Red was overdue for his shots. I checked the phone book to find the number of a local vet, Dr. Rebecca Nearside, called, and made an appointment.

Red, for all of his laid-back laziness at home, was not exactly a model patient, which made trips to the vet nerve wrecking experiences. He protested vigorously all attempts to provide for his health. The day of the appointment, I tried to explain to Dr. Nearside about Red's attitude.

When the technician tried to take Red's temperature and encountered a lion, Dr. Nearside stepped in. "Let me show you how to do it." She put a move on Red I'd never seen any Vet use before. "I've never met a cat I can't handle." She then attempted to insert the thermometer in his posterior.

I was about to sigh in relief when Red pulled a paw lose, yowled loudly, slapped the thermometer against the wall breaking it into a dozen pieces and scratched Dr. Nearside's hand in the process.

The technician handed Dr. Nearside a gauze pad to place on her bloody hand. The Vet studied Red who was now scratching feverishly on the examining room door trying to get out. "You know," she said, "I think his temperature is about normal." She pivoted and left the room.

"Can't take you anywhere," I complained later as I put Red back into the car. He purred loudly at me and rubbed against the front door of the carrier. "Now you act like an angel. All we're trying to do is help."

Red blinked at me with sweet eyes and meowed.

###

"Becky was accepted to the fine art school she applied to," Belle said half-smiling when we met for coffee one evening at the Dinner Bell.

"That's wonderful." As I stirred cream into my cup, I sensed Belle's heightened anxiety level and that the news was bittersweet.

"It'd be more wonderful if I could see how she was going to go. Even with student loans, the out of state tuition is unthinkable. I've had such hope over these past few weeks, but now I'm getting a little shaky."

Belle paused as if trying to decide whether she should continue.

"What is it?" I asked placing my hand on her arm.

"I'm behind on my mortgage payments. I don't know how long the bank will be patient with me."

Stella zipped toward us with a coffee pot in her hand and screeched to a stop a few feet away when she saw Belle's face. I shook my head slightly, and she pivoted and rolled back to the kitchen.

I thought about the stacks of money found in my basement and wished I could just give them to her. What a waste if I never found the heirs.

Belle continued. "There seems to be nothing I can do to change the way things are going. The doctor says I can't start working another job anytime soon. He says I'll wind up in the hospital again." Belle squeezed the mug in her hands her knuckles growing white.

"Belle, Morris left me in an adequate financial situation. I'm not wealthy, but I have income from my writing. Would you let me loan you a few dollars to see you through this time? No interest. You just pay me back when you can."

"Absolutely not." Tension crackled as Belle plunked her coffee cup on the table. "My family is not your responsibility. I don't know what's going to happen, but I want to remind you of the verse you gave me at Christmas."

"Verse?" I asked.

"Don't you remember? Romans 8:28."

I'd almost forgotten.

"After you left Christmas night, I asked God to help me believe and trust Him. I may have weak faith, but I still have faith. No, I don't know what to do, and yes, I feel helpless, but I believe God knows what to do."

"You're right." I sighed. Why did I never learn?

###

"How lovely," Addie said from her chair as I entered the Mountain Gardens gathering room with a gloxinia in my hand. "Let's leave it over on that sideboard there so everyone can enjoy it."

I knew she was going to say that, and was already moving toward the sideboard with the plant. I crossed over and eased down beside Addie who had Misty asleep in her lap.

Something cold and wet brushed against my leg, and I looked down to see Virgil nuzzling me.

"Now, Virgil, don't bother June." Addie glanced at the pig and then at me. "He's seeking a little attention. Quite a pet, that one."

I couldn't remember ever scratching a pig's ear before, but I reached down and rubbed Virgil a little on the head. He nuzzled me with his snout.

I nodded to the doors. "Addie, it's quite spring-like outside. Would you like to sit on the front porch a while?"

"I don't mind if I do. Let me put Misty down in this chair here, while I get my cane." Misty rolled off Addie's lap on to the chair surprised by the sudden rearrangement of her sleeping situation. Together, we ambled to the porch and nestled in the west facing rockers.

For a few moments, we took in the vista before us, which included Currahee Mountain. "This is why I came back to Toccoa, to fill my senses with the sights, and smells, and sounds I knew as I child. Before I died, I wanted to live in this place again. It brings back such wonderful memories. My body is old but my spirit still feels like that eight-year-old girl tagging after Silas and Buford down along the Tugaloo River, picking blackberries, and chasing rabbits. Sometimes, my Daddy would let me ride with him to the fields. He'd hitch up the wagon and, I'd stay with him until dinner time."

As we rocked, a thought came to me that was so obvious, I couldn't imagine why it hadn't occurred to me before. "Why don't we go see those places you knew as a child? I could pull my car here to the front, and you could just hop in. Do you think you can tell me how to get there?"

"Mercy, yes. I'd never forget where I grew up, but I know you'll have to talk to the office here. They like to keep up with where their folks are. Since they know you now, I'm sure they'd let me go with you."

'When do you want to go?" I asked.

"Let's go right now!" Addie showed more excitement than I'd ever seen in her.

I made the arrangements, signed Addie out, and in no time we were on the way. Misty had seemed insulted to be left behind, but it didn't seem to stop her from curling up for another nap.

We headed out of town on the road I'd taken to Jubilee's house. We turned right, however, not far from town and drove past land that appeared to be still under cultivation. "This used to all be cotton," Addie said. "Cotton as far as the eye could see back in the days when cotton was still king. Everybody we knew grew cotton, and had a vegetable garden, too, so they could put up for the winter. My mama used to can shelf after shelf of tomatoes, green beans, corn, butter beans, okra, and she even made pickles—the best bread and butter pickles I've ever eaten. I can still taste them." Addie closed her eyes remembering and then opened them again and studied the landscape around her. "We should be getting close now. Our house was past the Edward's place."

After a few moments passed, she clapped her hands and pointed, "There it is! It's still there. Can you believe it?"

Standing under the shade of ancient oaks beginning to bud was a hip-roofed, white frame house with deep porches and tall windows. The metal roof, though new, was reminiscent of the tin roofs I remembered on old houses from my childhood.

I turned right, drove up the gravel driveway to the house, and stopped the car. Addie was already reaching for the door handle before I could even cut the engine off. "Let's see if anybody's home," she said. As we made our way along the daffodil lined walkway to the front porch, I wondered if in some way, Addie was expecting to see her mama come to the door.

"Yoo, hoo, anyone here," Addie called in a high-pitched voice as she knocked on the door. We heard footsteps falling on hardwood floors, rustling inside, and then a turn of the knob.

"Hi, who are you?" a blonde headed little girl about eight years old asked through the screen door.

"I used to live here," Addie said, "when I was about your age. My name is Addie, and this is my friend June."

"You lived here when you were my age?" the little girl asked with raised eyebrows.

"I sure did. This is my home place."

"Jillie, who's at the door?" a voice called from the back of the house.

"A lady who says she used to live here," Jillie turned and called back.

We heard more footsteps, and then a young woman came to the door wiping her hands on a cloth. "Can I help you?"

"I grew up in this house," Addie explained again, "I haven't been here in a long time. My name is Addie Braham, and this is June Callaway."

"Pleased to meet you both, my name's Cary Kendall and this is my daughter Jillie," Cary said. "Would you like to come in? I was just making blueberry muffins. My house has been cleaner, but you're certainly welcome."

"Oh, could we?" Addie scooted into the house light-footed almost not needing her cane.

The house, I knew was built in a style prevalent at the turn of the nineteenth century with a wide center hall and rooms off to each side. An obviously fresh coat of light yellow paint covered the walls in the hallway. Addie stopped and gestured toward the right. "Just here beside this door, my mama had what she called a library table, and she always had a vase of flowers on it when the garden was in bloom." Addie pointed to the end of the hallway, "And back there was an oak hall tree. We used to put our shoes in a little hinged compartment in the bottom."

The first door to the right, a family room was open. Addie navigated the uneven threshold. "We had a pot-bellied stove sitting right there," Addie moved to the wall and pointed to where the fireplace was. "I use to wake up in my bed under a big pile of Mama's quilts and hated to get out from under that warm cover. I'd run in here and stand by this stove to get warm. Mama and Daddy had been up early getting the coal burning stove going."

"Our heat comes from vents in the floor now," said Jillie.

"We use the fireplace some, but not often," said Cary. "Please feel free to wander around."

Addie started to navigate through a door to the left of the fireplace to an adjoining room when something caught her eye. She pointed with her cane. "That bucket over there on the floor, where ever did you find it?"

A large grey enameled bucket filled with magazines rested beside a chair. "In the crawl space under the house when we put in the central heat and air," Cary said.

"That was my mama's bucket," Addie boasted. "We used to gather the vegetables from the garden in it. I still remember it being so loaded I could hardly get it up the back steps."

Cary started taking the magazines out. "You're welcome to it."

"No, no, I don't have any use for it, and no one to pass it down to. It gives me pleasure to think of it being used again." Addie smiled at Jillie.

"What was your last name, again," Cary asked.

"Braham, Addie Braham. My mama and daddy built this house."

"Yes, I remember, when we bought this house the lawyer told us that when he checked the title there'd only been two other owners, the people we bought it from, and the Brahams who built the house. We searched and searched for a place we could fix up that had a little land with it. We wanted to get out of the Atlanta traffic."

I nodded. "I understand that goal completely."

"So you're from Atlanta, too?"

"Just moved here last year."

"A transplant like us. Yes, it's been slow progress, but we've tried to be careful with the renovations and be as true as we can to the original. Trying to remodel not re-muddle. How are we doing?"

"You're doing fine, I'd say," Addie said convincingly.

"Why don't you two stay for supper?" Cary asked. I have plenty, and I'd love for you to meet my husband Anthony. He'll be here in a few minutes."

"We'd love to." Addie hadn't even glanced at me, and then she realized her mistake and corrected. "I'm sorry June. I didn't ask to see if you had other plans."

"It would be a joy to stay for dinner," I said meaning it.

###

As we pulled up in front of Mountain Gardens, Addie turned to me. "June, I want you to know this has been one of the happiest days of my life. I never dreamed my old home place could be in such good hands, being brought back to life like it is. This has been a fine day."

We strolled into the gathering room to see Misty curled up on top of Virgil, both of them fast asleep. "Have you ever seen the beat in all your life?" Addie asked.

I smiled at the expression I'd only heard one other person use—my grandmother. I knew she was asking me if I'd ever seen anything like it."I can honestly say I haven't."

Chapter Nineteen

Suspicions

"... whatever is true, whatever is noble, whatever is right, whatever is pure, whatever is lovely, whatever is admirable—if anything is excellent or praiseworthy—think about such things. Whatever you have learned or received or heard from me, or seen in me—put it into practice. And the God of peace will be with you."
—Philippians 4:8-9

I felt pressure to finish the novel, but tried to remember that God's timing was perfect, and He was in control of when I had a breakthrough in my work. But still, I became anxious at times over the unfinished state of something I'd worked so hard on. Once more I pushed back the "what if's" that lingered perennially in my brain.

Easter was only a couple of weeks away, and I looked forward to Linnea and Jason coming home for spring break. There wouldn't be much writing that week, because I liked to be available to spend time with them. I saw them so seldom; I didn't want to waste a minute.

I lolled at the kitchen table pondering whether to have a big Easter lunch like the one I had at Thanksgiving.

Through the bay window, the viburnum, or "snowball bush" as my grandfather, an avid gardener, had called it, was loaded with cream-colored spheres of blossoms. The weight of the flowers on some branches almost pulled them to the ground. An heirloom plant I'd transplanted from Atlanta, it was rooted from a cutting of my mother's viburnum, which in turn was rooted from a cutting from my grandfather's plant. He'd died in 1966—my mother in 2001, which meant for more than forty years we'd kept his garden alive. I hoped to root a cutting for my children so the legacy would continue. This plant and others like the yellow irises from my mother's garden helped me feel connected to family members long gone who shared my love of nature.

I slipped out to the patio, and peonies profuse with buds greeted me. The Mr. Lincoln rose I'd planted in the fall was coming along nicely, too. An old growth weigela was so large and full of magenta blooms, I knew it'd have to be pruned this year. The cleome seeds Jed had given me emerged into green foliage, which bore a resemblance to something else I couldn't quite put my finger on. As I made my way around the side of the house into the front yard, I understood again why Addie thought of Toccoa when she saw dogwoods. Under a canopy of pines, the dogwoods had naturalized on the sloping hills behind the homes on the south side of the street creating a fairy tale look.

While I stood in the front yard, Jed's familiar "Weed and Seed" truck passed. Jed blew his horn, smiled, and waved. I threw up my hand as he went by.

I returned inside just in time to catch the phone.

"Gladys told me what's worrying her," Ted said.

"What?" I asked while perched on a chair in the study.

"Before I tell you what it is, I need to tell you Gladys is a naturally suspicious person, and watches way too many mystery stories on television. She once thought the meter reader had stolen her pantsuits off the clothesline, and wanted me to press charges. It turned out she'd put them in a different closet. Another time she accused her niece of taking her JCPenney hose card which had enough punches for a free pair. She found it in another wallet."

"That is a little over the top." I leaned back in the chair trying to wrap my brain around what Ted was telling me.

"Just wanted you to have the context. Now, she thinks Elmer and Jed are growing marijuana in Elmer's basement. She's seen lights on in Elmer's basement, which she suspects, are grow lights, and Jed's big truck has been backed up over there this winter. She thinks they're loading marijuana in it, and selling it out of Jed's office. She's going to confront them this week. I thought you'd better know since it could just as easily happen over there since she's working for you."

"You're making this up," I said.

"I wish I was," he responded.

"Does she know Jed helps Elmer with his plumbing business during the winter?"

"Sure, she knows that, but when Gladys gets something in her mind, the facts don't seem to bother her. She's been a fine helper around here, but sometimes..." Ted trailed off.

A thought came to me."Oh, no."

"What?"

"Call you back."

I darted through the house and out the kitchen door to where I'd planted the Cleome seeds. Could it be? Surely, he didn't get mixed up and give me the wrong seeds. If Detective William Rust came over here and saw this, I could be arrested. I started to pull the plants from the ground just as I heard the roar of a truck out front.

I rushed to the front yard, and when I did, Jed was already out of the truck and walking around studying my yard.

"Jed, I didn't expect you today . . ." I said flustered as he sauntered toward me.

"While I's in the neighborhood, I thought I'd stop and see how yer grass is comin' along." He smiled innocently.

His cell phone rang, and he excused himself to answer it. He paced off a few feet, and then Jed's smile dropped from his face and his expression morphed into one of shock. Jed yelled into the phone, "She thought we was what? Is she crazy?"

I pulled spent blooms off the camellia bush while Jed talked. In a moment, he said, "She's gone too far now," hung up the phone, and came back to me with a stone face, "'Excuse me Miz Callaway. I gotta go."

He stomped off to his truck and burned rubber getting out of the driveway. I didn't have to wonder what happened. He was plenty mad, but maybe this meant I didn't have to pull up the plants in my back yard after all. I did pray, however, that Jed would get hold of himself before he said or did something he'd be sorry for.

###

The fur flew.

It took days to settle the mess between Gladys, Jed, and Elmer. The bad thing was that Gladys had about convinced her niece, Helen, that Jed and Elmer were really growing marijuana.

I'm glad Ted told me about it, because sure enough, the next afternoon just as Gladys finished cleaning, and Helen came to pick her up, Jed came back to check on the grass. The next thing I knew, Jed called Elmer and they were all on my front porch hashing it out.

I called Ted who was just leaving the office. "On the way," he said.

Afraid the neighbors might call 911, I asked them to all come inside.

"How's I supposed to know he really was helpin' with the plumbin'?" Gladys protested as she took a seat in the study. Helen sat beside her.

Elmer politely took off his shoes at the front door. "If you'd stop watchin' all them mystery stories and such and stick to the truth, you'd be better off. Mindin' yer own business wouldn't be a bad idee either."

"Next time, leave me out," said Jed who declined an invitation to sit, saying he didn't want to soil the furniture.

Gladys went on."I couldn't. You were over there every day with that big old truck of your'n. I couldn't figure no reason for it bein' over there but that you two were up to no good. I figured you was using it to get the marijuana Elmer was growin' out of his basement 'cause he didn'have no other way to move it. It just added up. "

"What were we supposed to be putting it in, herbicide tanks?" Jed asked shaking his head in frustration.

"I don't know. I hadn't thought about that." Gladys smoothed out the wrinkles in her striped blouse. "So why was them lights on in your basement all the time this winter?" she asked Elmer.

"Well, if you must know, I got some plumbing problems myself that I hadn't had time to fix, and was tryin' to keep the basement good and warm so the pipes wouldn't freeze up and make the situation worse."

I nodded. Sure understood that predicament. What was that old saying about the plumber's pipes always leaking?

"At the beginnin' I tried to tell her y'all wouldn't do nothin' like that, but she got to soundin' like she knowed what she was a talkin' about," said Helen.

Ted slipped in the front door and stood in the doorway of the study.

Jed folded his arms in a defensive posture."My pick-up's been actin' up, and I had to drive the big truck. If you'd asked me, I could of told you. It'd been better than you thinkin' I was growin' pot." He paused a long moment. "This here just about killed Ethel. She never dreamed anybody could be so lowdown, and especially kin folk. You're one of her favorite aunts."

At last Ted interjected. "Gladys, had you given any thought to how this might make Ethel feel?"

Gladys grew pensive. "I never dreamed I'd be a hurtin' Ethel this way. She's a mighty fine girl, and I sure didn't aim to hurt her. I reckon I owe her an apology."

"What about me?" asked Elmer.

"And me?" Jed echoed.

"All right, all right I'm sorry. I should have knowed you two weren't up to nothin' like that. Sometimes, my imagination runs away with me. I'm sorry and ashamed of myself. I don't know what got into me. How can I make it up to you?"

"Jest don't let it happen again." said Elmer.

"Yeah," Jed agreed.

"Thank goodness," Ted exhaled.

Chapter Twenty

A Big Job and a Big Fear

"Only people who are capable of loving strongly can also suffer great sorrow, but this same necessity of loving serves to counteract their grief and heals them."
—Leo Tolstoy (1828-1910)

While in the kitchen pouring coffee one morning, a loud hum I hadn't heard before emanated from the general direction of Bertha's house. I went outside and peered over the fence.

Sure enough, Jubilee had the tiller plowing full speed in the garden. The earth black with years of amendments and mulch, spilled over in neat piles. The fresh turned smell of it told a story of long years of labor. In contrast, my yard hadn't had nearly the attention; so much of it was still red clay.

The morning sun rose warm in the sky, so I returned to the kitchen and placed cubes of ice in a glass, filled it with water, and took it back out to the fence. Jubilee saw me, cut off the tiller, and strode toward me.

"I'm beholdin' to you,' he said as he took the glass. " It gets awful hot workin' that tiller. Miz Bertha's got me puttin' in more rows than ever. She's gonna have enough vegetables to feed all of Toccoa. All that time she spent pourin' over those seed catalogs when her hip was a healin' is gonna mean a heap of plowin' for me."

He stopped and gulped half the glass of water. "I don't know if I can do it. It's about to kill me just puttin' in the rows, and I ain't even started the plantin' nor the weedin' yet."

I studied his lined face, and knew Bertha had gone too far, but if there's anything I learned through this whole mess with Gladys, Elmer, and Jed, it's that I need to be careful about nosing around in my neighbor's business. Bertha had a temper, too, which I'd seen her demonstrate on more than one occasion.

"Jubilee, you have your yard art hobby I know you enjoy. If the work gets too much, just talk to Bertha. There has to be somebody else that can help her."

Jubilee's eyes drifted behind me.

He pointed to the whirligig. "I see you've got the piece I made for you right by your patio."

"It brings me great joy every time I see it."

"Glad to hear it," Jubilee replied giving me a toothy grin.

###

"June, I'd like to take you up to a restaurant in Highlands that Robert Giles told me about. What about Thursday night?" Ted asked one evening on the phone.

"Great." The terrible dilemma again—what would I wear? I scanned my outfit and decided the yoga pants and tee shirt I'd been writing in all day would not be an option.

After we hung up, I clicked my mouse and stared at the flashing screens as my computer shut down. Once more, I found my thoughts returning to the stolen desk.

Though it was no longer in my possession, I still couldn't stop thinking about it. Why couldn't I let it go?

I found myself praying the same old prayer. "God, please help me."

###

I studied the menu illuminated by soft candlelight. "Ted, they have sea bass. I haven't had that in so long."

"Sounds delicious." Ted closed his menu.

After the waiter had taken our order, we both leaned back and gazed out the large bank of windows. Because the restaurant was situated on the side of a mountain, through the southwest facing windows, we could see the lights in the valley below come on one by one as the sun slid toward the horizon. For some time, as soft classical music played in the background, we watched as the twinkles increased eventually dotting the entire landscape much like the stars become increasingly visible as the night sky darkens. But after a while, Ted leaned forward, took my hand, and fixed his eyes on me with great intensity. "June, you look beautiful tonight, but then you always look beautiful."

My cheeks stung a little under the attention.

"I've wanted to speak to you about something, and haven't felt the time was right."

I nodded concerned.

"I've tried hard not to push you in these past few months—with Morris' death being so recent."

Oh, no, where was this going? I squirmed in my seat and held my breath. He paused and his eyes wandered back to the windows. "I've had longer to deal with the death of my wife. These past months have been blessed—I've had a companion to share meals with. But I was wondering . . . "

My heart skidded like a car hydroplaning on a wet mountain road headed for a cliff.

He leaned forward again. "What I mean is, I don't just want to be your legal counsel, or the person you bounce problems off. I love being friends with you, but . . ."

Not ready to hear this. Trying to stop the slide.

". . . is there a chance for something lasting?"

Can't find the brakes.

He stared at me waiting for me to speak. He wanted some sort of commitment. I didn't know what to say.

Moments passed.

I fumbled with my water glass, trying to get it to my lips, and in the process knocked over both it and a vase of white roses on the table. Water spilled from the vase and the glass—a wet spot spread across the crisp tablecloth and dripped onto the floor. I jumped up quickly to avoid it staining my silk dress. The waiter rushed forward to catch the waterfall with a towel.

"I'm sorry," I said.

"Happens all the time," the waiter explained. "Don't give it another thought."

But as Ted, dimple-less and defused, made vain attempts to catch the water with his limp napkin, I knew that not giving it another thought wouldn't be an option.

###

As I circled the bubbling fountain at the Paul Anderson Park, I read the words inscribed in stone around the base: "If I, Paul Anderson, The World's Strongest Man, cannot make it through one day without Jesus Christ, how can you?"

The Olympic Champion and Toccoa native had left quite a mark on the world what with his boys' home and inspirational messages.

Waiting for Iris to arrive, I stood a moment, reflecting on Anderson's words, and staring up at the bronze statue of the muscled Anderson. The sculpture of the strongest man in the world contrasted sharply with my trembling and fear, but His words brought me comfort and reminded me of others from I Corinthians about God's strength being perfected in our weakness.

"Why are you afraid," Iris asked a few moments later.

I plopped down on a bench, and tied the loose strings on my walking shoes. "I don't even know. Maybe I'm afraid of making a mistake, or change is hard, or I'm not through grieving Morris, or I don't know what my children will say… how's that for a start?"

Iris grew quiet. A cardinal chirped from a nearby tree. "At some point you have to move on with your life."

I stiffened. "I think moving here was a pretty huge step in that direction."

"Of course, I didn't mean to indicate you weren't taking steps. I know it was hard to move here. I do." She paused again. "But your heart, June? What about moving on in your heart? You obviously have feelings for Ted, and he for you. But you seem, I don't know, stuck, somehow. Just because you've geographically moved doesn't mean you've made any progress in other ways."

The chirps in the trees multiplied, and I glanced up to see a female and a male cardinal singing, and then the female flew off.

"I need time," I said crisply.

Iris studied me a moment and nodded.

But I had to ask myself if more time would, in fact, change anything.

###

Palm Sunday dawned clear and a little cool.

On this morning a friend of Tom and Joe's, Tyler, a gifted young trumpeter played the introduction to the hymn accompanied by piano and organ. Pushing past my heavy heart, I joined the choir as we sang, "Hosanna, Loud, Hosanna," which rang from the rafters at Emmanuel Church.

The trumpet swelled as the congregation lifted their voices with us on the first verse, and the children's Sunday School classes filed down the aisle waving palms. From my vantage point in the choir, I could see their sweet faces as they deposited their offerings along the altar area, and then returned to sit with their parents.

After the last verse, the liturgist began: "Hosanna to the son of David!"

The congregation responded: "Blessed is he that cometh in the name of the Lord; Hosanna in the highest!"

I remembered the words Jesus spoke to the Pharisees when they complained about the disciples joyful praise, "I tell you," he said, "If they keep quiet, the stones will cry out."

This morning it seemed the same was true. Even through the cloud of so much not knowing, and wondering, about my relationship with Ted, about the desk, my heart still longed to praise.

I felt if we did not sing praise to God, if I did not sing praise, the sheetrock walls might do it for us. How often it seemed we were called on to hold opposites in our heart. Praise and sorrow. Joy and pain. Certainty and uncertainty.

Linnea and Jason sat midway down on the right in the congregation, and Belle, Joe, and Becky were beside them. As soon as Belle could manage, she'd started coming to services at Emmanuel.

I'd seen a change in Belle. I sensed that whatever lay ahead for her now, she would not be alone. For the first time, her despairing eyes were gone, and though I knew she was in pain, she bore a new light, and it seemed a weight had been lifted. She had hope not based on what she could see was going to work out, but based on what she could not see. I supposed that was the essence of faith.

I found her a true inspiration. I needed an increase of hope myself. Her trust and surrender challenged me and made me wonder if Iris was right? Was there something that sat like a stone in my own heart dragging me down?

Later in the day, I lounged on the patio with Jason and Linnea.

"How are you doing with the book, Mom?" Linnea asked.

"I'd say I was more than halfway there, I'm at a point where I need a breakthrough in the plot. I'm writing this by the seat of my pants. No outline." It was kind of like walking on water, and now, I seemed to be sinking some.

"What's it about?" asked Jason.

"I'm not telling yet." I'd read somewhere that if you talk too much about what you're writing it can get away from you.

"How about emailing it to us when you get through? We want to be the first ones to read it," said Linnea.

As we were talking, I became aware of birds flitting in and out of a gardenia from which I hadn't had the heart to pull the honeysuckle. I loved the smell of the sweet vine, and since I had more than one gardenia, I was willing to sacrifice one to keep the honeysuckle.

I rose to have a look after the bird left the bush. When I pulled apart the brush, I spotted three speckled eggs in a nest. In no time, I'd have baby birds.

"Jason, come see," I called knowing I could count on him to be excited about any kind of wildlife discovery.

He joined me and peered over my shoulder. "Song sparrow," he declared. They love to build in brush like this.

"Do you think your cat is too lazy to attempt a bird kill?"

"I'll have to have a talk with him to make sure he doesn't make a snack out of these little fellows when they hatch."

"You do that." In the mean time, I'd better keep an eye on that cat.

###

Ted and I strolled across the courthouse lawn and stood for a moment studying Currahee, which would soon be mostly eclipsed again by the leaves of budding trees. As I guessed earlier, the mountain was more visible in the winter from this location due to the loss of foliage. I took a deep breath. Ted and I had agreed to meet for a few minutes to clear the air, but I was unable to think of anything new to say. "I just can't talk about it right now, Ted."

He nodded.

Would the man who had the patience to restore a piece of dilapidated machinery to new life have the same patience with me? I didn't know, but I wasn't going to ask. The world seemed to wobble a bit, and I fixed my gaze on the steady mountain.

Ted took my hand and squeezed it. Oh, how I hoped that squeeze meant he would wait.

###

I thought Addie might enjoy an Easter lily, so midweek, Jason, Linnea, and I took one by Mountain Gardens.

"See you have your children with you again." Addie's eyes brightened.

"Jason's hoping he can get a glimpse of Virgil while we're here," I said as we approached her.

"I saw Virgil just a minute ago. He's really taken a liking to Misty, and almost every day he comes out here to check on her." Addie pointed to her right. "I believe he went back towards the dining hall." Jason followed Addie's directions and disappeared from view.

"For you." I handed the flower to Addie, but as usual, she pointed to a table by the front door. I gave the flower to Linnea, and she set it down. She returned and plopped down on a loveseat beside me.

"Glad you folks dropped by, because something came to my mind about that desk mystery. I told you Buford married, and had a little girl named Doris, who grew up and married a man named Robert. I believe I received a card from them, a birth announcement or such years ago, that had a picture of a baby girl, but I still don't remember where it was from or their last names. Does that help you any?" Addie asked.

It was of no help, but I didn't want to say that. I smiled. "Who knows?" is all I could think of.

Addie smiled. "Well, you never know. Maybe, there'll come a time when it does help you."

When she said that, a strange sensation came over me—one that I was at a loss to explain. What was it?

Chapter Twenty-One

Messages from the Past

"Do all the good you can
By all the means you can
In all the ways you can
In all the places you can
To all the people you can
As long as ever you can."
—John Wesley (1703-1791)

Thursday of Holy Week found things in full swing over at Bertha's house. Melissa sent a chipmunk family packing as she swooped by on her mower. Jubilee had already planted five rows of vegetables before noon and had five more to go.

Bertha decided she wanted a perennial bed by the fence, so late in the afternoon, Jubilee had to get the tiller out again to plow the bed.

Bertha had told me earlier, she planned to put Bath's pink, purple coneflower, and a butterfly bush in the ground.

As I held out water for Jubilee who was working in the heat of the day, he said, "I've done made up my mind. When Miz Sally's book comes out next month, I'm gonna need to be at my own place to handle folks comin' to get a look at my work. Miz Bertha's gotta find somebody to help me with this garden. There'll be a heap of weedin' here that'll need doin' about then."

"Have you told Bertha?" I asked as he drained the water from the glass.

He wiped his mouth and handed the glass back to me. "Yes ma'am. I wanted to be fair. I been with Miz Bertha a long time, but I ain't no spring chicken myself. We need help. Here we're puttin' in all these seeds. What I wanna know is who's gonna take out?"

Jubilee definitely had a point

###

Good Friday morning, I started the day by reading the story of the crucifixion. In this culture, it was too easy to insulate oneself against the terrible agony Jesus suffered on mankind's behalf, on my behalf. It was hard to read, and I had to force myself to move through it.

I lingered for a while on the patio pondering the implications for my own life—how sacrifice leads to redemption. How suffering leads to joy. How out of dark places like tombs, amazing things can happen.

In my mind, I was back standing at the cemetery by Morris' casket, so aware of the dark hole beneath it, so sure that when that box was lowered into it, I might as well be inside it, too.

Yet, here I was, alive, sort of.

A song sparrow darted in and out of the honeysuckle covered gardenia bush.

I rose and gently pulled apart branches. There in the nest, three beaks opened up to me—three just emerged from their own capsule of darkness, now unfolding to the uncertainties of life beyond the shell.

I stepped back and gently allowed the branches to envelop them, hoping the Mama bird had not seen me breaching her space.

I turned my thoughts to my plans for the day. Emmanuel's Good Friday service wasn't until that evening, and since Belle was off today, and my kids were otherwise occupied running errands, I'd asked her to have lunch with me.

I arrived early at The Dinner Bell and scanned the specials on the menu board.

I couldn't believe what was listed.

Belle entered and seated herself across from me.

"They have tomato aspic today." I pointed in excitement to the specials on the menu board.

"Tomato aspic?" A blank expression came over Belle's face.

"Don't you remember? I served it at Thanksgiving. It's a red congealed salad, with tomato juice, olives, Worcestershire sauce?"

She grimaced a bit. "June, I didn't want to be rude at Thanksgiving, but when I took a bite of it, I thought it was going to be strawberry Jell-O. It turned out to be all congealed tomatoes and olives. I'd never tasted anything like it before."

"Did you like it?" asked June

"I didn't want to hurt your feelings, but I don't know how you eat it."

"So, you weren't the one to clean your plate?" I asked laughing.

She shook her head and grinned. "Uh, no, you can be sure of that."

Stella swerved over to get our orders. "Sorry to keep you two waiting, but we got ourselves a big catering order today. Ain't had a chance to hardly take a breath." Stella started reeling off the specials. "Now today, your chicken salad plate's been popular, with your walnuts and grapes, and Lucille's brought back the pimento cheese on your choice of artisan breads." Stella leaned way over. "Let y'all in on a little secret, but Lucille's had some pretty big offers for her bread recipes. Don't nobody have a way with bread like Lucille."

"I haven't tasted anything that Lucille didn't have a way with," I mused.

Stella nodded in agreement. "Oh, and I almost forgot, we got your spinach quiche today."

I threw down the menu. "Quiche for me."

"Chicken Salad," Belle said.

After Stella left, Belle grew more serious.

"What is it?" I asked.

"I might as well tell you. The lender is foreclosing on my home. They've been patient, but I only have two more weeks."

"I wish you'd let me help you." I extended my hand to her.

Belle wrapped her fingers around mine. "I'd never be able to pay you back. I have to let God do this—to trust Him. Somehow, we'll make it."

I was at a loss for words, but it was just as well, because I knew that nothing I could say was going to change the circumstances or the way Belle thought about them. But still, me with the money I found in my basement just lying around when it could be put to good use. Such a shame.

Stella flew up to our table and stopped so short, I was sure the food would go flying off the tray and land on the people in the booth beside us, but it didn't. "Got your lunch right here." She placed the plates on the table, which appeared undisturbed from their trip of near sound barrier speed. The delicate sprigs of rosemary nestled on my plate seemed to be exactly as they'd been originally placed.

I took in the wonderful aroma of the quiche."Thank you, Stella. By the way, do you run?"

"I run, all right. But, just at The Dinner Bell. I've been told I'd make a good sprinter, but from here to the kitchen seems about all the distance I'm able to cover right now."

I nodded.

"If y'all need anything else, just let me know." Soon, she was gone in a fashion any athlete would be proud of.

As Belle reached for the pepper, I noticed she wore a lovely ring. I pointed to her hand. "What an unusual piece. I haven't noticed it before."

"I never wore it to work at the clock factory, because I was afraid I'd lose it. I don't wear it to school now, because I get my hands dirty so often. It's special, though."

She peppered her food.

"Special?" I asked as she handed the pepper to me.

"My mother used to wear this ring. I've been praying about selling it. I don't want to, but it's about the only item I have of value that I could liquidate to help with expenses." Belle twisted the ring off her finger and handed it to me.

I took the ring and examined it—a lovely estate piece, platinum with a small center diamond. As I held the ring between my fingers and examined it closely, my head began to spin.

###

The doorbell rang that afternoon, but spying through the peephole, I didn't recognize the elderly woman standing on the porch. I hesitated a moment, but then opened the door. Dressed in a skirt, cardigan sweater, and a brooch at the neck of her crisp white blouse, she held a large canvas bag in her right hand. Beyond the woman, a truck with the motor idling sat in the driveway, a middle-aged man at the wheel.

"Can I help you?" I asked wondering if they were lost, somehow. Not everyone had GPS these days.

"I believe I'm in possession of something you'll be interested in," she announced.

What did she have in that canvas bag? Oh, please, I hoped she wasn't selling cosmetics, plastic ware, or cleaning products. I had plenty of all of them.

"My name is Edwina Jones. I used to live in this house as a young girl." I wondered if Edwina was like Addie trying to reclaim a part of her childhood. I was pleased to be the one hosting such an event today.

"Miss Jones, please come in." I pointed to the truck. "Do I see someone with you?"

"Yes, my nephew, Henry, is in the car." She motioned for him to come. Henry exited the truck with head down and hands shoved in pockets.

I motioned for them to seat themselves in the study, and after I'd offered them tea, Miss Jones, very erect in her chair, cleared her throat to speak. "I know you had a desk stolen from you a few months back. I want you to know it's in the back of my nephew's truck."

"Excuse me?" These people did not seem like robbers.

"The desk is in the back of the truck."

"But how? Where'd you get it?" I asked stunned at the revelation.

"I'm sorry to say my beloved nephew stole it." Miss Jones diverted her eyes toward Henry. Henry bowed his head even more and stared at his shoes.

I couldn't believe what I was hearing.

"You may call the police." Miss Jones said. "We are prepared to suffer the consequences of these actions."

I tried to process what I'd been told. "What's this all about?"

"It's a lengthy story, but I will try to be brief." She gestured to the room around her. "As I told you earlier, I lived in this house when I was a young woman. Buford Braham used to court me."

Now it was coming back to me, I remember Ted mentioning the Jones family as prior owners of the house. Henry never raised his head.

Miss Jones continued. "We were quite serious. When Silas lost his wife, Anne Marie, Buford was desperate for a place to put the desk. He wanted to place it in a location where'd it be safe, and Silas wouldn't have to see it for a while. He thought perhaps Silas would change his mind about it. My family and I were trying to help Buford by offering our basement as a storage place. However, though Buford kept going back to him, Silas never wanted to see it again."

I knew Buford had not married Miss Jones, so this story was bound to have a sad ending.

"Just as I thought Buford was about to offer me a ring, he met someone else while on a trip and married her a short time later. Doris, I believe was her name. I was so humiliated and heartbroken; I had to move away from Toccoa. When my parents died, I sent for a few of my parent's things and left the disposal of the house to the realtor. Someone bought it for rental property, and I never went to the trouble of cleaning out the basement."

If Miss Jones had only known the worth of the desk, she could have drowned her sorrows in a couple of around the world excursions. About that time, Red lumbered into the room and studied the gathering. Unperturbed, he strolled over to the bay window, hopped up and sprawled in the sunshine.

Miss Jones went on not acknowledging the cat. "All my relatives knew the story of Buford's abrupt departure and my broken heart. I never found anyone else like Buford."

She sighed and folded her hands in her lap. "A few years ago, though, I did move back to Toccoa. Recently Henry, who is the groundskeeper at the local high school, overheard Tom Reynolds and Joe Mathews talking on the soccer field about some desk they'd found in the basement of this house."

I remembered Tom and Joe had mentioned the desk at soccer practice.

Miss Jones studied her nephew a moment. "Henry couldn't believe the desk was still here after all these years. He thought it might make things right if he retrieved the desk for me. He felt

Buford owed me and that the desk was mine, so he took it. He became frightened of what he'd done when he saw the report of the burglary in the newspaper. It took him all this time to get the nerve to tell me what he'd done. We're here to return it, and he's ready to face the consequences."

At last, Henry raised his head, his eyes as sad as any Basset Hound I'd ever seen.

"Let's wait about consequences," I said to Henry. "How did you get in?"

Henry wiped his face with his hand and shook his head unable to speak.

Miss Jones continued, "With a key of course. Henry knew I never disposed of anything. After all, I paid close attention to the stories of my parents who'd lived through the Great Depression."

My grandparents had shared similar accounts.

"I have a drawer with keys in it. I used to tell the nieces and nephews when they were growing up where I'd used each key, and Henry remembered I had a key to this house. He couldn't believe the locks had never been changed."

I leaned back in my chair shaking my head. "This is amazing."

Miss Jones gasped. "Amazing? It's horrible. My beloved nephew thought of as a thief. I never could have imagined Henry would have such a lapse in judgment. Henry is not a common criminal. Because of his love for me, he was trying to do something to rectify what he perceived as an injustice."

Henry dropped his head again.

Miss Jones cleared her throat again, took an antiquated shoebox from the canvas bag at her feet, and extended it to me.

"This should go with the desk. I've kept these things all these years hoping someday I'd be able to give them to the right person."

I held the box on my lap and took off the lid. On top lay a faded picture—the edges rough as if the picture had been carried around in a pocket. Even with the water spot stained edges, I could make out the image of a lovely young woman. I turned the picture over. "To my beloved Silas," it read, "with all my love, Anne Marie."

"Oh, my," I sighed.

"That's Anne Marie," said Miss Jones.

"What are these?" I held up bundles of letters tied with ribbon.

"The letters Anne-Mare wrote to Silas while he was an army paratrooper—some of the most beautiful things I've ever read. Evidently, Silas gave them to Buford to put with the desk. After Buford departed town, and just before I left, I was in the basement one day and became curious if there was anything in that desk. I opened the drawer and saw them. I thought, what could be the harm in reading a few. At the time, I thought I was so moved by them because of Buford abruptly marrying someone else, but now I know, I would've been moved by them, no matter the circumstances.'"

I untied a faded lavender ribbon on one of the stacks, took an envelope off the top, opened the yellowed letter inside inscribed with delicate pen and ink handwriting, and read:

"My dear Silas,

I have at last found my parents who were staying with friends in a neighboring village. They are thin and shaken but alive.

They send thanks to you and all the paratroopers for your valiant work in liberating our country from the aggressors.

They would love to meet you themselves, but feel they should stay and help rebuild our country. They say they send their very heart to you by sending me, and they give us their blessings.

Silas, I miss you more with every breath.

I can see you now on that distant shore waiting for me. You will soon see me running into your open arms.

"Je t'aime,
"Anne Marie."

I stopped a moment to compose myself, retrieved a tissue from my pocket, and wiped away tears.

"They're all like that." Miss Jones pointed to the stack in my lap. "No matter which one you read, you wind up in tears. I'm glad, at last, I can take care of this unfinished business of my life, even under the circumstances."

I stood and regarded the top of Henry's bowed head. "Let's forget consequences, Henry. I don't believe you meant harm."

Henry dared to look at me, a spark of hope in his eyes.

"Are you serious," he asked.

"I'm serious," I said. "I'll call Detective Rust and tell him about the situation, and that I don't want to press charges. No harm has been done."

"I'm so sorry, Mrs. Callaway." Tears rolled down Henry's cheeks. "Thank, you."

"You are very gracious, Mrs. Callaway," Miss Jones extended her hands to me. "We are indebted to you."

Henry easily brought the quilt-covered desk into the house on a hand truck. Too bad we didn't think about that when Tom and Joe originally found it in the basement. We could've carted it out the basement door around to the front a lot easier than lugging it up the stairs.

I escorted Miss Jones and Henry to the door. After we'd said our goodbyes, I went back into the study and picked up the picture again of Anne Marie. By the worn appearance of it, I suspected Silas might've carried this picture around with him while he was in the war.

I just had to tell Ted about it. I picked up the phone and punched a button. "You won't believe this."

After filling Ted in, I made another call to Detective Rust. I needed to speak to Addie as well, but since she didn't have a phone, I'd have to make a quick trip over tomorrow.

I took a seat and started reading through the letters. Every so often, I'd turn to my computer and type in a few of the words that I'd read. When the kids came in from visiting with their friends, I went through the whole business with them, too.

"This is quite a story, but aren't you ready to come to bed, Mom? It's midnight." Linnea asked.

"I'll be along shortly. I have a bit more work to do."

At 2:00 a.m., I still sat at the computer. I pulled the last tissue from the box, blew my nose, threw the tissue in the trashcan with a dozen others. I didn't think I could cry anymore, but I couldn't wait until a more convenient time. I resorted to jotting down an outline that formed in my head, because I knew I wouldn't be able to get everything written this weekend.

As it turned out, I was having everyone over for Easter lunch.

After all, what could I do to a ham? Especially a spiral sliced one from Colonial Store, which I planned to serve cold. Once again, everyone was pitching in with his or her own dishes, but I did have one special thing I wanted to do. Linnea agreed to help me. But, for now, I wasn't quite ready to turn off my computer.

###

Jason, Linnea, and I huddled around the table in the kitchen.

"Mom, how do you expect me to cut bunny ears out of cake?" Linnea asked.

"I don't know, but there has to be a way. My mother didn't cook any better than I do, and she managed to do it." I turned the mixer off hoping the white frosting would serve as the glue that held the bunny cake together.

Linnea started to carve. "What are we going to do with all these crumbs?" she asked as rows of yellow morsels mounded on the cutting board.

"Cover them with coconut and icing, I guess." I lifted the frosting from the bowl with a spatula and tested its consistency with my fingers.

"I don't know. I'm not sure this is going to work," Linnea complained as she guided the knife through a layer of yellow cake.

"It'll work." One way or another, it'd work. It had to. I didn't have a backup dessert plan.

Linnea compared the two appendages she'd cut against one another. "One ear's longer than the other."

"That occurs in nature, as well." I'm sure I'd seen a lop-eared bunny or two.

"What's that you're using for whiskers?" Jason asked.

"Licorice cut into strips," I explained.

Jason shuddered, "I hate licorice."

"Well, don't eat the whiskers, then." Linnea remarked as she arranged the ears in an artistic way.

Jason studied the landscape we'd prepared to place the rabbit in. "How'd you get that coconut to look like grass?"

"We tinted it with food coloring," Linnea said.

"Does that make it taste any different?"

"Not at all," I replied.

"I'll try it then," Jason stated.

I slathered frosting on the bunny's body. "Glad to hear it."

Chapter Twenty-Two

Revelations

"It is a breath-taking experience to place oneself completely at the disposal of God. No one can foresee through what vicissitudes he might be led, what heights he may gain, what victories may be his. Unaided by man, he might be called upon to charge the citadel of the enemy—or go forward in the strength of the Lord, working out miracles unbelievable!"

—Founder of Toccoa Falls College, Dr. R. A. Forrest

Chimes rang out the hour.

The liturgist lifted his voice, "The Lord is risen!"

The congregation responded, "He is risen indeed!"

So began the Easter morning worship service. Earlier, I'd torn myself out of bed to make the Sunrise Service at 6:45. It was no small feat, but I kept reminding myself that despite my sleep-deprived condition, it was going to be worth it.

I was not disappointed.

Something about singing "...up from the grave he arose" while watching the sun come up gave me goose bumps.

Here again for the service at 11:00, it was good to have Jason and Linnea in the congregation as well as Belle, Becky, and Joe. Even Ted came over from his church to join us, in addition to our special guest, Addie Braham. Jason and Linnea had picked her up on their way to church earlier because I needed to warm up with the choir.

I'd pushed aside what was weighing heavy on my heart—the tension of my relationship with Ted. I'd hardly slept in days, and of course, the preparation of a meal always taxed me, but it was Easter—a time for celebration.

Again, I had to choose only joy this morning. Especially today.

The choir had a special number we'd rehearsed for many weeks because of its difficulty. Once more, I was amazed at the sound that came from the front row.

As we were taking our robes off after the service, Debbie approached and wished me a wonderful Easter.

"Thank you. Are you having family over today?"

"Mark's brother and his wife are coming with their children. We should have a great time hunting Easter Eggs this afternoon with four children under eight."

"Sounds like fun," I said.

Rhonda Kay overheard the conversation and bounced over in her hot pink dress with floral pumps. "Cletus and I hid 1000 eggs in the front yard yesterday. I'm about wore out from all that bendin' over. We got every child in the neighborhood coming over to hunt them eggs this afternoon, but before they pick up one egg I'm gonna read the Easter story. I got eggs with the different symbols and all to help me tell it. We're gonna have a fine time."

I was reminded again that Rhonda Kay had a wonderful heart. I'd never asked why she and Cletus didn't have children, but I was sure she'd make a splendid mom.

###

As planned, Belle, her family, and Ted, gathered for lunch with Jason, Linnea, and me. Addie also joined us.

True to his word, Jason did eat the bunny cake. "This is good." His eyes widened.

"Give me one of those ears, too," Joe extended a plate toward me as I stood at the sideboard to serve. Overall, the lunch was a nice success. The cold ham and stuffed eggs were both hits.

When we moved to the study for coffee, everyone was amazed to see that the desk was back. "How did it get here?" they questioned.

"I'll tell you shortly, but first there's other business to attend." I turned to Addie and gestured toward the desk. "This is the desk I've been telling you about."

Addie stood leaning on her cane taking in its fine workmanship and elaborate details. "It's as beautiful as I imagined it would be."

"Mrs. Callaway, does Miss Addie know about the desk?" Joe asked in a puzzled way.

"Yes, Joe, she knows more than any of us. She was the answer to my many prayers about the desk."

"Addie, why don't you tell your part of the story?" I asked helping her get situated in a chair.

"Well, my part begins a very long time ago, before any of you were even born." As we'd prearranged, without revealing Buford and Silas' names, she held us all spell bound as she told about her nephews.

I followed her by retelling my tale of the desk, about finding the will, searching for its heirs, and finally coming upon Addie through the doll dress she had made. I pushed ahead by revealing how Jed and Elmer found money in the basement, although I didn't say how much or how old. Finally, I concluded with Edwina Jones showing up with the stolen desk.

"Wow, that's some story." Joe leaned forward in his chair. "But you still don't know who the desk belongs to."

"I'm pretty sure I do." I felt as if my joy might burst its bounds.

"You haven't told us any names yet," said Joe.

Becky punched him. "Be quiet."

Belle had not said a word throughout all the explanations. I directed my eyes toward her. "Would you tell us what the inscription on your ring says?"

She twisted the ring on her finger. "My ring? It says, 'For my beloved, with all my heart'." Her face reflected her lack of understanding.

"So?" Joe questioned.

"Shh, let her say what she needs to say." Becky glared at her brother.

"The note on the federal reserve band around the money says, 'For my beloved, with all my heart'."

Joe smirked. "Is that all? I bet a lot of old folks said that."

For a boy that hardly spoke a word the first time we'd met, he'd sure grown comfortable with speaking up.

Becky looked at him in a threatening way. "Joe, please, be quiet." She turned to me. "Mrs. Callaway, is there more?"

Belle was starting to tear, maybe as a twinkle of realization set in. "Belle, what was your mother's name?'

"Doris," she cried.

"And your grandfather's name?"

"Buford Braham."

"That's it," I exclaimed as I turned to Addie.

One of her hands flew to her mouth as her face became awash with joy.

"We were right. They're the ones. All these months of wondering and searching, and it was Silas' own great, great nephew that helped discover the desk."

"No, way." Joe sprang from his chair. "We're the ones that own the desk. I knew my great, great-uncle was a war hero, 'cause Mom showed us in a history book. I can't believe he's the same person as the hero in Miss Addie's story. Cool. Now we have a desk that belonged to him. I can't wait to tell Tom. Does that mean we get the money, too?"

"Joe, don't be rude." Belle motioned for Joe to sit down again. She rose and moved toward the desk, running her fingers over it cautiously as if it might turn to dust before her, and I knew she wondered if it could possibly be true.

"June, I don't know what to say. I had no idea this desk even existed. I think my grandfather must have died before he shared all of this or maybe he wanted to forget all the sadness surrounding it."

She held up her hand. "The only way I have this ring is my mother found it in my grandfather's things. She had no idea where it came from."

"A question before I go on with this story," I said. "How did you come to Toccoa?" I'd never asked her about this. It seemed we always had other things to talk about when we got together.

Growing more comfortable with the desk, Belle rested a hand on it. "Harold and I met in college at USC. I still can't believe that out of all the guys that were there, Harold and I found each other. He was from Toccoa, which I guess is one of the things that made him first attractive to me, because, although I grew up in California, I knew my grandfather had grown up here. I had a yearning to return to my roots. Of course, that was fine with Harold because he wanted to come back to Toccoa to live all along. He said he wasn't cut out for California life." It was the first time I'd heard her speak much about Harold.

Belle's eyes met Addie's. "That means you and I are related, doesn't it Miss Addie."

"It sure does, Sugar. I can't tell you how good that feels." Addie seemed ten years younger as if something had been lifted from her. "I thought my only family was Misty."

"Who's Misty?" asked Joe looking around.

"A great cat," Jason explained. "I'll introduce you later."

Belle crossed over and embraced Addie, "We can't wait to get to know you better, although I feel I've known you my whole life."

Addie smiled. "I can't wait either." She shook her head. "My, hasn't this been an exciting day. Why I've had more excitement in the past couple of weeks than I've had in years. I'm going to have to start taking my blood pressure medicine again, if this keeps up."

"We're not even through with the story yet." I was anxious to go on since I knew that Belle, Joe, and Becky still had no idea what the desk would actually mean for them.

"Belle, I think you'd better sit down for the next part. Ted, would you hand me that letter out of the desk drawer?"

Ted reached in, pulled out the only letter in the drawer, and handed it to me.

"Belle, this is the official appraisal I had done on the desk." Robert Giles had made a special trip down from Highlands the day before so I could have this to give to Belle. I handed it to her, and immediately Joe and Becky ran to stand behind their mother. Belle unfolded the paper and they all read it together. Joe started yelling and fell back on the floor. "475,000 dollars. That's enough to buy a couple of Lamborghinis."

Belle seemed not to know whether to laugh or cry.

A stillness came over Becky. Her voice a whisper, she said, "Mrs. Callaway, is this for real?

I nodded, and tears began their course down her cheeks.

Belle sobbed and clasped Becky's hand.

"There's still more. The money Jed and Elmer found was $5000 worth of $100 bills. However, because they're from 1934, they're worth twice that much."

Belle cried even harder, and her breathing and sobbing became so erratic, I was afraid she might hyper-ventilate. It seemed like we ought to give her water. I didn't know why people gave water to folks that were hysterical, but we needed to do something, so I told Linnea, "Run and get a glass of water for Belle, and a box of tissues."

When she came back, Belle took the water, stopped crying a little, and sipped it. Finally, she recovered enough to speak. "I can't believe it, I can't believe it. God did answer my prayers in a way I could have never imagined."

I knelt beside Belle. "Do you know what this means?" I asked. "It means everybody gets to go to college, even you."

This precipitated another eruption almost equal to the one that had preceded it. More water was needed.

"Of course, it means you'd have to sell the desk, but maybe that's why it's been in the basement for so long, so that it would be here when you needed it." I marveled at the wonder of it all.

Addie was crying now, and I passed her the tissue box. "Are you going to need water, too?"

Addie shook her head and wiped her eyes. "It's wonderful to see something good come out of such a sad story after all of these years."

Belle exhaled, seemed to pull herself together, and held up her hand. "June, did this dawn on you when you read the inscription in my ring?"

"Addie told me Silas had bought a ring for Anne Marie and had it inscribed with the same words he'd written on the Federal Reserve sleeve of the money. She thought it might be in the basement with the desk and the money. Of course, I thought we'd never find the ring because it was so small, and it'd been so long, but when I read the inscription on your ring I thought that had to be it."

"One more thing." I lifted packages of ribbon bound letters from the desk. "These are the letters Anne Marie wrote to Silas when they were separated by the war. You should have them, but don't read them now. I don't know if we have enough water or tissues in the house." I placed the letters in Belle's outstretched hands.

Ted hadn't spoken a word the whole time, but he gave me a dimpled smile, moved to my side, and put his arm around me. I fought the urge to pull away and for a moment, allowed myself to enjoy the closeness.

###

"So, Mom, how did the will get in the desk to begin with?" Linnea asked just before she left to go back to school on Sunday.

I shook my head. "The only explanation I can think of came from something Addie told me."

"What's that?" Linnea picked up her backpack beside the front door.

"She shared that she thought Silas could have died of a broken heart. I wonder if Silas gave Buford the will, because he'd despaired of life. And Buford put it in the desk because he didn't know what else to do with it."

"If only he could've known the good that would come from what he left behind," Linnea marvelled.

I kissed her goodbye, and she opened the door and left.

If only . . .

Chapter Twenty-Three

Oblique

"How desperately difficult it is to be honest with oneself. It is much easier to be honest with other people."
—Edward White Benson (1829-1896)

A reporter had called, and I needed to bring Bertha up to speed before the whole town buzzed with the story of the desk. It was just a matter of time before Bertha read about it in the newspaper. So, when I was out on the patio and heard her poking around by the fence a couple of days later, I thought that as good a time as any. I leaned over the pickets, and there, despite the hip surgery back in the winter, she was down on her knees putting mulch around little plants and talking to them at the same time.

"Now, you fellows have to hang in here. We have a cold snap coming tonight, probably our last. Can't have you wilting on me. I'll cover you up, good, though, so don't worry."

"Bertha?"

She peered up from her discourse. "You caught me. Sometimes, you have to send out a little encouragement to growing things. Helps them hang on."

I nodded. True enough, but I never knew Bertha was a plant whisperer.

I told her about what had gone on at my house in the last few days.

She stood to her feet, wonder dawning in her eyes. "I remember Buford Braham, now. I sure do. The Braham name seemed familiar when you asked me months ago."

Now, it came back to her.

Bertha took off her work gloves, put them in her jacket pocket, and grew thoughtful. "Before Fred and I bought this house, we rented one down the street—the little house next to the one on the corner, the one the Baker's live in now." She pointed to her left.

I followed her finger, trying to recollect which house she meant and shook my head. The next time I passed, I'd have to check it out.

"Well, anyway, we'd be sitting on the porch and see Buford coming to call on a girl who lived in your house, that was your Edwina Jones, I believe. He had a medical discharge from the army, something wrong with his feet I think, and he worked down at the hardware store. Edwina was real cute."

So intriguing to have someone else's perspective on Edwina Jones. If you'd asked me, I would've guessed she'd been just as business like when she was a girl as she is now. A familiar squirrel darted up a tree in Bertha's back yard, I'm sure with a plan to bomb me from on high with some of his bounty. I scrutinized him as he jumped from limb to limb and climbed into the nest just above me.

Bertha went on. "We thought they were going to get married. But I heard that on a trip to visit a relative in California, Buford met somebody else. That must have been Belle's grandmamma, `cause it wasn't too long before he married her and moved out there. I guess he left the desk in the house during the time he was dating Edwina. I wonder if Belle's grandmamma ever knew about Edwina?"

"I have no idea." Still keeping an eye on the squirrel, I thought she probably didn't.

Bertha leaned toward me, her voice a whisper. "I bet Buford wanted to keep Edwina a secret. Might not go over too well. That's probably why he didn't fuss much over the desk. It does look like he would've tried to get the money back, though. I guess people do funny things when they're in love."

A nut dropped to the ground two feet away from me, and I decided the squirrel needed to work on his aim.

Bertha continued, "I bet nobody but Buford even knew that money was there. Imagine that desk and the money being down there all this time with renters moving in and out, and nobody finding it."

"It is quite a story," I agreed.

"Somebody ought to write about this," Bertha observed.

"Somebody should," I said as a nut conked me on the head and bounced to the ground. Bull's-eye, I thought as I felt to see if I was bleeding. Again.

###

I met Ted at the Dinner Bell for coffee and cake the next Tuesday night. As we both exited our respected cars, the pressure inside me burst its bounds. Now or never, I thought. "Skydiving. He died skydiving." I burst into tears.

He rushed to my side and took me in his arms. I nestled close and caught a whiff of his after shave. After a moment he spoke.

"I know."

I pulled away. "How?"

"When we went to the library benefit, you obviously avoided giving too much information. I didn't want to ask, so I searched for your husband's name. It was all over the Internet in several online Georgia newspapers with it being such a terrible tragedy."

I felt relieved and something else, maybe violated—like he was a cyber-stalker. I took a step back. "That feels kind of weird, like an invasion of my privacy."

Ted appeared surprised. "Invasion . . . no, no, I didn't mean that at all. I wanted to save you from having to tell me. It helped me understand why you've been hesitant to move forward."

"Hesitant to move forward? Isn't that what I've been doing? Didn't I move here? Haven't I been living my life every day?"

He backed away from me. "Well, yes, I didn't mean it as an insult." He wiped his hands on his pants. "I was just trying to help, June. Just trying to help."

Some help.

###

Later that evening, still unsettled by Ted's foray into my past, I slid for the last time behind the lovely desk. Belle had borrowed a truck to take it to her house, and they were picking it up in the morning. She knew she'd have to sell it, but she wanted it to spend just a few days at her house before it left them forever.

I ran my hands across the gilt finishes. Poor, Silas. Crushed, heartbroken, and chained to the past.

Chapter Twenty-Four

Turning a Page

"There are some prayers that are followed by a Divine silence because we are not yet ripe for all we have asked; there are others which are so followed because we are ripe for more. We do not always know the full strength of our own capacity; we have to be prepared for receiving greater blessings than we have ever dreamed of."
—George Matheson (1842-1906)

He turned the page of the newspaper with hands he felt were still amazingly steady for his age and read the heading of an article on page ten, "Miracle in Toccoa, Georgia."

Toccoa?

It must be a remarkable incident for a newspaper here in Massachusetts to have picked it up from the wire service, even if it was on page ten. He found it impossible to read the fine print these days without glasses, so he only read headlines unless a piece especially interested him.

Where were those glasses?

Now, he remembered—in the kitchen. He reached for the cane beside his chair and slowly covered the few short steps to the kitchen table. Yes, just where he'd left them. He put the glasses on and read:

After decades, an antique French desk discovered by a Toccoa, Georgia resident in her basement has been restored to the rightful owner. June Callaway of Tugalo Street discovered the desk in the basement of a house she recently purchased. Relegated to the basement for nearly sixty years, the desk is estimated to be worth nearly a half million dollars. Through the diligence of Mrs. Callaway, and a will discovered in the desk, the beneficiary, Mrs. Belle Mathews, has been located.

He dropped the paper on the table. French desk? Beneficiary? The phone rang, and he reached over and picked up the cordless lying on the table.

"Silas, are you coming over today? Some of the men were counting on seeing you."

Silas checked his watch. How had he let the time slip up on him? It was happening more and more lately. He'd always felt if you weren't fifteen minutes early, you were late. "Be there soon." He hung up the phone, and wrestled with whether to finish reading the article or just leave. His curiosity won out. He turned again to the newspaper.

Mrs. Mathews states she believes the desk is the answer to her prayers for her children's as well as her own education. She plans to become a public school teacher.

Anne Marie's desk? The memories flooded back into his mind. Did Buford put her desk in a basement? Could this Mrs. Callaway possibly have discovered it after more than sixty years and might Belle Mathews be related to him? It didn't seem that long since he'd seen Anne Marie, but on the other hand it seemed an eternity. Sixty years of heartache.

Enough of this, he thought. He had people waiting on him. He laid the paper on the table and went to the hat rack beside the front door, lifted a plaid cap, and placed it on his head. With the cane in one hand, he reached for the doorknob with the other.

Later, as he eased into the driveway of the Hero's House residential hospice facility for veterans, he tried to put the newspaper article out of his mind. He was not here to talk about his life. He never talked to anyone about Anne Marie, and he was not about to start now. He came to visit with these men, these ones who served their country well, but wound up with a terminal illness and no place to go.

"Silas, we thought you forgot about us!" a voice called out as Silas came through the door.

He scanned the common room filled with the bunch of men he'd come to know over the past few weeks. Some had lost hair due to chemotherapy, and others had those telltale sunken eyes from the effects of their illness. But they faced this part of their lives with the same courage with which they'd always lived. Often Silas went away feeling they'd brought more encouragement to him than he had to them.

"No, no, lost track of time, that's all. What have you guys been up to?"

"Playing hearts and talking about how long Ed's hair is getting," Leo answered from a group gathered around a card table.

Silas studied Ed, also sitting at the card table. His gray hair hung over his ears and down on his forehead, one of the few who still had hair. Very unmilitary. "How about you and I going into town tomorrow, Ed? We'll see about your hair then."

"Yeah, Ed," said Leo, "You want to keep yourself looking sharp for the nurses."

Silas took a seat at the card table. "Deal me in"

###

The coffee dripped through the filter, and I stood in the kitchen on Thursday morning, lost in thought, staring at it as if it was the most fascinating thing I'd ever seen. I was thinking Ted and I had already planned to attend the downtown art festival together on Saturday. I'd looked forward to it for so long, and now I dreaded it. I hated to cancel, so I guess I had a decision to make about whether I was going to let this business about Ted snooping around in my history put a wedge between us.

My thoughts drifted back to one summer when Linnea started dating a guy that Morris and I didn't like very much. I don't know what it was about him—he put his feet on the furniture when he visited, and didn't use "sir" when he talked to Morris. Linnea wasn't forthcoming about his family, so I checked him out on the Internet—along with his whole family. Turned out he wasn't a convicted felon after all. His dad ran a non-profit in downtown Atlanta. I felt kind of bad after I did it.

Just like I was feeling now for storming at Ted about something I'd done myself.

I called Ted, and we met downtown in a new coffee shop for muffins on Saturday, as I knew Stella would notice our falling out if we went to the Dinner Bell.

We took our seats at a table, and I looked into his eyes. He reached over, touched my hand, and I felt a tear welling. His face showed compassion as I confessed my own foray into someone's past.

After I finished, I squeaked out, "I'm so sorry."

He handed me a napkin to dry my face and gave me a dimpled smile. "Aw, that's okay," he said as he extended a hand to me. "Let's just forget it."

I squeezed his hand, grateful for his kind nature.

We finished our breakfast, and as we left, the tone of the day took on a decided uptick. Ted and I let a blue grass group put a bounce in our step as we browsed through the arts festival held in Toccoa every spring. The lead singer belted out:

"Well, I've never been to Atlanta or to Nashville, Tennessee
"But I lived along the Tugaloo with the mountain close to me.
"I remember when I was little my mama used to say to me
"Son, don't you go so far you can't see the top of Currahee.

"And this has been my home now for so many years
"It's changed a lot and grown a lot from what it used to be.
"But the Tugaloo is still flowing and the mountain's standing strong.
"And I'm so glad I still live in the shadow of Currahee."

Local color saturated the entire day. Potters, jewelers, and artists filled booths up and down Main Street. The Toccoa police had blocked off the street, while folks milled around exchanging their money for handcrafted items of all kinds.

I took in the wide array of offerings. "I never knew so many artists and craftsmen worked in the Toccoa area."

"Perhaps the mountain acts as a muse. I do think there's something to it. As the song says living 'in the shadow of Currahee' seems to help the creative flow. Every year I see a few more new faces at this festival," said Ted.

As we navigated to the other end of Main Street, the Stephens County High School jazz band played their version of Glenn Miller's "In the Mood."

I felt an impulse to jitterbug right there on the center line of the street.

We took the long way home that evening, holding hands all the way. I kept thinking about the words in the song and what Ted had said about "living in the shadow of Currahee."

What was it about the mountain, anyway?

Just before Ted left that evening, he pulled me close and whispered, "You are very dear to me, June." He kissed me, leaving my heart spinning like one of Jubilee's whirligigs.

Chapter Twenty-Five

The Eagle

"These are thy wonders, Lord of love,
To make us see we are but flowers that glide:
Which when we once can find and prove,
Thou hast a garden for us, where to bide."
—"The Flower," George Herbert (1593-1633)

Jason secured an internship with the Chattooga Ranger District in Northeast Georgia, which meant he'd be staying in Toccoa all summer. It was the oddest sensation for me to gaze up at the mountain and know my son was often working at the Ranger station at the top.

Linnea delayed an opportunity to study abroad until the next year, so she too could spend the summer in Toccoa. I only hoped my kids didn't choose to stay at home because of me, but they really seemed to want to be here. Linnea picked up her paintbrush to capture the local scenes, and was invited to hang them in a small gallery in the center of town frequented by quite a few tourists. One of those tourists owned a gallery in Atlanta and was delighted to discover Linnea's work. Linnea could hardly keep up with the demand for the paintings the Atlanta clientele demanded.

"Mom, can you believe it? A gallery in Buckhead wants my paintings!" Linnea shared one evening at dinner. "I can believe it."

I swelled with pride that the gallery in one of Atlanta's most elite areas saw my sweet daughter's talent. I spooned steamed squash from Bertha's garden onto my plate. "I'd be surprised if they didn't want your paintings."

"Spoken like a true mom." Jason grinned at me as I passed him the green beans. "By the way, I spotted a mountain lion early this morning on Currahee. It's the first time I've ever seen one in the wild. I was scanning some brush through my binoculars and spotted movement. I zoomed in and there she was."

A little chill rippled up my spine. "Exciting, but please be careful."

Red roared into the room and yowled at the top of his lungs.

Simultaneously, we all turned to him.

"Must've overheard, and gotten a little jealous," Jason observed.

That cat could be weird sometimes.

###

I stood up, arched my back after working in Bertha's garden all morning, and watched as Tom and Joe approached Jubilee. "Do we need to water the green beans?" Tom asked.

The boys were Jubilee's new helpers in what promised to be a nearly commercial undertaking in Bertha's backyard.

"I think they'll be fine. We've had a lot of rain this week. Some years it's real dry though, and we have to water about every day." He studied Tom and Joe a minute as if he wasn't sure they understood. "Every day, if we don't get no rain. You have to do it early, like 5:30 in the mornin'. You can't shock plants with no cold water in the middle of the hot afternoon."

Tom and Joe looked at each other wearily. Somehow, through their internship under Jubilee's supervision, they'd managed to keep up with the work in Bertha's garden—that was until the time came for harvest. Here it was July, and it was taking nearly everyone Bertha knew to help cut the okra, pull the corn, and pick the tomatoes and beans.

I had no idea what Bertha was going to do with all that produce.

Jubilee wiped his forehead with a red bandana and turned to me. "Why'd that woman have to go and plant so much? Somebody's gotta have a talk with her. We can't handle no more of this. She's out of control."

"I have to agree with you." I rubbed my arms, which stung from picking okra and examined my dirty fingernails. I'd experienced an aching back from sitting long hours in a chair writing, but this was an entirely different kind of pain. I didn't think I could bend over and pick one more squash. "I'll try to talk with her about next year, but, we're going to have to do the best we can right now."

I stepped into Bertha's house to get a drink of water. Bertha bellowed, "He's the Lily of the Valley, the bright and morning star, He's the fairest of ten thousand to my soul," and buzzed around the kitchen like a twenty-year-old. She gazed out the window over the backyard and chirped, "Wouldn't Fred be proud to see his acre of land being used like this?"

I found it hard to confront Bertha with how much her happiness was costing her friends. Her face brightened even more. I'd known her long enough to discern when Bertha was about to give birth to a new idea, so as her eyes grew wide, I braced myself.

"June, I don't know why I didn't think of this before. Let's share all this bounty. We'll give all this good produce away to the soup kitchen, and help make some fine lunches for folks."

It was just like Bertha to come up with something that would make me have to repent of my complaining. I managed to turn the corners of my mouth up into what I thought might seem like a smile. "That's nice, Bertha."

###

In the days ahead, we loaded our trunks with bushel baskets and carted all that extra produce downtown to the soup kitchen. We not only took the produce down there, we worked several days preparing the vegetables.

Bertha was not able to stand for a long time. We found a chair for her to sit in so she could peel and chop and boss, which she was better at than just about anybody I knew. Jason and Linnea broke away when they could to help, as well as Eunice, Tom, Joe, Belle, Iris, Ted, Jubilee, and I who all took shifts for several days to prepare and serve the food.

"Ted, will you hand me one of those hair nets?" I asked while on my shift.

He reached into a box, pulled an elasticized piece of plastic out and handed it to me. "Very glamorous," he said after I'd put it on.

I checked out the little white cap perched on his head. "You're pretty stunning yourself."

"All for a good cause." He cut up more tomatoes and added them to a large pile to his right.

Bertha leaned over from her roost on the stool and scrutinized how I cut corn from the cob. I'd become used to her evaluating my efforts.

I shaved an especially large ear. "I have to hand it to you Bertha, folks seem to really enjoy these fresh vegetables."

Apparently satisfied I had things under control, she went back to shelling peas. "If I hadn't had all that time on my hands after I fell, I would've never thought about planting such a big garden. And look what good has come out of it."She waved in the direction of the doors. Through the exterior glass doors, folks waved back. A long line of people going through hard times had formed to get the green beans, peas, corn, sliced tomatoes, and chicken strips The Dinner Bell had donated.

As I threw another pile of corncobs in a sack for a mulch pile, I sensed the wheels in Bertha's brain at work.

"Next year, I'm going to have fifteen rows," she said.

I lifted my eyes to Jubilee who was snapping more green beans, and I could see he almost fell off the stool. What could we say?

"You folks need to stop what you're doing and get ready to serve. They're opening the doors now." Iris called from the dining area. "Looks like a record crowd, too."

The doors opened and the first of the patrons came to the serving line. "I ain't had nothin' this good in a mighty long time." He took the plate with a "thank-you ma'am" and went to the drink table.

Bertha cut her eyes over at me, and I saw tears had welled in them. "See what I mean."

###

Sally Philips' book, *Yard Art in the South,* quickly made Jubilee a celebrity. He was featured on the cover of the book right next to members of Congress, the ones in his yard that is, and had to set up regular hours in the afternoon at his place for tourists who wanted him to sign the book and buy a whirligig or yard ornament.

My phone rang early one morning. I answered and heard, "You won't never believe who this is?"

I thought hard. Who was it? It sounded like Jubilee, but he didn't have a phone. "No, I don't know who this is."

I heard loud cackling on the other end of the phone.

"It's me, Jubilee, and I got me one of them there cell phones. How am I soundin'?"

"Sounding fine, Jubilee. How'd you get a cell phone?" I asked, curious how he'd broken through the barrier into the twenty first century.

"Tom and Joe helped me get it, then they showed me how to use it. I can call anywhere I want from this gadget. Them boys even got it so's I can call folks by pressin' one little button. I just gotta remember which one to push."

Between Bertha's garden, working at the soup kitchen, and the demand for whirligigs, Jubilee had to hire Babs Lawson's son to help him keep up with his woodwork.

"Jonah working out all right?" I asked.

"Right well, once I showed him a few things." He paused a moment. "I feel like one of them there CEOs." Another pause. "Now, how do I cut this contraption off?"

###

I was so tired with all the manual labor on top of trying to write as much as I could, I didn't know if I could even make it to choir practice, but I went and as usual was glad I did. I would've hated to miss the big announcement.

"May I have everyone's attention?" Laura asked before choir practice began.

We stopped our usual pre-practice jabbering and focused on Laura.

"I sent an audition tape of Rhonda Kay in to the Georgia Symphony."

Rhonda Kay gasped. "You sent a tape of me?" she asked. "Why?"

Laura grinned sly. "They've selected you to sing in their Fall concert."

The whole choir room erupted into a celebration: Cheers, clapping, hugging and general merry making ensued.

When things finally quieted down Rhonda Kay said, "They don't know what they're gettin' themselves into."

Debbie disagreed. "Sure they do. They couldn't have made a better choice." To which everyone agreed.

"We're all going to be there for the concert, Rhonda Kay," someone said from the back.

"You all are going to make me so nervous, I'll never be able to get out a word," Rhonda Kay replied.

"That could never happen," someone else shot back to more laughter.

###

I hadn't heard much about Gladys Pickens lately nor had I seen her at the library on my days to volunteer. Since Jason and Linnea were home, they were helping me around the house, which made Gladys' services unnecessary.

One day I spotted the Pickens Plumbing truck on my street. I slowed down as I passed, and to my surprise found Gladys riding shotgun.

I stopped and hit the electric window button on the passenger side. "Hi, Gladys, how are you?" I couldn't believe she sported a green jumpsuit with a Pickens Plumbing logo on it.

"Got me a new job helpin' Elmer. I don't know nothin' about plumbin', but all Elmer needs is somebody to hand him tools and hold pipes and such. I get to meet such interestin' people, too."

"It keeps her from gettin' crazy idees," a voice from the back of the truck said. Elmer slid up beside my car, stuck his head in the open window and nodded at Gladys. "Keepin' my enemies close."

Gladys laughed. "I ain't your enemy."

Elmer raised his eyebrows at me. "Could've fooled me, but I'm trying to keep her too tired to be curious."

Gladys slapped her knee and nodded. "This with the cleanin' jobs I have keep me plumb wore out. I never even have a chance to watch any mystery stories."

###

The rain that helped Bertha's garden so much also helped Jed Turner. Jed was busier than ever because of all the precipitation, and sin in the form of weeds abounded in Toccoa.

Jed found great pleasure in conquering it.

"Miz Callaway," Jed called out one day as I rested in the shade on the patio with a notebook in my hand trying to work on the acknowledgements for my book.

"Jed, I didn't even know you were here." I turned to see him stomping into the backyard.

"Sorry, didn't mean to surprise you," he apologized, "but I stopped by 'cause I got somethin' to tell you."

Lately, my front lawn had drawn several comments from the neighbors on the street including Bertha. That was no small feat with her being the local garden club queen. So, I couldn't imagine my grass needed a thing.

When Jed approached me, I spotted a funny little grin on his face.

"What is it?" I asked putting my writing aside.

"Gonna be a Daddy. Ethel and I are having a little Jed Junior." His grin widened.

"How exciting. Is Ethel doing all right?"

He placed a hand on his sizable belly. "Little sickly right now, if you know what I mean, but she's fine. I've taken her out of the field. Strictly office from now on. Yes, Ma'am, strictly office. I'm probably gonna be huntin' for more field help. This is a busy time. Let me know if you hear of anybody wantin' a job."

"I sure will, Jed."

After Jed left, I looked back on what I was writing—the last task to accomplish before the book was finished. Had I mentioned everyone who needed to be included? I'd hate to leave anyone out. I'd been making a list for weeks now. At some point I had to say, "Done." This book might not be the literary masterpiece I wanted it to be, but it was simply the best that I had to offer.

Next, I'd prepare a proposal to send to an agent I'd known for years.

I thought about the forthcoming rejections. Like every other writer in the world, I hated them, but they were an inevitable part of this life I lived.

What if everyone rejected it?

There it was again, that ugly fear that always threatened to hold me back.

###

Silas relaxed in Hamby Duncan's barbershop reading a magazine occasionally checking to see what was happening with Ed's much-needed haircut.

"A little more off the sides," Ed said to Hamby.

Hamby stared at Ed's head. "If I cut any more off the sides, you're going to have a Mohawk."

"I like a neat look," Ed shot back

"You're going to have a weird look if any more comes off above your ears." Hamby sighed and turned to Silas. "How are you adjusting to life back in the states?" He asked clipping on the top of Ed's head.

Silas closed the *Boston Globe* he was reading onto his lap. "Pretty well, for an old guy, I guess. I've come to know folks like Ed, and that's made it an easier transition."

"Yeah, Silas has been a big help over at the Hero's House these past few weeks." Ed said.

Silas wondered if this was Ed's last haircut. His diagnosis was not good, and he'd already been in hospice care at the Hero's House for some time.

Silas found it odd that at nearly ninety, he was the one taking these men on errands, and trying to cheer them up. He'd always had good health, and didn't take a pill except a Centrum Silver vitamin every day. Good grief, at this rate the doctor at the VA said he might make it to one hundred. He was older than almost every one of them, but for him, serving these men made life worth getting up for in the morning.

"That cottage you living in pretty comfortable?" Ed asked.

"It's fine for now. I wouldn't want to weather any Massachusetts snows in an un-winterized summer cottage. If I stay, I'll have to search for something warmer in September."

"Do you think you'll stay?" Hamby turned Ed around to get at the front of his head.

"Don't know," Silas replied taking the paper from his lap and putting it on the table beside him.

"Sure would like it if you did. Where'd you say you moved from? England?" Ed asked squirming in his chair.

Hamby dropped his scissor hands to his side. "You have to be still, or I'll lop off one of these elephant ears of yours." Ed glared at Hamby, and then settled back in his chair.

Silas drifted off for a minute. After Anne Marie died, he'd stayed busy with work trying to forget, circling the globe to run from his memories.

When he retired, he chose to live in England, away from anyone who could ask questions, but yet, he had to admit, close to the place he last saw her. In the last few years, he began to have a longing to return to the States.

Living in Wesley's Orchard, Massachusetts was nowhere near home, but at least he could see the American flag flying at the Post Office, and feel he was doing something worthwhile with his remaining days.

He sure hadn't expected to live this long

"Silas, Silas, are you still with us? Didn't you move here from England?" Ed repeated.

Silas came back to the present. "I lived there quite a few years, but I started feeling like I should come back to the States. I saw the North Shore while I was in the army and decided I wouldn't mind spending some time here, and of course, I'd heard about the Hero's House. I'd always wanted to help out in a place like that."

Ed smiled at Silas."Glad you came."

###

A dark grey mist surrounded Currahee just before dawn, but gradually dissipated as a simmering July sun rose on the towering short leaf pines of the mountain. A tawny mountain lion circled underneath the shade of a chestnut oak in dense vegetation to prepare his bed for a rest after his nocturnal wanderings. He nestled in, having just drifted down from the mountains further north. He thought his presence remained undetected by the locals who never would have guessed he'd have come this far south.

Above him, from a lookout in one of the pines, a golden eagle took to flight in a now cloudless sky. After some time of cruising above the northeast Georgia tree canopy, he soared over the tin roof of Jubilee Johnson's house, and eyed the whirring of Jubilee's hand crafted whirligigs. He sailed past Jed's Weed and Seed, just as Jed's souped up truck thundered into the parking lot.

The eagle glided over the roofs of several downtown stores, and then breezed by the steeple of Emmanuel Church as Pastor Grady unlocked his office door. He finally found a resting place on the top limb of a magnolia in Bertha Henderson's front yard.

From his vantage point, he eyed my house, almost as if he could see through the walls with his penetrating gaze

I woke with a start, sat up in bed, and checked the clock. 6:30.

What kind of dream was this? I'd have to ask Jason, but I didn't even think there were any eagles on Currahee. Why would I have a dream about one coming to my house from there?

Chapter Twenty-Six

A Lot of Living to Do

"We must not limit the mighty grace of God."
—D.L. Moody(1837-1899)

I leaned back in my desk chair and spoke into my cell phone. "Ted, didn't you get my message?"

"What message?"

"The one I left with Tracie, that new administrative assistant of yours. You forgot your cell phone again, so I had to call her. Belle and I have been trying to contact Robert Giles to see if he would help her sell the desk, and we can't reach him. We wondered if he was out of town." It still thrilled me that the desk would help Belle and her family. I checked the battery on my phone. Almost dead. I fumbled to get it plugged into the wall charger.

"I do remember him saying something about making a buying trip to England. In fact, I believe he goes every year about this time."

I finally snapped the charger into my phone but had to lean way over toward the wall as I tried to scoot my chair closer to the outlet. "How long is he gone? The bank is working with Belle to extend her credit based on the appraisal I had done of the desk, but she needs to sell it."

"He's usually gone about three weeks. I wonder why I didn't get the message from you."

Three weeks. Belle was so anxious to take care of her obligations. This wasn't good news at all. "I have no idea. Tracie told me you were in a conference, and she'd give you the message."

"She must've forgotten. It's been pretty busy today."

"If you hear from him, could you let us know?'

"Sure, and by the way, would you like to go to the Cardiac Association Gala? It's three weeks from this Saturday. You'll love it. It's black tie."

"Black tie?" I jerked straight up and pulled the phone cord out of the wall.

Bathrobe without a doubt.

###

When I finally found a break from Bertha's garden, the soup kitchen, and writing, I stopped by to see Addie. She was holding court as usual in the gathering room at Mountain Gardens.

I gladly eased into a chair beside her. "I'm sorry it's been so long since I've been here. It's been a huge undertaking getting all of Bertha's produce picked and taking it to the soup kitchen. I'm also making the final changes on the book. Tell me what you've been doing lately."

Addie patted me on the knee and laughed. "Honey, don't worry about me. Have you forgotten I've found family here? Joe, Becky, or Belle come by here several times a week, and I've already been to their house for supper I don't know how many times."

Addie fairly glowed. "Plus, the Kendalls want me to write down everything I can tell them about my home place. I asked them why they wanted to hear all my old stories."

She paused and leaned forward. "You know what Cary said?" Not waiting for me to answer she went on. "She told me my stories are their stories. Said the stories made their place come alive and helped them see it like it was when I was a little girl. That's what they want it to look like now."

She swelled with pride, "Besides, they told me Jillie's grandparents are all gone, and I'm like a grandmother to her."

One doll dress and a ride in the car opened up a door neither of us could've imagined.

"I was out there last week, and when I came through the front door, I could hardly believe my eyes. A library table with an aqua pottery vase filled with flowers rested in the front hall. It was like Mama's." Joy danced in Addie's eyes.

I tried to take it all in. "It's all so amazing."

"I came back to Toccoa to die," said Addie. "But it seems I'm going to be doing a lot of living here before I pass on. If that little girl needs a grandmother, I can't leave her. Becky and Joe, I'm the only relations they have besides their mama. I have responsibilities now. Yes, ma'am, I have a lot of living to do."

I laughed. "It appears that you do. Where's Misty?" I searched for the cat in the gathering room of Mountain Gardens.

"You haven't heard, have you?" Addie asked.

I shrugged.

"Remember that day we returned from the Kendall's and Misty and Virgil were curled up with each other? Well, they've become best friends. In fact, someone told a reporter at the newspaper about it, and he came over here yesterday afternoon to do a story on those two. I'm going to have a famous cat on Thursday when the paper comes out."

Sure enough, when I removed the plastic sleeve from the paper, the first article that caught my eye was on the bottom of page one: "Unlikely Couple Finds Friendship at Mountain Gardens." Below the heading was a picture of Virgil and Misty curled up beside one another in the gathering room.

I could just make out something else furry in the picture and determined it was the cat slippers we'd given Addie last Christmas.

###

"Mrs. Callaway, I understand you've been trying to reach me," I heard Robert Giles say as I clicked my cell phone on. I sure did spend a lot of time with the device in my hand these days. I took a break from sweeping the patio and slipped into a chair.

"My friend Belle Mathews is in desperate need of your assistance in selling the desk you appraised," I responded.

"I'd be happy to handle that for her, at a percentage of course."

"Of course, but we do need to expedite things. She's in some financial distress." That'd be an understatement.

A squirrel poked his nose out from the chrysanthemums by the patio and chirped at me in an impertinent way.

My old buddy.

"Certainly. I remember you explaining that the day I appraised the desk. What's her number, and I'll call her immediately," Robert Giles said.

I gave him the info and switched off the phone. I felt a certain relief in knowing that finally, the desk would be handled properly and Belle would be getting the money she desperately needed.

The squirrel switched his tail, shot about twenty feet out into the back yard, and up a Virginia Pine. I didn't feel like being a target today, so I headed for the house.

As I did, I directed my thoughts to a much less important, however, difficult problem. What was I going to wear to the gala? Everything in my closet was too heavy for a summer event. I'd have to go shopping, and oh, how I dreaded it. It was bound to take too much time, and I had a book proposal still to write and send to my agent. But I did want a nice dress. Where would I go to find it? I hated to make a trip to Atlanta.

The next week after choir practice, I was discussing it with Rhonda Kay. As she nodded, her gold spangled earrings twirled causing me to be distracted and almost made me lose my train of thought.

"Honey, you have the right gal. I know exactly where you need to go shoppin'. In fact, I gotta find somethin' for my concert this fall; I'll go with you."

I was sure that my taste and Rhonda Kay's did not run in the same vein or even the same quarry for that matter, but it would be nice to have company on this shopping excursion. "Great. Would this Saturday be all right?"

She smiled a lip-gloss smile. "See you then."

###

"You're gonna love this place," Rhonda Kay said when I picked her up on Saturday. "They've got the most darlin' dresses you've ever laid your eyes on."

We traveled a few miles to a neighboring town to reach a shop called Roberta's. I hoped this was not a mistake fearing it might be one of those shops with a lot of tulle and sequins. I like things a bit simpler. When we pulled into the parking lot, I loved the window displays, though. After entering the store, Rhonda Kay took my arm and guided me to a room filled with "after five" type apparel.

"You check out this rack." Rhonda Kay pointed to a round rack directly in our path, "While I go over to the wall and look at somethin' that's catchin' my eye."

I noticed Rhonda Kay pulling a long sixties-type print in hot pink and turquoise off the rack. She gazed at the dress with longing in her eyes. "Wouldn't this go fine with my hot pink stilettos?" She held the filmy chiffon dress up to her shoulders.

"Rhonda Kay, I thought black was the usual concert apparel," I offered.

"Black?" Rhonda Kay shot a look at me as if I'd slapped her. "I hate black. I don't even wear black to funerals. No ma'am. I'm not standing up there lookin' like a vulture. If I'm singin' I'm gonna look alive."

She turned her back to me as if to say the subject was closed.

I shrugged and returned to reviewing the rack in front of me. The next dress I plucked from the rack, I knew was the right one—an elegant red jersey with a small drape over one shoulder. A diamond pin I inherited from an aunt would be fabulous with it.

"Rhonda Kay, what about this one?' I held up the dress up for her to see.

"Looks just like you," Rhonda Kay said curtly.

I was not sure whether her comment was a compliment or not, but I tried the dress on anyway, and it fit perfectly. When I went to pay for the dress, I discovered, however, that my wallet was not in my purse. I remembered I'd left it by the computer at home when I'd ordered a pair of shoes on line.

"Oh, no. I'll have to come back. I've left my wallet at home."

"We can only hold it for you until the end of the day," the sales woman said.

"No problem, I'll be back later."

Even though she was mad, Rhonda Kay offered to loan me the money, but I didn't want to stretch things between us, and told her it was no problem to come back.

I noticed Rhonda Kay's empty hands. "Didn't you get the dress you liked?"

"I decided I'd better ask the symphony what they want me to wear." Rhonda Kay sounded disappointed.

I knew this was a perfect time not to say anything in response.

I called Ted on the way home, "I found a great dress for the gala today at Roberta's—a lovely red."

"Red is my favorite color," Ted said.

"I didn't know that, but I forgot my wallet, and had to put the dress on hold. I have to run back over there this afternoon."

"You can't go back to Roberta's today. Have you forgotten we agreed to go to the lake this afternoon with Iris and Sam? If the dress is on hold today, I'm sure it'll still be there when you go back on Monday."

"Sure, Monday's fine."

Chapter Twenty-Seven

Going Somewhere?

"Rely on His faithfulness, not on your own."
—Hannah Whitall Smith (1832-1911)

I hated to cry right in front of the sales woman at Roberta's. "When did you sell it?" I moaned plunking my purse down next to the cash register.

"Someone came in early this morning and bought it just as we put it back on the rack." She put a yellow blouse down on the counter. "If you'd called we could have worked something out."

"I know, I know." I sighed and trudged back over to the "after five" room.

After an hour of trying dresses on, the only one I found to fit was in taupe.

Grandmother of the bride, I thought. Taupe drained the color from my face and made me appear as if I were coming down with the flu. I felt about taupe the same way Rhonda Kay felt about black, but I bought the dress fearful I wouldn't find anything else.

Sure enough, I checked online and at several other stores, but inventories were low with everyone changing from summer to fall stock, and I didn't find anything else that would work. I finally resigned myself to taupe, but I was not happy about it.

###

Silas lowered himself into his chair, let go of his cane, adjusted his glasses, and pulled out the article from his pocket. Again. He unfolded it and reread the headline he'd read so many times, "Miracle in Toccoa, Georgia."

If the person who found the desk, this June Callaway, had located the beneficiary, that meant that Buford must have had a grandchild, and even great-grandchildren. That meant he himself was a great-uncle. He had relatives. How strange he'd spent years running from those in his past. Now, he was wondering what it might be like to call someone family again.

He refolded the article and put it in his wallet. He picked up the train schedules from the coffee table that he'd gotten Conner at Hero's House to print off the Amtrak website. He'd spent enough time in airplanes in the army. He was ready for a mode of transportation that more fit the stage of life he was in.

"Going somewhere," Conner had asked when he'd requested the schedules.

"I'm not sure," Silas replied shuffling from one foot to the other.

"Looks like you might be going south if you need the Crescent Schedule," Conner observed.

"Could be," he had said taking the schedule from Conner's extended hand not wanting to get into the details.

As he studied it, he found he could take the Northeast Corridor Express from Boston and get into New York around 12:45. That would give him time to get his baggage, grab lunch and still board the Crescent at 2:15. It had been a long time since he'd been on the Crescent. Back in the day, the train was called the Southern Crescent before Amtrak bought it. Maybe he would go when the weather turner cooler and catch the changing tree foliage as he went south.

That would be about right. He'd have to move out of the cottage anyway, so taking a little trip before he settled into a more permanent situation would work well. What would it be like to see Currahee Mountain again after so many years? In some ways, the mountain had always been with him, growing up in sight of it as he did. It remained to this day part of the wallpaper of his mind.

"Toccoa," he whispered aloud without even realizing it, and as he did, homesickness unlike anything he'd ever known before came over him.

He studied the schedule for the Crescent, again. The train would arrive at the Toccoa station around 6:15 in the morning. His first sight of the mountain in over sixty years would be in the light of the rising sun.

But, what would he do once he arrived? He couldn't just show up at this Belle Mathews' house and say, "Hello, I'm your uncle who's been missing for sixty years." What if she doesn't want an uncle? What if she's angry that he abandoned the family for so long? He didn't know if he could do this or not.

Maybe, he'd better stay here in Massachusetts and not risk it.

###

When the Cardiac Association Gala finally rolled around, I was no happier about my dress. I was even less happy about the fact that it'd started raining early that morning. The heat and humidity did what they always did to my naturally curly hair. By late afternoon, most of it was standing at a right angle to my head accompanied by a halo of frizz. I'd used every hair product in the house to no avail.

It was not going to be much of a gala for me.

Ted arrived to pick me up, and found me still searching for one earring that'd disappeared.

"I'll be right back. I can't find my other earring."

"Are you ok? You seem a little harried," he called as I started back up the stairs.

I didn't even know how to respond.

When I came back down later, I found him reading *Southern Living* in the study. "There are some good recipes in here," he said.

I tried not to take it personally.

"Are you ready?"

"Not really," I replied, "but let's go anyway."

"I thought you were excited about tonight."

"I was until I had to wear brown and my hair went crazy."

"You look beautiful," Ted said with dimples.

Ted was kind, but I felt as frazzled as my hair.

###

When we arrived at the Gala, I saw several people I knew from Emmanuel Church—all milling around bidding on items for the silent auction before dinner. I was about to bid on a gift certificate to a local bookstore when a flash of red caught my eye. I looked closer and saw a young woman wearing the red dress I'd had on hold at Roberta's. This young woman was wearing *my* red dress.

"Tracie," I heard Ted call out from beside me, "there's someone I want you to meet."

The red dress woman approached, and Ted gestured toward her. "June, this is Tracie, my new administrative assistant."

Ted's assistant had bought the dress? How unbelievable.

"Nice to finally meet you Tracie," I managed to get out. "We've spoken on the phone, but it's good to put a face with a voice."

"Nice to meet you, too. I've heard many wonderful things about you." She wore a pearl pin in the same spot I'd planned to use my diamond one.

"Tracie came along just in time," Ted said. "Louise had to leave quickly because of her mother's fall. I didn't know what I was going to do, and then Tracie showed up."

"I remember you saying something about that." I studied Tracie's blond hair and the dress that was a touch too small.

"I'll see you folks later—there's a massage I want to bid on." Tracie slid away into the crowd.

"She's lovely," I observed.

"I suppose she is." Ted lifted a bid sheet from a table for a set of golf clubs.

"And young, and . . . she has on my red dress." My eyes dropped to the ocean of muddy water fabric in which I was swimming.

Ted studied me in a puzzled way, no dimples, and then focused on the bid sheet. "What do you mean she has on your dress?" He jotted a few numbers down.

"The dress at Roberta's that sold before I could get back to buy it."

"That's a strange coincidence." He placed the bid sheet back on the table.

I glanced at Tracie across the room. Quite a coincidence.

###

Summer pressed into September, but seemed to lose heart somewhere around the tenth of the month, bringing a noticeable and welcome change from the almost one hundred degree temperatures we'd had in early August. Around the patio this morning, even the flowers seemed a little brighter and not quite as wilted as they were a few weeks back. A squirrel barked somewhere in the distance, and a monarch butterfly made what I knew would be one of its last stops here for flower nectar. Jason had told me they'd be heading toward Mexico before the end of the month. Pleasant this morning, yet I struggled to focus on the email I'd been working on so long. I put it aside for a few moments.

I couldn't get Tracie and the red dress out of my mind. Ted was unaware of how attractive he was and probably didn't even know a young woman like Tracie would be interested in him. Could she really have bought that dress out from under me?

How silly. I shook off the question, picked up my laptop, again, and turned my attention to the email on my computer screen. *The email.* I'd attached my manuscript and proposal and was ready to press send.

As I put my finger on the button, I prayed. "God, please let this agent see the possibilities here. I give it to you."

As I watched the send icon light up indicating the message had gone, rustling sounded from Bertha's side of the fence.

"Who's over there this morning?" I called as I moved to the fence.

"It's me, ma'am," Jubilee said from the direction of the green beans. "I'm tryin' to figure out what Tom and Joe need to do to clean up this garden."

I peered over the fence, and he pointed to a row of cabbages.

"We still got these to tend, but the worst is over. There'll probably be okra 'til frost, but glory be, most of the other vegetables is playin' out."

He stopped and mopped his brow with a bandana. "Weather's cooler, but still hot when you start workin'. I need a break from this place. I got so much to do, I don't know whether I'm a comin' or a goin'."

"Your yard ornament business going well?" I asked

"The custom work's about to kill me. Somehow, folks found out about that whirligig I made that looks like you, and they all want one to look like their mama, or their grand pappy, or some other kin. Why, I got enough to keep me busy `til sometime next year. But I'm a chargin', yes ma'am, I'm a chargin'. What's surprisin' to me is how much folks is willin' to pay."

"Your work brings a lot of folks great joy when they see it. That must be fulfilling."

"Yes ma'am it is. Don't tell nobody this, but truth be told, I'd do all this and not charge nothin', I love the work so much. But, I got an employee to think about now. I gotta charge to pay him."

"Your work is worth every penny you receive for it and more."

"Thank you, ma'am." Jubilee flashed his toothy grin as his cell phone rang.

"Jubilee Johnson at your service," he answered.

Chapter Twenty-Eight

Fearless Ed

"The greatest thing in my life is being a Christian."
—Paul Anderson, Olympian and Toccoa native (1932-1994)

In late September, I received a phone call from Belle while I was volunteering at the library. "Hold a minute." I stepped into the area where we prepared new books for circulation and repaired others which had grown shopworn.

I perched on a stool, and on the counter lay a copy of *The History of Stephens County, Georgia,* the spine of which I intended to repair later in the day.

"I received a check for the desk," Belle said.

Oh, how I hoped it would be enough to take care of Belle's expenses, but I couldn't read her voice. "I hope it's a lot."

"$479, 000." Belle squealed into the phone sounding as if she were exploding on the other end.

It all seemed surreal. "Really? 479,000?" I guess I didn't think it'd actually fetch as much as Robert Giles thought it would. It seemed so . . . I don't know . . . too good to be true.

Over the phone, I could hear Belle's simultaneous laughter and tears. "Can you believe it? I'll be able to pay off the house, the bills, and help my kids with their education. I can't believe I'm crying again. I didn't think I had any tears left."

I pulled a tissue from a box on the desk beside me and dabbed the tears running down my own cheeks. "I'm thankful to God that all this happened the way it did. Robert Giles must have expedited the sale in order for you to get the money this fast."

"He tells me the desk was purchased for donation to a museum."

Museum? "The next time you talk to him, ask him which one. Wouldn't it be great to visit it again, sometime?"

"You won't believe the other new development. Roger Wood is going to help me invest. In a few weeks, I've gone from financial disaster to needing an advisor to help me handle the extra money."

I had to laugh.

"June, Ted told me that legally you had no obligation to part with the desk. Thank you."

"That will contained the last wishes of a man who did so much for our country. I couldn't ignore it. The desk has always been yours."

"Wouldn't it be wonderful if Uncle Silas wasn't dead but still alive and knew what a blessing he's been to us?"

I sighed. After all the dead ends I'd come to regarding Silas Braham, I didn't hold on to much hope for finding him. What age would he be now anyway? Close to ninety I supposed. "I guess we have to let that go. We have to remember that it was because of a will that I found you. What if he wanted the money back?"

Belle's breath caught on the other end. "I hadn't thought of that." Another pause. "Still, I'm going to pray."

"There's been no trace of him for over forty years. He never showed on any of the searches I did. He probably died overseas long ago." I hated to be such a killjoy.

"Still praying," Belle declared.

###

"What's on your mind?" Leo asked Silas. "It's certainly not on the card game. You didn't even deal the right number of cards." Silas had joined several men gathered in the common room at Hero's House to play cards while others read or reminisced.

"What did you say?" Silas mumbled.

"Your mind's not on the game," Leo shouted.

"My hearing's not that bad; you don't have to yell." Silas shifted in his chair.

Leo put his cards down on the table and leaned forward.

"I have to yell to get your attention. Listen, we haven't known you for that long, but we can tell something's bothering you."

Silas didn't know what to say.

"See, you clam up when we try to talk to you about anything but sports or cards. We appreciate you visiting with us, but for a change, why don't you let us do for you? Make us feel needed. None of us are going to be around long." Leo gave him a forlorn look. Ed put his cards down and did his best puppy imitation. Others in the room followed.

Silas recognized a manipulation tactic when he saw one. This was low, using the sick man ploy. He put his cards down, too, and sighed.

"We all know you've been asking about train schedules to the south. Conner told us, so you can go ahead and tell us what you're thinking about," Leo said while others around him nodded in agreement.

What was this, a conspiracy? Silas again didn't know what to say, but finally pulled out his wallet and took out the newspaper article he'd been saving and pushed it across the table toward Leo. Those around the table leaned over to read. Someone sitting on the sofa yelled, "Read it to us," so Leo read the entire article aloud.

"That's a nice story, but what does this have to do with you?" Ed asked.

Silas ran his hand through his thin hair. He moved his cane around. "That woman Belle Mathews might be my great niece. I don't know."

"What makes you think that?" Ed asked. "I thought you said you didn't have any family."

"I didn't think so, but that desk they mention in the story sounds a lot like a desk I once had," Silas said. "Hard to believe there'd be more than one of them in a town that size."

"You had a desk worth almost half a million dollars in a basement, and went off and left it?" Leo asked incredulous.

"Not exactly." He'd never explained this to anyone before.

"What does not exactly mean? We've been asking a lot of questions, but I don't think we're even close to what you don't want to tell us." Ed grabbed the cards on the table and put them back into the deck as if through playing cards. He folded his arms defiantly.

Silas studied his cane handle intently trying to decide what to say next. "I was married once—to a French girl during the war." He still didn't trust himself to say her name aloud.

"You never told us you were married. We thought you were a tough old ex-military guy who never stayed in one place long enough to get serious," Leo said.

Oh, the plans they'd had."She was coming to America after the war. We were going to get a little house, but she . . . she died on the passage over."

Ed's face was lined with compassion. "That's rough Silas. I lost my wife after forty years, and I thought it would kill me."

"I guess I did die," Silas said. "Stayed in the military, and never went back home. It's been sixty years."

"Sixty years?" Ed said. "You haven't been home for sixty years?"

"No, I didn't even know I had any relatives left until I read this article," Silas explained.

"You trained on Currahee Mountain near Toccoa, didn't you?" Leo asked.

"Yes, but I grew up in that area, too." The memories of home flooded back to him.

"You don't sound like a southerner," Ed said.

"Lost the accent in England."

"Looks like you might be thinking about going back since you're getting those train schedules."

"No, not really," Silas said.

"Wait a minute, what about the desk?" Ed asked.

"The girl I married brought the desk with her on the boat. When I learned she died, my brother Buford took it and the rest of her things and stored them. I never knew where. I had a will drawn up. I was sure I wouldn't live long, because I felt like I might die any minute. Buford took it, must have put it in the desk and after all this time, June Callaway probably found it. Buford moved to California years ago and died there. This Belle Mathews might be his descendent."

"What was the girl's name?" Ed asked.

Silas looked at Ed, and then back down at his cane handle. "Anne Marie."

"Pretty name," Leo said and directed his gaze to the cane handle as well. He lifted his eyes and steadied them at Silas. "Nobody asked my opinion, but I think you ought to go. You're getting old like the rest of us, and a man ought to be able to go home before he dies."

"What if this great niece of mine doesn't want to see an old ghost like me? They think I'm dead. I haven't talked to any relatives since my brother Buford died."

Leo smiled. "I bet she'll be real excited to see you. This article says she has children. They might need a grandpa. I bet they'd be glad to take you on."

"I don't know." Silas lowered his eyes. "Sounds risky."

Leo slid the article back over to Silas. "When you jumped out of that airplane sixty years ago, that was risky, wasn't it? But look what good came of it. You're a hero to this country. You can't let fear get you now. It seems like to me you're a whole lot more afraid of living than we are of dying."

Ed sat large in his chair. "I'm staring square in the eyes of death, but I'm not afraid. No sir, I've got Jesus on my side, and I'm not afraid."

Others around uttered a collective, "that's right."

Silas nodded. He hadn't thought much about God in a long time.

His mama always made him go to church when he was young and to the yearly Camp Meeting in Poplar Springs. It was so hot during the July Camp Meeting services, the perspiration would run down his legs into his shoes. But, one night as the preacher was preaching he realized he needed Jesus. He walked that sawdust aisle in his squishy shoes and gave his life to the Lord. God seemed real then, but over the years, the experience faded, and when Anne Marie died, he wasn't even sure there was a God. He still wasn't sure. This close to the end, and he just didn't know.

Chapter Twenty-Nine

Something to Think about

"There are joys which long to be ours. God sends ten thousands truths, which come about us like birds seeking inlet; but we are shut up to them, and so they bring us nothing, but sit and sing a while upon the roof, and then fly away."
—Henry Ward Beecher (1813-1887)

I entered The Dinner Bell and knew right away Ted hadn't received the message I left earlier with Tracie. Crumpled up napkins and sweetener packages littered his table as if he'd been encamped there for days.

I took a seat across from him, and skipped the niceties. "I left a message with Tracie saying I needed to go out of town this afternoon, and that I'd be late for dinner. You obviously didn't get it. How long have you waited?"

"Not too long." I guessed that Ted only pretended to study a menu.

"How many glasses of tea have you had?"

"A few."

I picked up a dozen empty sweetener packages and held them up. "You have waited. This is a problem. If you could just remember to keep your cell phone with you." I put the packages down, picked up a menu, and scanned it tryng to check my annoyance.

"I know it's been a little bit of a problem," Ted said.

"I think I know why Tracie is doing this."

"Why?" Ted seemed genuinely mystified just as Stella whooshed up to the table.

It took her about half a second to read our faces. "I can come back." And with that, she peeled off toward the kitchen.

I leaned forward and whispered, "You really don't know, do you?" I didn't wait for an answer. "Tracie has her eye on you, and is trying to cause trouble between us."

Ted laughed. "You have to be kidding, June. I'm at least twenty years older than she is."

"That makes no difference these days. She's attracted to you and that's that."

Ted's smile grew wider and showed his dimples to their best advantage. Even with my feelings of aggravation, my heart seemed to skip a beat. He leaned forward and raised his eyebrows. "And this bothers you?"

"Well, I…I just think it's rude, that's all." It was rude. It was.

He leaned back in his seat appearing a bit self-satisfied.

"You should ask her why she doesn't give you my messages."

"I guess I could ask her if there's a problem." Ted studied me curiously.

"You certainly could."

I didn't know Stella was capable of the slow pace with which she tiptoed to our table. She stood with her hands on her hips and eyed us both. "Y'all gonna order tonight, or do you need to take it outside?"

###

"June, you sound pretty jealous for a woman who says she's not ready to get married," Iris said when we met at Sherrino's for lunch.

"Jealous, I'm not jealous." I crunched down on my bread.

"Just telling you how you sound." She twirled her fork in spaghetti. "I'm your friend, right?"

"Well, of course." I wondered why she had to ask.

She hesitated a moment, as she steadied her eyes on mine. "It seems for some time, you've been finding petty reasons to be annoyed with Ted. Just enough to keep him at arm's distance. Just enough to keep your relationship from moving on. Now, you're annoyed with him over the possibility someone else is interested in him. It wouldn't bother you if you didn't have strong feelings for him. Think about it." She put her forkful of spaghetti in her mouth.

Well . . . I never. I hadn't been finding reasons to keep Ted at a distance. Why would I do that? There was that phrase again—"moving on." So tired of hearing it.

Iris interrupted my thoughts. "Changing the subject, do you know how college is going for Becky?"

I tried to focus on her question. "Having a wonderful time. Belle says it's hard, but she's dancing a lot and learning so many new things." I put my fork down. The appeal of my lasagna had dimmed, somehow.

Iris put her head in her right hand, which rested on the table, and a dreamy expression crossed over her eyes. "Such a miracle you found the desk and Belle, otherwise Becky would never be able to attend that fine school. So amazing." She shook off the dreamy look and went back to twirling spaghetti. "I've been thinking. I know it was hard for you to leave your home, and friends in Atlanta, but see what's happened since you came here."

"I didn't know if I could do it or not, but then that person or angel or whatever he was at the writer's conference said 'Do it afraid,' and I thought I had to make the move, that God was telling me to do it. I guess now I know why."

"Maybe, this isn't even the end of the story," Iris said. "Maybe there's more for you than you even imagined. Maybe—just maybe, there are some other things you need to 'do afraid.'"

I couldn't miss her implication.

###

Rhonda Kay had an uncharacteristically glum expression on her face when she shuffled in for choir practice the next Tuesday night.

"What's wrong," I asked as we headed for our seats.

"Black. I gotta wear black. This symphony stuff is not all it's cracked up to be if I gotta stand up there wearin' a funeral suit."

"Maybe, it's the price you pay for being such an amazing vocalist." I pulled my music out of my folder.

Rhonda Kay perched on the front row. "That don't make me feel no better."

I searched my brain for any encouragement. "You can still wear stilettos!"

She seemed to brighten a bit. "That's true. I can go shopping for a new pair of shoes. Yes, ma'am, shoe shopping. Just the thing." Seeming more satisfied, she went on, "Hey, what did you ever wear to that gala to-do?"

"I wore brown accompanied by fuzzy hair."

"Brown, I thought you was gonna buy that red dress you found at Roberta's."

"Someone bought it before I could get back."

"Too bad. I wouldn't want to be wearing brown to no party. Sorry."

"Me, too."

###

The doorbell rang, and I rose from the computer to answer it. Red flew ahead of me as if it was a competition, and I almost tripped over him and his ball before I reached the entry.

"Howdy, Miz Callaway," Jed said as the door swung open. "I got me some new help I want you to meet." He gestured toward a young man approaching on the walkway. "Miz Callaway, this here is Eugene West. He's the newest addition to Jed's Weed and Seed," Jed beamed.

I extended my hand. "Pleased to meet you, Eugene."

With his right hand, Eugene tipped his baseball cap emblazoned "Jed's Weed and Seed." "Pleased to meet you, Mrs. Callaway," and he held up that same hand before he took mine. "Hand's clean—first stop for the day."

"Eugene's just moved to Toccoa," Jed said. "His cousin's at the police department."

"I've had some recent dealings with the police department. Detective William Rust and Cletus Smith were a big help."

"Cletus is my cousin," Eugene explained. "Good man."

Jed nodded toward Eugene. "He ain't married. Stayin' over at the Toccoa Motor Lodge for the time bein'. Huntin' for a permanent place, though." Jed scanned the front yard. "Well, we got plenty to do. We're here for the monthly maintenance, but I'm thinkin' we might overseed this month to get a real good stand of grass for next spring."

"Whatever you think, Jed." I closed the door and headed back to my desk. I'd no sooner settled in my chair than the doorbell rang again. Once more, Red shot to the door like a bullet, this time carrying his ball in his mouth. I opened it to find Bertha's daughter, Melissa, smiling from ear to ear.

Melissa pointed to Red. "I can't believe you both answered the door."

Red sat at my feet with the ball in his mouth, the absolute model of feline obedience. No one would've ever guessed he'd just about knocked me down only seconds earlier.

"I have great news." She appeared to hold a letter of some sort in her right hand.

I gestured for her to enter."Can't wait to hear it. Come in and have a seat."

After we took our seats, Melissa began. "Remember when I took that video of Red retrieving his ball?"

I'd almost forgotten. It seemed at least a decade ago with all the desk developments following after. "Yes, back around Thanksgiving."

"Right. I thought it was so good, I sent it to the 'Celebrity Cats' television show. They've selected it to be in their competition." She unfolded the paper in her hand. "See, here's the email."

I took it from her and scanned it. "What does this mean?"

"To continue in the competition, Red has to go to Hollywood with you or Jason and appear on the show."

Traveling a couple of thousand miles with Red? My recent experience with him at the vet came to mind. No way. "Jason will definitely have to take him. Red is his cat, and he should go." I took out my cell phone. "I'll call him right now."

I checked the time and saw Jason would be out of class, so I pulled my cell phone from my pocket and dialed. I told him about the development.

"Celebrity Cats, woo hoo." I heard voices in the background. "Hey guys, I'm going to have a famous cat, `cause we're going to Hollywood."

I laughed, said good-bye, and put the phone in my pocket.

I studied Jason's tiger-striped cat and picked him up. "Well, boy it seems like you're destined for stardom." Red dropped the ball in his mouth on the floor and peered at me in a self-satisfied way.

Melissa stroked the tabby. "It appears he already knows that."

Chapter Thirty

A Lot of Doings

"Let the past sleep, but let it sleep on the bosom of Christ, and go out into the irresistible future with Him."
—Oswald Chambers (1874-1917)

I settled in my chair at Mountain Gardens.

"Celebrity Cats?" Addie asked.

"That's what it's called," I said.

"I don't watch much television; I didn't even know there was such a show, but I'll have to see it, if Red is going to be on it. It seems like every animal we know is getting to be a star." Addie glanced at Misty who was curled up again with Virgil.

"Quite amazing." I paused a moment before I spoke wondering if I should say what was on my mind. "Addie, Belle believes Silas could still be alive. Do you think it's possible?"

"Looks like if he was alive, we would've heard from him. But then, he might think we're all gone, too."

Misty jumped in her lap. Addie stroked her. "Prefer me over the pig, now? I guess you're hungry. I'll get your food." Addie started to get up.

"I sure hate to see Belle get her hopes up only to be disappointed." I took Addie's arm to assist her. "What if he were to be upset, and want the desk back. Wouldn't that be horrible?"

"Now, June, you can't do a thing about it. The best we can do is pray."

I wondered if Addie and Belle had been talking to each other about this. Of course, they were both right.

###

"Are you going?" Conner asked Silas when he came through the door of Hero's House the next Thursday.

Silas pushed the door shut with his cane. Knowing exactly what he meant, he still asked, "Going where?"

"South. The guys told me the whole story. I think you should."

Silas paused in the entryway and sighed. Didn't they understand he couldn't just barge into someone else's life? "I appreciate you telling all of them about the train schedule. Now the whole place is talking about this—exactly what I've tried to avoid all these years."

"You've been running too long, Silas. The guys are trying to help. Give them a break." How old was Conner anyway? Here he was not even half of his age trying to tell him what to do.

Silas shuffled into the common area. "I hear you people have teamed up with Conner to try and run my life."

"Sure have," Ed said from his place at a card table. "We told you what we think you should do, and it didn't seem to have any effect. So, we went to Conner to bring him in on the deal."

Silas collapsed in a chair at the table.

Across from Silas, Leo leaned forward on his elbows. "You ought to go."

From the other side of the room, someone spoke up. "What are you waiting for?"

Silas rapped his cane on the floor. "Okay, Okay, I'll go. I'll never get any peace here if I don't." He hoped they were prepared to hear about the possible negative consequences.

"You're right." Leo slapped the table for emphasis and sported a big smile on his face. "We agreed we were going to give you the business until we wore you down. It didn't take as long as we thought it would." Leo took a deep breath seeming pleased with himself. "Now, when are you leaving? I say the sooner, the better. When does your lease run out at the cottage?"

"I'm paying month to month. That's not an issue."

"Good," said Ed. "That means you can leave right away. Get your train schedule out tonight, and let us know tomorrow what your plans are."

"Anything else you want me to do?" Silas asked. Bossy, these people.

Leo pointed to a card deck. "Yeah, deal."

Silas shook his head, picked up a deck, shuffled, cut, and started flinging the cards out. "Ed, before I go, I'm taking you for one more haircut. I've never seen anybody as old as you with hair that grows so fast. I can't leave you in a mess."

Ed rolled his eyes, "Aw, just play cards."

###

Later that night Silas sank into an arm chair, and studied the train schedule, again.

If he took the Crescent and changed his mind about stopping in Toccoa, he'd just go on to New Orleans.

Wait a minute, those were the thoughts of a coward.

That old feeling he had before he jumped out of the C-47 in 1944 was stalking him. In many ways, fear had driven him to his restless wanderings. Fear of being reminded of the pain of losing Anne Marie.

It was time to stop wandering.

All the guys at Hero's House were counting on him. These dying men were teaching him how to live. He had to face this. If he couldn't do it for himself, he would do it for the guys who believed something good could really happen. He sure hoped they were right. He picked up the phone and dialed a number, "Hello, is this Amtrak? I'd like to make a reservation."

###

Laura Goodhay stood at the podium and leaned forward. We all grew silent. "As you know, next Friday is the Symphony concert. We want to support Rhonda Kay in force. How many of you are planning on going?"

I turned to see that every member of the choir raised their hand.

"Well, with this response we'll need the church van. I'm sure some of our parishioners will be joining us as well." Laura turned to Rhonda Kay. "How do you feel?"

Rhonda Kay seemed a bit pale and uncharacteristically reticent. "I got to be honest. I'm gettin' nervous. The practices have been goin' well, but we still got the dress rehearsal Thursday night. I ain't never sung in front of so many people before, but I'm prayin'. I keep rememberin' that verse in Philippians, 'I can do everything through Him who gives me strength.'"

Laura stepped over and put her arm around Rhonda Kay. "We're praying, too." Laura bowed her head. "Lord, please be with our friend, Rhonda Kay. Help her to lean on you, and to sing for your glory. Lord, we give you thanks for the talent you have placed within her. We leave this concert in your hands, Amen."

"Amen," the entire choir echoed.

"Double Amen," Rhonda Kay said.

###

Tracie had apologized for her lapse of memory in communicating messages, but it didn't seem to help.

"She did it again," I said as Ted finally answered his cell phone.

"What did she do?" Ted asked.

"She didn't give you my message. Because you never keep your phone with you, I leave messages with her. I wanted to tell you Iris and Sam invited us over for dinner tonight, but since I never heard from you I told them no."

"June, I'm sorry, I had closing after closing today."

"Couldn't she have slipped you the message between them?"

"Tracie has gone for the day, something about a hair appointment. But I'll talk to her tomorrow. Now, what can I do to make it up to you? What if I take you out to Sherrino's tonight. You love their ravioli."

"That's true." I remembered Iris' words and tried to be more pleasant. "It's a deal."

"I'll pick you up in thirty minutes," he said.

###

Silas dropped his cane on the floor, put his cap on the table, and folded into one of the card chairs. "October fifteenth. Is that soon enough for you people? I'm beginning to think you guys are trying to get rid of me."

"So you booked your reservations, then?" Ed asked putting the deck on the table.

"I'm set to go," Silas said.

Leo appeared thoughtful. "Now, we'll need to have a report on how things are going. Why don't you get one of those cell phones so you can call us every day and keep us posted."

"Yeah, make sure you get nationwide calling. It's cheaper, I think," said Ed.

"Have you folks thought about becoming travel agents or maybe social directors? Seems like to me you might've missed your calling?" Silas could not even imagine having a cell phone. He had tried to avoid technology as much as possible. "A cell phone might be going a bit far. I'm too old to learn how to use one."

"Afraid of moving into the twenty-first century, huh?" Ed leaned back in his chair. "You owe it to us to keep us informed. We're the ones who talked you into going, remember?"

How could he forget? Ed appeared a bit more washed out than usual. "You're not going to give me a choice are you?"

"No, we're not," Leo agreed.

"I'll get one tomorrow." Silas shook his head in resignation, as he picked up a deck of cards and held them up. "Whose turn is it to deal?"

###

I stared at the calendar on my desk. Friday was going to be a wall-to-wall day. Jason was coming home Thursday night, and I would take him and Red to the Atlanta airport early Friday so they could catch their flight to Hollywood. I'd stay in Atlanta and visit with friends. Then, I'd attend the Symphony concert downtown that night and drive back to Toccoa afterward.

Ted and I had talked about Ted riding the church bus to Atlanta that evening and riding back with me that night. All this business with Tracie had left me feeling a little off kilter, not sure of exactly where I was anymore.

Iris was right. Because of my reluctance to make a commitment to Ted, I knew I didn't have a right to make demands of him or his time, but it was all so exasperating. I kept thinking about what Iris told me—that I was finding reasons to keep Ted at a distance, all the while being annoyed about Tracie's behavior. Conflicted continued to be the best word to describe my state of being.

Maybe Iris was right about some other things, too. Maybe I was jealous. Maybe my feelings for Ted were deeper than I knew. He'd been patient with me. I didn't want to lose him.

Red hopped up on my desk with a ball in his mouth and nuzzled my hand. I stroked the tabby. "You don't have these problems, do you boy? All you have to worry about is being a star these days. I hope you don't let all this attention go to your head." I scratched him under his chin. Red dropped the ball, which I threw, and Red retrieved. I scooped up Red and hugged him. "You've always been a celebrity in my book."

###

On Wednesday night, Silas stopped at the Hero's House for a final visit before his departure the next morning. He ambled into the common room to visit with the men.

When he opened the door, a loud cheer greeted him, and he dropped his cane.

Balloons and banners filled the space. "Bon Voyage, Silas," read one. "You Can Go Home Again," read another. A big cake in the shape of a mountain sat on one of the card tables. He shuffled over to the cake. Currahee was written along the base, and a little toy train was sitting next to it.

"Are you surprised?" Leo asked obviously proud of himself.

"Surprised? I'm in shock," Silas said. "Nobody's ever given me a party in my whole life."

"It was our idea, but Conner and some of his staff put it together," Ed announced from his place in an armchair. He strained a little to speak, and his face appeared gray, his clothes looser than ever. "We wanted you to know how much you've meant to us these past few months, and how much we believe in what you're doing." He coughed.

"I don't know what to say." Silas had always been a man of few words, but now he was almost speechless.

"Say you're leaving," Leo laughed.

"I am, first thing in the morning."

"And your cell phone?" Ed asked.

Silas pulled a phone out of his pocket and held it up for all to see. Another cheer filled the room.

"Can you . . . use it?" Ed tried to smile.

"I have one with real big numbers. I can read it even without my glasses, and Conner programmed the Hero's House number into the phone. I think I'm set."

"We'll be looking forward to our first report," Conner spoke up from the doorway.

"I hope I don't disappoint you people," Silas managed to say. He hoped he didn't disappoint himself either.

Ed pushed up on the arms of his chair to stand. His knees buckled at one point, but he managed to straighten himself to his full height. "I want to do something very unmilitary," then he reached out his arms to Silas.

Silas stepped forward and he and Ed embraced, "God go with you, my friend," Ed whispered.

"Thank you." Silas felt a tear start down his cheek which he quickly whisked away with the back of his hand.

Others came and offered their best wishes to Silas, and then one of the staff began serving cake. After about thirty minutes, Silas knew he had to leave so he could finish last minute packing.

"I'll take care of returning your car to the rental place tomorrow," Conner offered.

"I appreciate all you folks have done for me." Silas picked up his cap.

"Thanks for all you've done for us," Leo said.

Silas waved, and turned around for the door.

"See you later, Silas," he heard Ed say from behind him.

Chapter Thirty-One

Do It Afraid . . . Again

"Jesus Christ teaches men that there is something in them which lifts them above this life with its hurries, its pleasures and fears. He who understands Christ's teaching feels like a bird that did not know it has wings and now suddenly realizes that it can fly, can be free and no longer needs to fear."
—Leo Tolstoy (1828-1910)

As Silas stood on the platform waiting for the train, he wondered who would take Ed to get a haircut. Who would play cards with Leo? But then, Conner was pretty resourceful. He'd probably find a volunteer with not so many miles on him. One thing was sure—he'd miss those men.

A whistle blew in the distance as the train approached from the North. The rumble of steel on steel grew closer, and the train slowed to a stop. Silas took his time boarding, pulling himself up by the handrails. He found a seat on the right side of the train, and as he peered out, he spotted Conner and Leo getting out of a car at the station. They waved, and he waved back touched by their presence. The train pulled away.

Was he really going home?

###

"Did you read the paper yesterday afternoon?" Bertha said as I picked up the telephone.

"No, I'm too busy getting ready for tomorrow night, I haven't had a chance." I put the cordless under my chin as I zipped the garment bag, which held my clothes for the symphony. "You have to see the society section. There's a picture of that Edwina Jones that lived in your house. It says she's marrying some retired psychology professor from Alabama. They're going to have a church wedding and everything." Bertha audibly sighed.

"I think it's very sweet, Bertha. After all these years, she's finally met someone besides Buford. Sounds romantic. Maybe all the stolen desk business helped her say a final good-bye to that part of her life." I laid the garment bag aside and put my shoes in an overnight case by the bed.

"At their age," Bertha said.

I moved to defend Edwina and her fiancé. "I'm sure it was scary for them to make such a commitment, but sometimes you have to be brave and plunge ahead."

"You don't really believe that, do you?" Bertha asked.

"Of course I do."

"So, why haven't you married that nice Ted that's always coming to see you and taking you to eat?"

There she went meddling. I placed a bag of toiletries in the overnight bag. "I don't know, Bertha." I hung up the phone and sank down on the bed.

I thought about Silas and his broken heart holding him hostage. I didn't want that to happen to me. I was trying my best to move past my fear, but was there something else, too. Could that heavy thing in my heart be closer to anger than fear? The minute I thought it, I knew it was true. I knew anger was a stage of grief, and I'd been openly angry for awhile—angry that Morris died and left me alone. Angry that my children were fatherless. But maybe, it was more than being angry about the situation. Maybe, somewhere deep inside, I was secretly angry with God and didn't want to admit it—hiding my distrust, lest if I give him my heart again, he might let it break once more. I guess that same distrust had spilled over onto others. Staying mad at God hadn't helped anything, and I knew my lack of confession kept me trapped in it.

I felt weary—so very weary of the thing that I denied so much.

I was stuck.

I dropped my head in my hands, and cried, "Oh, God, I don't want to be angry with you or be in bondage to my own tragedy. I surrender this to you. Help me trust you completely for my future. Forgive me, Lord. I give you my heart."

I wiped my face with the back of my hand, stood, and started to pick up my suitcase. I always over packed and knew my case would be heavy, however, for the first time in years, inside me, a load had been lifted, and I felt so light I might have floated out of the room.

###

After switching trains in New York, somewhere just past Manassas, Virginia, Silas made his way to the dining car. The steward seated him, and a short time later a young man with dark hair, neatly dressed in a golf shirt and khakis joined him. He'd forgotten how one shared dinner with total strangers on the train. "Good Evening," Silas said.

"Good Evening," the young man responded. "Where are you headed?"

"Toccoa, Georgia," Silas replied.

"I know that area, it's quite lovely. I'm Mike." He extended his hand.

Silas shook it. "Silas. Nice to meet you. I remember Toccoa as a beautiful place, but it's been a while since I've been there."

"How long?

"Over sixty years."

Silas felt the young man's eyes on him, studying him, and was relieved when the crisply attired waiter approached to take their order.

"What may I get for you this evening?" the waiter asked directing his question to Silas.

He'd love to order the Amtrak Signature Steak with the Morel Wild Forest Mushroom Sauce, but he'd better stick to something lighter. The VA Doctor had warned him about too much fat—the same doctor who said he might make it to one hundred if he ate right. One hundred. Who would've thought? But still, he complied. "I'll have the Healthy Option pork tenderloin."

"Excellent choice, Sir. And to drink?"

"Since I'm headed to Georgia, how about a glass of sweet tea?" The waiter jotted down the request and turned to Mike. "And you, Sir?"

"Give me the steak," he said.

Caution to the wind, thought Silas.

After the waiter left, Silas could feel the question coming from Mike. "So, why are you going back, now?"

He didn't know why, but he felt he could trust Mike, besides he'd probably never see him again. So after keeping everything a secret for so long, here he was again spilling the whole story from Anne Marie, to wandering the globe, to Hero's House, to June Callaway and the desk—this time to a complete stranger.

Mike listened attentively. Sometime during his ramblings, the waiter brought their food, but Silas' grew cold as he continued to talk.

When Silas finished, Mike said, "That's quite a story," and stirred cream into a fresh cup of coffee. "You sound a little anxious about going back, though."

"I am. What if they don't want to see me? After all, I'm as good as dead to them." Silas studied the pork tenderloin on his plate afraid he'd lost his appetite.

Mike leaned forward. "You of all people know, Silas, sometimes you have to move past your fear. You have to do it afraid."

Silas studied Mike. Powerful wisdom from such a young man.

Mike continued, "One more thing, God cares about you. He always has."

###

He hadn't slept much. Even in the dark, he knew from the stops they were making that outside his passenger car window, the Blue Ridge was becoming more and more evident. Charlotte, Gastonia, Greenville, Clemson. Silas' heart began to pound—almost there. He could just see in his mind's eye the forested rolling hills whizzing past him occasionally dotted by a house or pasture.

He'd only planned his first move. He'd go to June Callaway's house, speak with her and find out if the desk had been Anne Marie's.

If it was, he needed to know if Mrs. Callaway thought this Belle Mathews might be open to seeing him,

Though the sun still had not come up yet, he could imagine the ever-changing kaleidoscope of foliage in russets, golds, and reds that would welcome him back to the scenes of his childhood. At 6:15, when the conductor announced the Toccoa station, Silas stood up and pulled his bag from the overhead rack. He placed his cap on his head, and as the train rolled to a stop, he made his way with his bag in one hand and his cane in the other to the exit and stepped down.

He stood alone on the platform of the Toccoa station. He noticed a sign to his left which read, "Currahee Military Museum." Seemed they'd converted the old train depot into a museum. Impressive. He'd have to come back later and see it.

After the train, which had obscured his view of the mountain, pulled away to the west, Silas caught the first golden streams of the rising sun on the iconic mountain of his early life. After all these years, he found it unchanged from the memories he had carried so long.

Finally, he turned to look down the street and recognized the building still standing where Rothell's Feed Store used to be. His family had bought farm supplies there when he was a boy. Looked like a radio station might occupy the building now.

He'd have to wander around and ask where he might get breakfast this morning. Next, he'd get a cab and go to June Callaway's house. He didn't know what he'd do then. He'd deal with that later.

###

The alarm went off at 5:30, and as I put my feet on the floor, I realized I'd had that dream again last night—the one of the Eagle in Bertha's magnolia staring down at me with his piercing gaze. So strange and a little unsettling. Again as he was perched on high, the mighty eagle seemed as if he wanted something from me. Needed me somehow.

I slid my feet into my slippers. This was the third time I'd had this nocturnal image, and I thought that attributing it to too much

Sherrino's pizza just wouldn't work anymore. But there wasn't really time to put much more thought into it.

When Jason, Red, and I left later to get to the airport, I made a detour through downtown because I needed to visit the ATM machine. As I passed the train depot, I spotted an older gentleman with a plaid cap holding a suitcase in one hand and a cane in the other. How peculiar for him to be all alone at the station this early in the morning. I'd heard the Crescent whistle earlier, and knew he'd just arrived. Why was there no family to greet him?

But we pressed on to the ATM, and on our way out of town, we spotted a familiar sight.

I pointed to a whirligig placed by a mailbox. "It's one of Jubilee's pieces. I've not seen that one before. Who does it depict?"

Jason turned to see when I slowed the car to a stop. "Best Wishes Rhonda Kay" he read from a sign posted underneath the whirligig. He looked at me and asked, "I think it's a nice likeness, don't you?"

I took in the big blonde hair, the stiletto pumps, and what appeared to be an orange pant suit. "That's definitely her. As my mother used to say, 'Will wonders never cease?'"

###

Silas finished his scrambled eggs and bacon at the Dinner Bell and relished the last of his huge biscuit. Delicious.

The waitress with the Stella nametag zoomed up to his table and whisked away his empty plate. "Looks like you enjoyed yourself."

"You can't imagine how much."

"You're new in town, ain't you?"

"Yes and no," he said. "I wonder if you might call a cab for me?"

"Happy to, but you might as well know we just got your one cab company: Elvin's Cabs. I'll try to get him to come pick you up. Nice guy, Elvin, but he needs to quit smoking cigars. You can smell him coming a mile away."

"Never have minded a little cigar scent. Kind of like it actually."

"Well, Elvin's your man then. I'll call him right now."

With that, she shot away at such a speed, Silas wondered if she left traction marks on the linoleum. She must run, he thought.

In a moment, Stella returned at the same warp speed. "Elvin said he'd be here in just a few minutes. He's got a fare he has to drop off at Mall Market and then he'll be on. Where you headed?" she asked as she refilled his coffee.

He'd forgotten how everyone in small towns wanted to know each other's business. Of course, the very reason he was here was other people pushing him into it. "A residence in town."

She cleared the rest of the table. "Got family here?"

Silas smiled and held up his cup, "Could I get one to go?"

Stella blinked at him. "Coming right up." She appeared to take the hint, pivoted and sprinted back to the kitchen.

###

"Tugalo Street," Silas announced as he loaded into Elvin's minivan turned cab.

"Tugalo, huh?" Elvin said. "Done been over there one time this morning to take a tourist to the Paul Anderson Park. That where you going?"

"No, 5210 Tugalo." Silas closed the door and rested his cane on the seat. "It's a house." Although, he wouldn't mind visiting the park, sometime. That Olympian Paul Anderson had really been something with his extraordinary strength.

Elvin nodded and they were off. As promised, cigar smoke enveloped him as they headed away from The Dinner Bell, but it reminded him of card playing nights back in England.

As the cab wheeled down Sage Street, Silas tried to find landmarks that remained of the place he once knew.

The county courthouse still stood sentinel over the little town, and just as he passed, the clock struck 8:00. He closed his eyes and the resonance of the chimes carried him back thousands of yesterdays.

He wondered what happened to Addie—the shadow that he and Buford always had with them—the one they teased about being their aunt, the youngest child of their grandparents.

Probably gone like the rest of his family.

###

"5210 Tugalo Street," Elvin announced to Silas as they pulled up in front of a white frame house with glass paned front door. "Shall I wait?'

"If you don't mind," Silas said.

Silas exited the car and advanced up the walkway to the front steps of Mrs. Callaway's house wondering how these few steps might lead to changing his life. He grabbed the handrails and pulled himself up on the porch. He took a deep breath and rang the doorbell.

Chapter Thirty-Two

Very Curious

"...but those who hope in the LORD
will renew their strength.
They will soar on wings like eagles;
they will run and not grow weary,
they will walk and not be faint."
—Isaiah 40:31

Silas listened for movement inside the house. Nothing. He rang again. Silence. He knocked. Again, he only heard birds singing in the Magnolia next door. Finally, he turned and shuffled back to the cab.

"Where to?" Elvin asked.

Silas thought a moment."I don't know."

Elvin turned around in his seat and stared at Silas. "We can't sit here on the street the rest of the day. The meter is running."

"Ok, I'm thinking, I'm thinking." Silas took his cap off and ran his fingers through his hair. "I probably need to get a room."

"A room, huh? Let me think. There's the Willingham Bed and Breakfast. It's convenient. You can walk to most everything downtown from there. Nice place."

"Take me there, then." He didn't know what he would do or how long he'd stay, but he'd at least have a place to relax.

###

I arrived at the concert hall parking lot to meet the group from Toccoa at the already agreed upon time and place. The Emmanuel Church van pulled in, and I exited my car to meet Ted. As I waited at the open van door, Ted stepped out, and our eyes met. It was almost as if I was in one of those corny commercials where a man and a woman run toward one another in a sunlit field. I wanted to run into his arms. I took a step toward him, but then . . . Tracie appeared in the doorway. My eyes darted from Ted and back to Tracie. He shrugged his shoulders and gave me a smile, but I could tell he was concerned about Tracie's presence.

As we moved side by side into the concert hall, a battle raged inside of me. I was sure Tracie probably found out there was an empty seat because I'd driven to Atlanta, and asked Ted if she could go. It was a church van, though. Who was I to say she shouldn't be on it? God, please help me sort this out, I prayed. Help me not to let this color my whole evening.

As we took our seats and the lights dimmed, the symphony began to play, and Rhonda Kay took her place on the stage. I already thought Rhonda Kay was an extraordinary vocalist, but tonight she dazzled us.

When she reached the crescendo in the last chorus of the evening, the goose bumps rolled up my arms. The standing ovation lasted several minutes.

Rhonda Kay had arranged for the folks from Emmanuel to meet her in her dressing room, and as she opened the door, she asked, "What did y'all think?"

After hugs all around, Laura Goodhay said, "Outstanding."

"Extraordinary," Debbie offered.

"Rhonda Kay, it gave me chill bumps," I said. "You were very striking in your black dress."

Rhonda Kay smiled, looked down at her feet and lifted her floor length dress about six inches.

The entire choir erupted into laughter as they beheld Rhonda Kay's red stilettos with gold heels.

"I can't believe you got away with wearing those," Debbie observed. "I'm surprised the conductor didn't make you take them off."

"He never saw them." Rhonda Kay admired her shoes. "But they sure made me feel good."

"Rhonda Kay, Rhonda Kay." Laura shook her head. "You are one of a kind."

Cletus, who'd stepped aside to the back of the crowd, now joined his wife who he regarded with admiration. "That's the truth if I've ever heard it."

Just as we all prepared to leave, Rhonda Kay touched me on the arm. "June, Laura's done told me that you're the one that let her know about the auditions with the Georgia Symphony. You were the connection to me even singing with the group."

I smiled. "The symphony conductor and I have a mutual friend, and I knew you had a rare talent. All I did was link a couple of people. Laura and you did the rest."

"Still, I owe you. Anytime you need to borrow a pair of stilettos, I'm you're gal." And we both burst out laughing.

###

Silas plopped on the edge of his bed frustrated. He'd gone over to June Callaway's house again after his dinner at Sherrino's, but just as before, there was no one at home. The upside was he and Elvin were getting to be pretty good friends.

He hadn't called Hero's House since he'd arrived in Toccoa, because he didn't have anything to say. He hated to disappoint the men there.

Music sounded from the chair in his room. What was that? He rose and moved to the chair, and then remembered it must be his cell phone. He fumbled in his jacket pocket lying on the chair and pulled out the phone.

He managed to push the answer button. "Hello."

"Is that you Silas?" he heard a voice he recognized as Conner's.

"It's me."

"What's going on? We didn't hear anything from you, so we thought we'd call."

"Nothing to report."

"What do you mean nothing to report? You're there aren't you?"

"Yes, I'm here, but June Callaway is not. She's not been at home all day." Definitely a frustrating turn of events.

"Too bad. What are you going to do?" Conner asked.

"Try again tomorrow, I guess."

"We're hoping for the best," Conner said.

"I appreciate it."

###

I kept quiet on the way home from the concert as I tried to decide how to respond to the Tracie situation. I just stared straight ahead as if concentrating on my driving and gripped the steering wheel with vigor.

As if reading my mind, Ted interrupted and broke the glacial silence. "She heard me talking on the phone about going to the symphony, and asked if there was an empty seat in the van. I knew there was, because you had to drive your car to take Jason to the airport." He turned to me completely unruffled. "I think Tracie is lonely."

I relaxed my grip on the wheel.

Ted appeared to concentrate on something outside the passenger window, something beyond the darkness.

We continued home in silence. *God, if Tracie is lonely, help her find a friend.* Though, I would have normally been more annoyed, my heart grew lighter as I remembered that singular moment by the van when Ted and I stood facing each other and even in the midst of a busy parking lot, for the first time, it was just us. Not me and Ted and Morris. Just me and Ted. In the light of that moment, I reached over and took his hand.

###

Saturday was another early morning because Tom and Joe's soccer team played at 8:30. I barely made it to the fields before the game started. When I found Iris, I pulled my chair out of the bag, and put it down beside her.

"Some night last night wasn't it?" Iris asked.

"Some night," I agreed.

Tom blocked a shot from the opposing team and the Toccoa crowd went crazy. Since I'd attended a few soccer games now, I had a better idea when to cheer. I embarrassed myself a lot less than I used to thanks to *Soccer for Blockheads,* but I still had my moments.

The referee signaled off-sides against Toccoa. "Why did he do that?" I asked Iris. Several different people had tried to explain off-sides to me, but I still didn't get it.

I thought Iris bore a long-suffering expression. She adjusted her sunglasses. "June, when one of Toccoa's offensive players moves toward their goal past the other team's last defensive player, off-sides is called on Toccoa."

Why couldn't I get it? I turned back to the field.

At that very moment, Joe kicked a ball into the net. The Toccoa crowd cheered. At the half, Toccoa was ahead 2-0.

At halftime, as others around us left the sidelines for the concession stand, the players headed for the Gatorade. Iris grew still, as if she wondered whether to speak. "I saw Tracie last night. How are you feeling about that?"

I shook my head. "I'm at a loss. Ted thinks she's doing all this because she's lonely."

"Lonely, huh?" Iris asked. Her eyes brightened, and I sensed she might be having a light bulb moment.

"I have an idea," she said.

"Tell me."

"I think I'll wait until I know a little bit more about how it turns out before I tell you what it is."

I couldn't stand it. "You can't keep me in suspense like this."

"It's for your own good," she responded.

###

Silas dialed the number again for June Callaway's house. *Ring, ring, ring, ring, ring*. No answer. He couldn't leave a message. She'd think it was a prank. "Hello, I'm the man you thought was dead." No, he couldn't do that. So, what would he do today? Maybe he'd go back to the Military Museum at the train depot later. That was bound to be interesting.

He picked up the Toccoa Record lying on the bed and scanned the front page. He couldn't believe the same newspaper his parents read was still around. Somehow, it gave him a sense of belonging.

Music played again. This time it came from his stomach. He stared at his mid-section a moment and then remembered the cell phone in his jacket pocket. He took it out and answered.

"Well?" a voice asked.

"Well, what?" Silas answered.

"Well, did you talk to her?

He recognized the voice as Leo's.

"She's still not at home."

"You think she's gone on a cruise or something?" Leo asked.

Silas hadn't thought about that. That's just what he needed, for June Callaway to be on a Caribbean Cruise. "Don't say that," he told Leo.

"Conner says I can't run his minutes up on his cell phone, so I'll talk to you later. How about you call us?" Leo asked.

"I will, I will," Silas said and hung up.

###

Near the end of the soccer game, my cell phone rang. I rummaged around in my purse and finally found it. The caller ID showed it was Jason. When I answered, Jason was talking so fast, I could hardly understand him.

"Please slow down. What?"

"Mom, they're airing the segment on Sunday night. Maybe we can get a crowd together to watch it on television."

"I can't wait, and I'll be at the airport on Sunday. I love you Son!"

I hated to miss church, but I wanted to be at the airport when Jason arrived Sunday morning. I couldn't wait to hear the whole story of Red's performance.

I'd no longer hung up the phone with Jason, than my cell phone rang again. "June, I'll pick you up about noon to go up to Highlands," Ted said.

"I'm at a soccer game right now, but I'll go home, jump in the shower, and get ready." We'd accepted an invitation to Robert Giles' house to visit and have dinner with him and his wife. He'd been a big help to Belle. I was glad for the opportunity to thank him for all he'd done.

I made up my mind, I wouldn't say a word about Tracie.

Instead, as we drove to Highlands, I told him about my eagle dreams. "So, what do you think?"

As the fall foliage zipped by, and the sun began to dip towards the mountainous horizon, Ted grew quiet. "I don't ever remember many of my dreams. It is curious that you've had three of them."

"Very."

I slid my eyes sideways to Ted remembering again the moment we had at the symphony concert, and as if reading my mind, he turned his head toward me. We didn't speak, but I think both of us knew, at last, something hard and heavy had been lifted.

Chapter Thirty-Three

Plans

"'For I know the plans I have for you,' declares the Lord,
'plans to prosper you and not to harm you,
plans to give you hope and a future.'"
—Jeremiah 29:11

Silas entered the Dinner Bell mid-morning, as he'd decided to forego the light breakfast at the B and B in favor of a late one here, after which he would skip lunch to have an early supper.

Stella screeched up to his table. "Now, we got your smoked sausage today. You're going to want to try that if you ain't had ours before." She pointed to the menu with the pencil in her hand. "And, when you was here the other day, I forgot to tell you that your muscadine jelly here was made by Lucille, the proprietor of The Dinner Bell. She's done won I don't know how many awards for it. Been written up in the local paper and all."

What could he say? Turned out to be the best breakfast he'd had since he was a boy. Scrambled eggs, smoked sausage, grits, biscuits, and the best preserves he'd ever put in his mouth, that is besides his mama's blackberry preserves. She made hers from the blackberries he, Buford, and Addie used to pick down along the Tugaloo River.

Stella didn't ask any more questions about his business there, and he was grateful for her restraint. He tried after noon to reach June Callaway, but once more was met with no response. He ventured over to Sherrino's again for supper, and tried to reach Mrs.

Callaway again as soon as he returned to the Bed and Breakfast. Still not home.

This wasn't working, and he was beginning to think Conner had been right about her being on a cruise.

He visited the military museum, and especially enjoyed the original WWII barracks the museum had moved from England and set up almost exactly as they were back during the war.

He later strolled around the courthouse lawn reading the memorials, and saw his name on the one from D-Day. Nice to know he was remembered in some small way here in his hometown. Such a strange feeling to be in a place where everyone thought he was dead. Felt like attending his own funeral.

He returned to his room and read the newspaper from cover to cover. As he readied for bed, he tried to decide what he would do. If he didn't find her at home the next day, he'd leave on Monday. Maybe he would visit New Orleans after all. He couldn't stay here indefinitely. Now, when did that train come through here? He had a schedule somewhere. He rifled through his coat pocket hanging on the back of the chair but didn't find it, and then wondered if he might have put it in the bedside stand. When he pulled open the drawer, he noticed the Gideon Bible inside.

He forgot about looking for the train schedule as he remembered Ed's pep talk when Ed tried to persuade him to come to Toccoa. Ed talked of "having Jesus" and not being afraid. He reached down, picked up the Bible and it fell open to Jeremiah twenty-nine. He read verse eleven: "'For I know the plans I have for you,' declares the Lord, 'plans to prosper you and not to harm you, plans to give you hope and a future.'"

As old as he was, he couldn't imagine God having plans for him. It seemed all he had to look forward to was death and what then? Nothing? But hadn't that Mike he met on the train said God cared for him? He flipped a few pages in the Bible. He read verse three from chapter thirty-three: "Call to me and I will answer you and tell you great and unsearchable things you do not know."

Did God have great things to tell him?

He sank down on the bed still holding the Bible, and the phrases ran through his mind.

"Call to me."

"I know the plans."

"Hope and future."

He put the Bible down, finished undressing, put on his pajamas, turned out the light, and went to bed. But he lay there a long time wide awake.

###

"Hey, Mom," Jason called waving to me when he arrived at baggage claim.

I ran to him and threw my arms around him, "Good to see you." Next, I kneeled to peek into Red's carrier. "Good to see you, too, boy." He meowed loudly ready to get out of the enclosure.

Jason said as I stood up, "I'll tell you about the trip, but I'm not telling you anything about the show. You're going to have to wait until tonight to see what happened."

"This is torture. You won't even tell me if Red won the contest?" So secretive.

He moved his thumb and forefinger across his lips as if zipping them.

I shrugged."All right, let's go then. We have a few folks coming over to watch it with us."

Jason picked up Red, and I wheeled his overnight bag toward the exit.

"Sounds great," Jason said. "But let's find a drive-through. I'm starved."

###

Since The Dinner Bell was closed on Sundays, Silas ate breakfast downstairs at the inn, and then came back up to his room. He'd slept later than he'd planned to that morning. He pushed aside the curtains over his window, and from his top floor vantage point, he had quite a sweeping view of the town. As he gazed out over the panorama, The Emmanuel Church bells signaled the worship hour simultaneously as the Courthouse clock began to ring.

A thought came to him. Why not? He knew the exact location of the Church. He could walk. He'd be late, but that was fine. There'd be less folks to ask questions about who he was.

###

Silas took off his cap and slipped in the back door of Emmanuel Church as the last notes of "How Great Thou Art" were sung. He found a seat on the back pew and rested his cane against the seat. He must have been later than he thought, because the pastor stood to read the text for the morning. Silas couldn't believe it when the pastor told them what it was: Jeremiah thirty-three, verse three. Quite a coincidence.

As he listened, he felt a tugging at his heart. The words of the preacher and the phrases from the night before filled his mind: Call to me. I know the plans. Hope and a future.

He breathed a prayer. "God, I call to you. I don't have much to offer, not in years or strength, but here I am."

Almost immediately, inside of him, all of the things he'd done to shield himself from hurt seemed to be melting. What was happening? In the place of the old familiar pain he'd carried, a deep peace began to settle in.

By the end of the service, he didn't want to leave. He didn't have a name for this, but he was pretty sure it had something to do with what Ed had told him. "I have Jesus, and I'm not afraid."

Whatever was happening made him sure of one thing. Though he wasn't afraid of dying, now, miraculously, for the first time since Anne Marie's death, he wasn't afraid of living either.

###

The crowd gathered early in anticipation of watching "Celebrity Cats" and crammed into my den. Jubilee, Bertha, Melissa, Tom, Joe, Belle, Ted, and of course Jason, as well as Addie and me. Even Linnea came home from school to watch the show with us. Everyone brought his or her favorite snack food to share.

We cheered when Red and Jason were introduced as contestants and watched intently as the competition began.

Jubilee slapped his knee."I ain't never seen no cat jump like that. That Red's a sight."

I agreed.

"To think, it was my Melissa that helped him get on the show." Bertha proudly gazed at Melissa.

Joe pointed at the television. "Look at him retrieve."

"Yeah, better than a Labrador," Tom said.

"I wish Misty could do that," Addie chimed. "But I guess I have to be content that my cat is famous for loving pigs."

Everyone laughed, and Belle added, "Misty is quite a star in her own right."

At one point, I thought I heard the doorbell, but there was so much cheering and clapping for Red, I wasn't sure. As the time for the winners to be announced approached, I wasn't leaving the room for anything. Out of the seven contestants, third place went to a dog that could Hula-hoop. I didn't know how in the world the owner taught him to do that. Second place was a monkey that made potholders.

"I need some new potholders. Wonder if they sell them?" Bertha asked. "Be a real conversation starter in the kitchen."

I didn't think Bertha needed any conversation starters, but if she did, monkey-made potholders would probably do it. I plucked the remote from an end table and turned the volume up on the television.

"The first place winner," the emcee announced, "is Red Callaway, the Retrieving Cat." The house went wild. Everyone cheered, clapped, and hugged Jason.

All the while, Red perched on the back of the sofa licking his lips and paws as someone had left an unattended bowl of cheese crunches, which were his favorite of human foods. He looked around at all the commotion and went back to the more pressing matter of removing orange crumbs from his glossy fur.

As the celebration waned, loud banging on the front door caused us all to turn toward the sound.

"What in the world is that?" Bertha asked.

I went to the door, and as it swung open, in front of me stood a man who looked much like someone I'd seen before. Who was it? Oh, yes, the man I'd seen at the train station Friday morning. He pulled off his plaid cap, and put it in the same hand with his cane.

He tipped his head to me. "Good evening, ma'am. I'm looking for June Callaway."

"I'm June Callaway."

"Well, ma'am, I'd like to speak with you if I may."

I nodded toward the back of the house. "We're having a little celebration right now. It's not a very convenient time. What's this about?"

"Mrs. Callaway, I've traveled an awful long way. It will only take a few minutes."

"Well, all right then; we can step into the study a moment."

###

Ted popped his head into the study. "June, what's going on? Everyone is wondering where you went." I peered at him from what I knew were red-rimmed eyes, but couldn't speak.

He stepped in, appearing concerned. "Is something wrong?"

I still couldn't say anything. I pointed to the older man sitting next to me on the sofa.

"June, what is it?" Ted glanced between the two of us.

I finally managed to get out a few words. "Let's move to the den."

In a minute or so, Ted, Silas, and I entered the den. Everyone turned to us with "What's going on?" expressions on their faces. They studied the man standing beside me now leaning heavy on his cane.

Addie glanced at him, and then at me, and then back at him. The genesis of recognition dawned in her eyes. She slowly rose from her seat and stretched out her arms. "Silas, my nephew!" Addie cried.

"Aunt Addie," Silas said and made his way over and embraced her.

"We thought you were dead!" Addie cried.

"I know," Silas whispered. "I was dead, but I'm alive now."

"Silas?" Belle seemed awestruck and looked at Joe.

"Uncle Silas?" Joe asked. "The one the desk belonged to?"

Tears spilled onto Belle's face.

"Silas, this is your great niece, Belle and her son, Joe. You also have a niece, Becky, away at college."

"I'm pleased to meet you, ma'am." Silas let go of Addie and turned to Belle.

Belle dabbed her eyes. "I prayed for you to come back."

"That doesn't surprise me ma'am," Silas said. "If it weren't for your prayers I might not be here. I was afraid I'd scare you all to death, like I'd come back from the grave or something."

A streak of panic crossed Belle's face. "But the desk—I've already spent so much of the money we received for it."

Silas held up his hands. "Whoa. I'm not here for any money. I'm glad something good finally came of such a heartache. I don't have any need for the desk or the money you received for it."

Belle crossed over to Silas and threw her arms around him. "Do you know what you've done for my family? Do you know how close we were to being homeless before June discovered I was your niece?" she whispered to him through her tears. "How did you ever find us?"

Silas shook his head. Belle let go of him, he reached in his back pocket, took out his wallet, and removed a folded tattered newspaper article. He handed to Belle.

She read it aloud.

"Have you ever?" Bertha asked.

I hadn't and I doubted anyone else had either.

When Belle finished, Silas fumbled in his pocket and pulled out his cell phone. "There are some other folks who want to know what's going on here." Silas pressed a button. "Hello, Conner, I finally have news for you." Silas scanned the room. "I found her. I found all of them." He handed the phone to me. "Mrs. Callaway, would you tell this friend of mine what's going on? He knows my side of the story."

As Silas conversed with his newly discovered family, I left the room and returned a few minutes later and handed the phone back to him. "Amazing."

"Tell all of the guys what's going on, especially Ed," Silas instructed over the phone. He held it up the device so we could all hear.

From the cell phone, we too, heard the sounds of men cheering.

"I'll call you later, Conner," Silas said and hung up.

Silas scanned the room around him as if drinking us in. "It's a miracle. After all this time."

I edged over next to him. "Silas..." I touched his arm. "You're home."

"Right," said Ted. "It looks like the eagle has landed."

Chapter Thirty-Four

Life in the Shadow of Currahee

"To an open house in the evening
Home shall men come,
To an older place than Eden
And a taller town than Rome.
To the end of the way of the wandering star,
To the things that cannot be and that are,
To the place where God was homeless
And all men are at home."
—G.K. Chesterton (1874-1936)

One month later

At twenty-three pounds, I didn't want to risk dropping the turkey, and I sure didn't want to leave it in the oven and chance a rerun of last year's burnt bird fiasco. I called Jason to help me move it from the oven.

"Do you have it?" I asked him as we both grabbed the sides of the pan and lifted.

He grabbed it wearing his dad's old oven mitts. "I do."

"Let's put it here on the counter and then I'll carve it a little later," Jason said. We heaved the turkey up and lowered it to the granite surface. "Wow, is this a big one or what?"

"Mom, I can't believe the crowd you have coming today." Linnea stood at the kitchen table and with a flourish, put the finishing touch of mayo on the tomato aspic.

"I can't believe it either, but I was determined." I surveyed the Thanksgiving Day preparations with a bit of pride.

"Tell us what else we can do," Linnea offered.

"We'll have to have a card table set up in the foyer, because everyone won't fit at the dining table. You count while I name: Jubilee, Bertha, Melissa, Belle, Joe, Becky, Me, You, Jason, Ted, Addie, Silas, Eugene, and Tracie."

"Who are Eugene and Tracie?" Jason asked, frowning.

"Ted's administrative assistant and her new boyfriend," I explained.

"That makes fourteen," Linnea tallied.

"Ten at the dining table, four at the card table," I said. "Help me get it out."

Linnea and I moved to the hall closet and began wrangling the card table from it. We finally set it free just as the phone rang. We rested it against the wall, and I scrambled to the study to answer the phone.

"Happy Thanksgiving," I heard.

"Happy Thanksgiving, to you too, Iris."

"I hear you're having Eugene and Tracie over today."

"I'm still amazed at your matchmaking abilities."

"All in a day's work. Jed had introduced me to Eugene when he was over here on his last maintenance visit, and I knew Eugene was probably lonely because he was new in town, plus you told me Tracie was lonely. Something clicked in my brain and we invited them both to church that Sunday you picked up Jason at the airport, took them to lunch, and the rest is history."

"I'm looking forward to having them today. We'll talk later," I said and hung up.

Ted came through the front door as I was trying to set up the card table. "I'll help you do that," he offered.

"Thanks." After we popped out the legs, I went to him and kissed him on the cheek. "Happy Thanksgiving."

He took me in his arms and held me, then gazed into my eyes."Happy Thanksgiving to you."

When the whole crowd had gathered, I asked Jason to return thanks.

"Lord, we've had quite a year with a miracle desk, homecomings, a celebrity cat, a big garden for the homeless, and a new business venture. Thank you for all our blessings, especially these friends, and thank you we didn't burn the turkey this year."

We all snickered and after he'd finished, we echoed our amens. I studied the crowd now plucking turkey from a platter, scooping sweet potato soufflé from a bowl, and attacking a large pan of cornbread dressing. In only the year and a half since I'd been in Toccoa, so much had happened. I still couldn't believe it sometimes.

"Heard from Conner today. They're having the memorial service for Ed this Saturday," Silas said.

"I'm sorry you lost your friend, Silas," Belle sympathized and placed her hand on his arm.

"He knew before he died that all his prayers for me were answered. He was the one who encouraged me the most to come to Toccoa. So, though I'll miss him, when I think of him, I smile. He's finally home, too."

"All the ladies over at Mountain Gardens love Silas," Addie said. "They know he's a hero, and they fight over who's going to sit beside him when he comes to visit me." She cut up her turkey and took a bite.

"Did I tell y'all I'm doing bizness on the Internet?" Jubilee asked while he ladled gravy onto his turkey.

"No, you didn't," I answered, amazed.

"Internet? Since when did you get a computer?" Bertha wondered. "Would you pass me the gravy, please, Tracie?"

"Since Tom and Joe helped me get one. My daughter helps me, too. I'm livin' in the twenty-first century; I figure I ought to act like it. Tom and Joe got somebody to set me up somethin' called a website. Yessiree bobtail, I shipped me a whirligig to a customer in Australia last week." Jubilee laughed out loud. "I had to get a map to see how far away it is—clear on the other side of the world."

"I went to Australia once for a conference," Ted said. "Enjoyed it. Hey, changing the subject, but I stopped by the Dinner Bell the other day to pick up lunch, and Stella told me she decide to run in the Currahee 3K this spring. Said Lucille found out about it, and decided the Dinner Bell would help sponsor the race."

"I can't imagine anyone being a better contender than Stella."

Ted's eyes scanned the table, and he seemed to be searching for something. Ted, Jason, Linnea and I were sitting at the card table and having a bit of a problem getting the food over our way.

"Do you need something, Ted?" I asked.

"Sure do. Would you pass the tomato aspic, please?"

What a wonder. "Ted, you're having seconds on tomato aspic?" I asked, taking it from Bertha and passing it to him.

"One of my favorite dishes. Didn't I ever tell you that? In fact, I love it so much I suggested the Dinner Bell start making it. They even put it in their cookbook."

"That's where I found the recipe." I couldn't believe this.

"Sure enough?" Ted asked.

I thought it too good to be true. "Among all the other wonderful things that have happened this month, I heard from my agent about my book. He has a publisher who may be interested. I told him I'd like to write an epilogue."

"That's wonderful," Belle said.

"What's the name of your book, Mrs. Callaway?" Eugene asked.

"*The Writing Desk*. It's fiction, but based on a true story." I smiled as I surveyed the faces of Belle, Joe, Becky, Addie, and Silas.

"We can't wait to read it. To think I'll have a famous author living next door," Bertha chirped.

"We'll see about that," I laughed.

"I was sitting here thinking there was somebody else that encouraged me on this journey," Silas said.

"Who?" Addie asked.

"I ate dinner with him on the train coming down—a young man. You know what he told me? He said sometimes you have to move past your fear. 'Do it afraid,' I believe is the way he put it. He seemed wise for his age."

I almost choked on my green beans. I glanced at Silas and then at Ted. Ted shrugged and gave me a dimpled smile. Could it have been the same person I'd met at the writer's conference? I wiped my mouth with my napkin. "Silas, someone once told me that, too. When he said it, I felt it was confirmation that I should come to Toccoa."

Silas shook his head. "Really?"

"I only saw him once at a writer's conference. I never learned his name."

"Very strange." Silas looked at me questioningly.

"Yes, very," I agreed.

"I almost forgot." Jubilee jumped up from the table, went to the front door, reached for something outside the door, and brought it back in. "This is for you," he said to Jason. "Your mama had me do it."

Jason studied the whirligig in Jubilee's hand. It was a great representation of Red with a ball in his mouth. "This will look great outside my condominium in Athens. It'll give me a chance to tell everybody about my famous cat." Jason smiled broadly. "Thanks, Mom. Thanks, Jubilee."

"You're welcome," Jubilee and I chorused.

"Jed is so nervous about the baby coming, he's afraid to leave the house," Eugene said. "He has me making all the wreath deliveries tomorrow, and I'll have to man the Christmas tree lot as well. Jed wants to be right with Ethel all the time in case she goes into labor."

Tracie looked up from her green beans. "Does this mean we won't be able to go to the Christmas parade together?"

"No, way. I'm not missing the parade. We'll work it out somehow."

Tracie beamed at Eugene.

Ted swallowed the bite of aspic he had in his mouth."Sounds like a lot for you to do."

"Happy for the work," Eugene said.

"Who's ready for dessert?" I asked.

Everyone chorused, "I am."

Linnea and Jason joined me to help with the desserts, and for some reason, Jubilee went back out the front door. As we served German chocolate pecan pie, coconut cake, and fried apple pies,

Jubilee returned with another whirligig and gave it to Silas. "Welcome to Toccoa."

The signature plaid cap, the cane in the left hand all told that the whirligig was of Silas. Silas stood up and accepted the gift. "This will look fine in my front yard, whenever I get a front yard."

"But you're welcome to stay with us for as long as you like," Belle said. "No hurry."

After dessert, as everyone helped clear the table, I saw Belle take Silas aside. I eavesdropped a bit. "I have something for you." She pulled out bundles from her purse, and I recognized them as the money Jed and Elmer had found in my basement. "These are for you."

Silas peered at me with a wondering look.

I stepped toward them. "Silas, this is the money you were going to buy a house with all those years ago. Buford hid it in my basement and we found it this year."

Belle placed it in his hands. "You've given so much to my family already. We insist you have this back."

Silas took it and June saw him reading what he'd written so many years ago: "For my beloved with all my heart."

"Thank you," he whispered. "I might do something in memory of Anne Marie. I don't need the money, but I understand you want me to have it."

Belle hesitated a moment. "I've waited to tell you this and I don't know if you want to hear it, but we have Anne Marie's letters and her picture if you want them."

Tears welled in Silas' eyes. He reached over and embraced Belle. "This is all too much, more than I could ever imagine, having a family like this."

I smiled as I blinked back tears.

###

After we'd cleaned up and everyone had left for the day, Jason and Linnea went to visit friends, so Ted and I lingered alone in the study. We both leaned exhausted against the back of the sofa, and he eased his hand on top of mine. I grasped it and squeezed, and he pulled me close to him.

In letting go of my anger, my fear had also vanished. I snuggled closer to him, placed my head on his shoulder and dared to entertain the possibility of a future beside him.

We sat wordless for a time, the distant dongs of the courthouse clock striking the hour—the only discernible sound in the quiet early evening.

I closed my eyes, and in my mind saw Currahee standing sentinel over the town. I settled in comfortably and realized that just as Silas had found after so many years, God and the mountain had guided me home.

Recipes

Currahee Carrot Cake

1 ¾ cups sugar
4 unbeaten eggs
2 teaspoons baking powder
2 teaspoons cinnamon
3 cups grated carrots
1 ¼ cups cooking oil
2 cups plain flour
2 teaspoons baking soda
1 teaspoon salt
1 ½ cups chopped nuts (pecan is best)

Preheat oven to 375 degrees. Cream sugar and oil. Add eggs and cream until soft. Sift dry ingredients and flour and add to above ingredients. Mix well. Fold in carrots and nuts. Bake for 25 minutes.

Frosting
1 pack confectioners sugar
½ stick butter
8 oz creamed cheese
2 teaspoon vanilla
Cream together ingredients and frost cake when cool.

Grandmother's Peppermint Cake

June's grandmother never used recipes. June had to guess as to the ingredients of this cake. She chose a basic white cake recipe for the layers, which may be found in most cookbooks. She also prepared a seven-minute frosting.

These items finished her cake.

1 package of starlight mints
1 package of soft peppermint sticks
Fresh mint

Crush one-half package of soft peppermint sticks, then melt in the top of a double boiler.

Place the bottom layer of the cake on a serving plate. Perforate the top of the cake with a toothpick. Pour half of melted peppermint over cake until the melted peppermint saturates the layer. Frost only the top of the layer. Place the second layer on top of the first, perforate it, and saturate with the remaining melted peppermint. Frost entire cake. Crush remaining peppermint and sprinkle heavily on the top of the cake. Place starlight mints around the base and garnish with mint.

June's German Chocolate Pie

¼ stick butter
¾ teaspoon flour
1 cup sugar
¾ cup evaporated milk
pinch of salt
¾ cup chopped nuts
1 ounce unsweetened chocolate
½ teaspoon cornstarch
1 egg
½ teaspoon vanilla
½ cup coconut
pie shell

Preheat oven to 350 degrees. Melt butter and chocolate in top of double boiler. Mix flour, sugar, and cornstarch. Stir in egg. Add melted chocolate mixture. Mix until smooth. Gradually add milk, vanilla, and salt. Sprinkle coconut and nuts on bottom of pie shell. Pour in the chocolate mixture. Bake 40 minutes or until a toothpick inserted comes out clean.

Jubilee's Fried Apple Pies

Jubilee visits the apple farms in Northeast Georgia or across the state line in South Carolina so he can buy Rome apples. He dries them himself on screens in the back yard as June's grandmother did. June found that drying the apples in a hydrator according to the manufacturer's instructions works well when they are pretreated with a little lemon juice. June stores the apples in plastic bags and places them in tins.

Jubilee doesn't use recipes either, so June had to use a little guess work. She uses a biscuit dough recipe her family has loved for years. Use one of your family favorites, then knead the dough gently on a floured surface. Roll biscuit dough out to about ½ inch thickness. Cut with a medium size biscuit cutter. Roll each biscuit out again on a floured surface until a circle is formed. Spoon the mixture below onto one side of the circle and fold. Place in a pan preheated with hot oil or shortening and fry.

Apples

Place dried apples in a medium pan with enough water to cover. You may choose to add a couple of tablespoons of sugar. It is not necessary. Cook until apples are tender.

Makes about 7 or 8 pies.

"The Dinner Bell" Tomato Aspic

You're on your own with this southern favorite. The Dinner Bell decided to copyright the recipe, and Lucille wouldn't allow us to print it here. She's thinking of franchising The Dinner Bell and wanted to keep most of her recipes close.

If you're brave, you'll be like Julia Childs who started with a calf's foot. If you're not so adventurous, unflavored gelatin is your ticket to an aspic delight. Let us know how it turns out, and remember to invite Ted and June for dinner.

Acknowledgements

My many thanks…

To my husband Jerry, for your love and support through many long years of writing. I love you more. To Aaron and Bethany, you have my heart, and I am so proud of you as you move toward your own dreams. Thank you for encouraging your mom to chase hers. To dear Mari—so proud of you for that doctorate, to her husband Brent for much IT help, and to Walker and Sara Alden, the best grandchildren ever. To my sister, Tammy, who kept the vision for this story and wouldn't let me forget it. To her husband Foy, and my nephew, Christopher, whose music fills my heart.

To my dad and his wife, Irene, who share the love of Currahee. Dad, you have been as the mountain to me, strong and enduring my entire life. I love you so much.

To the young women who shared our home for years, Marni and Mandy, you will always be special to us.

To my mother, who still leads the cheer from heaven.

To many who helped with research: the staff at the Currahee Military Museum; the Toccoa-Stephens County Chamber of Commerce; Kathryn Trogdon for her History of Stephens County Georgia; Georgia Forest Watch; The Georgia Botanical Society; Ron with the National Forest Service; Fortson, Bentley, and Griffin Law Firm; The Metropolitan Museum of Art; my cousin Iris for the family genealogy that provided so many names for this story; Andy for a great line; Tara at Hero's Home; Whit at Clarke County Lock and Key.

A special thanks to Paula Anderson Schaefer for permission to quote her father, Paul Anderson, Podge Cross at Toccoa Falls College for permission to quote Dr. R.A. Forrest, and Mark Rodel at Letourneau University for permission to quote R.G. LeTourneau.

For my many beta readers, among them, Dr. Joel Cook who also provides medical advice to my characters, as well as Leslie Lynch, Christen Morris, Lilyan West, Tammy Todd, and Marion Bond West. To Gayle Roper, for her helpful advice. And to Connie Harding, who was one of the first to read this manuscript, and make suggestions. You have been a lifelong inspiration. And as always, to beloved Harriette Austin, writing mentor to many. To my own writing group, Mary, Maria, Carole, Lilyan, Linda, Paula, Evelyna, and Alli. So grateful for you all and our shared love of writing.

To a group of women at Gateway Church who prayed during the penning of the first iteration of this book many years ago: Jerri, Cathy, Marion, Amy, Claudia, and Lilyan. To the men of the Athens YMCA Bible Study and that special group of pastors who meet every Monday, the "Cronies": Howard, Lee, Mark, Morris, and Scott. You are all an extraordinary example of the love of Christ. To Andrew and my friends at Chick-fil-A for coffee and a second office.

To my spiritual mentors: Dr. Warren and Jane Lathem, Rev. Grady and Doris Wigley, Dr. Gary and Diane Whetsone, Rev. Walton and Martha McNeal.

To the people at Rays Church, who have loved me through many writing projects. You are so precious to me.

To my readers at One Ringing Bell, thank you for the gift of your time and encouragement.

In memory of friends I will never forget: Becky Carter, Debbie Parrish, and Dr. Jim Kilgo.

Special thanks to the brave men who changed the world on D-Day. Especially to Reed Pelfrey, who is no longer with us, but who once took the time to help me in the research for this story. A member of the 101st Airborne and a pathfinder, you were one of the first to jump that fateful day. Thank you for the legacy of freedom that you leave to the world.

About the Author

Beverly Varnado writes to give readers hope in the redemptive purposes of God. She has won numerous awards for her work, including being a finalist for the prestigious Kairos Prize in Screenwriting, a finalist in screenwriting at the Gideon Media Arts Conference and a semifinalist in Christian Writer's Guild Operation First Novel. She currently has a screenplay under option with Elevating Entertainment.

She has been featured in several Georgia publications, including *Southern Distinctions Magazine,* which recently highlighted her with a select group of Georgia authors.

Beverly's nonfiction credits include the *Upper Room Magazine* and blog, a Focus on the Family publication as well as a segment of *The World and Everything in It*, a World Magazine Radio broadcast.

She blogs at One Ringing Bell, bev-oneringingbell.blogspot.com, where you will find "peals of words on faith, living and writing". You may also visit her on her website, www.BeverlyVarnado.com

Beverly lives in North Georgia with her husband, Jerry, wonderful children, Aaron and Bethany, and their chocolate Lab, Lucy, who is outnumbered by several cats.

CPSIA information can be obtained
at www.ICGtesting.com
Printed in the USA
FSOW02n1907240916
25337FS

9 781629 523545